A HUSBAND FOR HARTWELL
THE LORDS OF BUCKNALL CLUB

J.A. ROCK
LISA HENRY

A Husband for Hartwell

Copyright © 2021 by J.A. Rock and Lisa Henry.

All rights reserved.

No part of this book may be reproduced in any form or by any electronic or mechanical means, including information storage and retrieval systems, without written permission from the author, except for the use of brief quotations in a book review.

This is a work of fiction. Names, characters, businesses, places, events and incidents are either the products of the author's imagination or used in a fictitious manner. Any resemblance to any actual persons, living or dead, or actual events is purely coincidental.

Edited by Susie Selva.

Cover Art by Mitxeran.

ACKNOWLEDGMENTS

With thanks to our beta readers, Bridget, Amy, Mia, and Heather.

ABOUT A HUSBAND FOR HARTWELL

He must marry, or risk his fortune.

The whole of London Society has long assumed Lord William Hartwell will marry his childhood best friend, Lady Rebecca Warrington. After two Seasons, Hartwell remains quite content with bachelorhood—his parents do not. When Hartwell learns they intend to cut his purse strings unless he makes a match this Season, he resigns himself to a marriage of convenience with Becca, and yet he can't help but be drawn to her younger brother, Warry.

He must marry, or risk his sister's ruin.

The Viscount "Warry" Warrington is used to being viewed as the tagalong little brother. Now a grown man about to enter his second Season, Warry is desperate to be seen. When Lord Balfour, a handsome older peer, takes Warry under his wing, Warry thinks his dream is finally coming true. Until Balfour reveals his true intent—to make public a letter that will destroy Becca's reputation, unless Warry agrees to marry him.

Time is running out for both of them.

When an injury forces Warry to recover at Hartwell House, the two succumb to a secret flirtation. But Warry's sudden announcement of his engagement to Balfour drives Hartwell near mad with jealousy—and right into Becca's arms. With the clock ticking for Warry to save his sister, will Hartwell discover the truth of Warry's feelings before it's too late?

A Husband for Hartwell *is the first book in the Lords of Bucknall Club series, where the Regency meets m/m romance.*

CONTENTS

Chapter 1	1
Chapter 2	14
Chapter 3	20
Chapter 4	35
Chapter 5	42
Chapter 6	50
Chapter 7	62
Chapter 8	77
Chapter 9	90
Chapter 10	101
Chapter 11	114
Chapter 12	123
Chapter 13	137
Chapter 14	155
Chapter 15	164
Chapter 16	174
Chapter 17	184
Chapter 18	198
Chapter 19	213
Afterword	227
About J.A. Rock	229
About Lisa Henry	231
Also by J.A. Rock and Lisa Henry	233
Also by J.A. Rock	235
Also by Lisa Henry	237

In 1783, the Marriage Act Amendment was introduced in England to allow marriages between same-sex couples. This was done to strengthen the law of primogeniture and to encourage childless unions in younger sons and daughters of the peerage, as an excess of lesser heirs might prove burdensome to a thinly spread inheritance.

CHAPTER 1

William Hartwell, arguably London's most eligible bachelor and certainly London's most melancholy marquess, was not entirely surprised to find a frog down the back of his shirt.

Perhaps he should have been. Nobody had put a frog down his shirt in a very long time. But once he'd shot to his feet, tugging his shirt free from his trousers in a flurry of panic, he heard Lady Rebecca Warrington's musical laugh behind him.

"Gentle!" she chided. "It is not the frog's fault. It is mine. I couldn't resist."

He turned to face his truest friend. As he did, the frog slid down his back and out the bottom of his shirt. It sat for a moment on the grass, its vocal sac inflating and deflating, and then it hopped away.

"Whatever possessed you?" he asked brusquely, seating himself again with what he hoped was a modicum of dignity.

She gazed at him for a long moment, the light catching in her golden curls. Hartwell could not read her expression. The early spring grass was warm under his palms, reigniting his irritation at the unseasonably sunny day. What right had the weather to be so fair when his mood was so foul? From several feet behind them came a cough, which only rendered Hartwell's countenance darker. He missed his childhood days when he and Becca could sit on her lawn without a chaperone.

"I could not stand to see your long face," she replied at last. Her cream-coloured afternoon dress had a grass stain near one knee, and her shawl lay discarded nearby.

"Put your shawl on. You'll catch cold."

"William Hartwell." Her low, lovely voice had sharpened significantly. "Do not harry me as though I am a child and you are my nursemaid. I am your oldest friend and confidante. I have been assaulting you with frogs since we were in leading strings, and I implore you to tell me what's wrong. Is it what my father said?"

It most certainly was, and her acuity pierced between his ribs with a keenness that lingered.

William, Marquess of Hartwell, was three-and-twenty years old and the only son of the Duke of Ancaster. He was more than aware that his dark eyes, chiselled features, artfully tumbled black curls and tall, muscular body—not to mention his vast wealth—attracted not only the, wholly welcome, attention of other sons of the nobility, but the sharp interest of aristocratic daughters and their parents. He was also aware that his parents were growing impatient for him to marry. He'd managed to fend off his mother's unsubtle hints last Season, but now they weren't so much hints as a battering ram taken to his—if his mother was to be believed—incomparably thick skull. The Hartwells needed an heir. Which meant William Hartwell, an only son, needed a wife.

Of course, Becca's parents would think him the logical choice for their daughter. His own parents thought the same. Their families had teased them about their future wedding throughout the whole of their childhood, prompting squeals of "Ugh!" and "Never!" from both. And yet, hearing the suggestion spoken aloud by Earl Warrington in utter seriousness had made everything feel so horribly real. Hartwell hadn't fully realised until Earl Warrington's rant last night that he and Becca were in danger of souring like milk left out too long. Or perhaps he'd always known but had done his best to ignore it.

"It is not the worst idea I've heard, William," Becca said softly. "I've no wish to marry, but if I must, I'd rather it be to you than to… well, anyone who made conversation with me last Season. Or the Season before."

He made no answer.

"There are worse fates, one supposes, than signing the paper and satisfying our families." She gave a wry twist of her mouth. "And in our future home, we will be as we are now. Friends. Frog catchers. Free to pursue our own lives as long as we employ some measure of discretion."

"What about an heir?"

"We will say we cannot conceive."

"That's not fair to you. They will say it is you who cannot conceive. Your reputation will be stained, and your parents will hire a physician to poke and prod you…I cannot bear it. The very idea makes me ill."

"I am willing to be poked and prodded if it means I keep some scrap of freedom."

"Do not speak that way, Becca. It is a fantasy world you live in. I am an only son. If we marry, we must have children—it is the only reason my father is pushing for a match! And if we have children, then our lives—"

"Are over," she finished with a sigh. "How strange that the man who thinks the solution is to bill himself an eligible *parti* indefinitely, letting half a dozen young ladies and gentlemen dangle after him without a thought for their feelings—"

"It is not my fault they dangle."

"—would call *me* a creature of fancy."

"I do think of their feelings."

"Just not as often as you think of your own," she said, not unkindly. She placed a hand on his arm. "If we did have children, I should think they'd at least be handsome."

He heard the grin in her voice, and in spite of himself, he offered a shadow of a smile as well. "They would be handsome."

"*There* you are," she whispered, letting her hand fall away. "I've missed you."

He made himself face her directly. "I'm sorry I've been such a great brooding donkey."

"You mean an ass."

"Be a lady."

A smile lit her beautiful face. "Never."

He smiled too, fully this time. Becca could always cheer him up. And truly, a life as her husband would not be any gruelling punishment. He wanted to spend each day with her as it was. It was simply that—

Her gaze had shifted to something behind him. "Warry! Where are you off to?"

Hartwell glanced over his shoulder and spotted Becca's younger brother, Joseph Warrington, skulking across the lawn. Warry had always been a skulker. And a tattler, and a gabster, and a damn bloody nuisance. As children, the only thing that could draw a truce between himself and Becca in their war of frogs and dried leaves down the backs of dresses and shirts, bonnet thievery, and cravat unknotting was to join forces to push her obnoxious younger brother into the frog pond or encourage him to climb a tree, promising they'd join him and then leave him stranded and bellowing at them in the branches.

Yet Warry had grown into such a serious young man of late. Hartwell could no more imagine the stony-faced lad trotting after them on their adventures, prattling animatedly about different types of ploughs and the workings of horses' digestive systems, than he could imagine himself light and free enough to grab a handful of leaves and stuff them down the back of Becca's dress.

"N'where," Warry mumbled. He dragged his fingers through his wheat-coloured hair. At nineteen, he was quite handsome, apart from his recent dourness. He was tall and slender and well made, as were all of the Warrington brood. He wasn't as striking as Becca, but he was handsome, with fine features, eyes the colour of a summer sky after rain, and a wide, generous mouth. "Got errands."

"Speak up," Becca urged.

Warry sighed. "I have errands," he enunciated as slowly and carefully as though Becca were deaf.

"You're supposed to be chaperoning us."

"Annie's here." Warry jerked his head toward Becca's maid, who was standing several yards away, her hands clasped in front of her.

Hartwell's mood was further dampened. "We are watched with more scrutiny than babes," he muttered.

Warry's gaze found his for a moment, but Hartwell couldn't tell what he was thinking, and the strangeness of the look made his stomach jump a bit.

"He is probably going to see his new friend *Lord Balfour*," Becca said knowingly, shimmying her shoulders slowly and catching the tip of her tongue between her teeth as she grinned at her brother.

Warry's gaze hardened, though his cheeks turned pink. "It is none of your concern."

"So you *are* going to see Balfour! What is it today? Will he teach you to drink as a man does? To spit as a man does? To prattle on endlessly about horribly dull subjects, on which you have no real knowledge, and to dismiss any contribution a woman tries to make to your conversation because her brains are very obviously made of crinoline, and her only worth is in how many sons she can produce?"

"I'm not going to see Lord Balfour today." Warry stared at her for a long moment. "And it is rude of you to think so badly of him."

Then he turned and stalked away.

Becca snorted softly. "Between the two of you, I feel like I am forever in the presence of sulking children. Do let me see you smile again soon, Hartwell, or I shall frog you relentlessly."

The implication that he himself might resemble the damnable brat in behaviour was nearly enough to wipe the sullenness from

Hartwell's face. Warry had barely spoken to him since their families had arrived in London in preparation for the Season, and Hartwell had even attempted to joke with him at the Gilmore rout, though, he recalled with a slight hint of shame, the joke had perhaps not been made in the friendliest spirit. And they hadn't spoken often last year either—Hartwell and Becca had been busy avoiding entanglements with overeager potential matches, and Hartwell had barely seen the younger Warrington—though he could still recall teasing Warry over tea and Warry responding with laughter. He had missed Warry's laughter more than he cared to admit.

The young man who had just stormed past him without a word looked as though he'd never laughed in his life.

Hartwell wrapped his arms loosely around his knees. "He has been so disagreeable of late."

"He does not like to leave the country in winter, and we arrived in Town this year just after Christmas."

"You think that is it?"

"Who can say?" Becca's voice held a note of sadness. "We were everything to one another, not so long ago. Now, I speak, and I can immediately feel him close some invisible door on me."

"Why do you tease him so about Balfour? Is it not fortunate that he has found a friend? He had always preferred the company of farmyard animals and books to people. He's never had close friends."

"He's always had us."

"We pushed him into ponds."

"I can't stand Balfour," Becca admitted. "He looks like a great wax sculpture. He fancies himself Warry's mentor, and yet he teaches my brother nothing of use. I am sure of it."

"Well, you do know everything."

"I do!" Becca agreed readily. "The whole world should listen to me."

Very slowly, Hartwell reached behind him, the movement subtle enough not to draw any attention from his companion, who was still staring after her younger brother.

He picked up a handful of leaves.

Her shriek of surprise as they went down her back was enough to make him laugh, genuinely laugh. And when she pounced on him, he pulled her over and they tumbled together on the grass. Not even Annie's series of increasingly disapproving coughs could stop him from reaching out to pinch Becca's arm while she yelped and tried to kick his shin. He lay there for a moment, staring into the most familiar eyes in all the world, and tried the words out in his mind: *Lady Rebecca Hartwell. My wife.*

∽

Joseph, the Viscount Warrington, hated William Hartwell. His loathing had simmered in him the entire afternoon, mercifully distracting him from his nerves regarding that night, as he studiously avoided going back to the house until he could be sure Hartwell had left. It was quite a turn-up for the books because not that long ago, he could recall quite liking the fellow and being happy to find himself in his company—even if it was only as Becca's tagalong younger brother and the target of all their mischief. But over the course of last Season—Warry's first—he had found himself, at first, mildly irritated by Hartwell's presence, then annoyed by it, and now, following Hartwell's cruelty toward him at the Gilmore rout, downright infuriated by it. It did not help that Warry mostly only saw him these days when he was supposed to be chaperoning Becca so that she and Hartwell couldn't do anything scandalous. Unless shoving frogs down someone's shirt was some sort of obscure French method of lovemaking that Warry was entirely ignorant of—and to be fair, he would be—he hardly thought his parents had anything to concern themselves about on that score. Sometimes he thought Becca and Hartwell were more brother and sister than Becca and himself. For all that, though, Warry did have a brotherly duty to Becca, as well as a duty to the entire Warrington name, and this entire dreadful mess was *his* fault to begin with. Which was why he found himself out of doors hours after the household had gone to bed, at midnight, alone, in the rookery of St. Giles.

Or, to be more precise, *not* alone. He was almost certain he'd been followed since leaving Oxford Street and was quite sure the fellows following him weren't doing so out of an abundance of care for his welfare. He was sure to end up in the pages of a newspaper, in an article that finished by stating that the details of his funeral arrangements were to follow. He straightened his shoulders, thinking of what Lord Balfour would say about his letting an overactive imagination get the better of him. He wished he were Lord Balfour right now. Confident, unafraid, and claiming the world as his own with every elegant stride he took through it.

A flash of heat went through Warry at the recollection of the imposing figure Balfour cut. Why a nonpareil such as Balfour had deigned to take a trembling mouse like Warry under his wing was beyond him, but he was grateful for the turn of fortune that had thrown Balfour and himself together. Why, just yesterday, Balfour had observed that Warry seemed not quite the thing and had asked what was the matter. The concern in his dark eyes had almost convinced Warry to spill the whole sordid tale. Balfour would quite likely have found a solution that didn't involve Warry wandering St. Giles alone in the dead of night. But Warry had been too ashamed of what he'd got himself into to confide in the fellow whose good opinion he sought above all others.

He peered at the sign on one of the street's many gin shops, hoping it was the one he wanted, but no, finding a specific gin shop in the rookery was apparently like looking for a needle in a haystack. A filthy, teeming haystack that smelled like literal shit. To keep fear at bay, he focused on his anger at Becca. How dare she disparage his friendship with Balfour at every turn. If she had any idea the lengths he was going to for their family…His heart lodged in his throat as he heard what sounded like muffled laughter. His head buzzing and his mouth dry, he hurried on determinedly.

It really oughtn't have been so difficult to pay a damned blackmailer. Warry could not help but think that putting one's victim in danger of his life wasn't the smartest way to ensure one received prompt payment, but what would he know? He'd never blackmailed anyone and could not confess any desire at all to ever do so. But he did need that letter back. And, once he got it, he needed to throw it in the nearest fire.

A woman lurking by the entrance to the gin shop lifted her skirts and offered to swive for what Warry could only assume was a reasonable rate of pay, and he stammered out a refusal as he hurried on his way.

"I've got a bruvver!" she yelled after him. "If you're looking for a Backgammoner!"

Warry suspected that she was not referring to the game, and also that the brother might be just as unappealing. Besides all that, there was only one man Warry was seeking tonight: Wilkes.

Wilkes had been employed as Warry's valet for several months before he'd been dismissed. Warry's father had been unhappy at what he'd considered the man's unreliability, and there had been an unresolved matter of some missing silverware. Earl Warrington had torn a strip off Wilkes before sending him on his way, but not before, as it happened, Wilkes had stolen the letter. The letter, which, if the contents were to be made public, would provoke a dreadful scandal. His desire to prevent such a scandal wasn't entirely selfless nor was it driven by some deeply rooted sense of morality. It was, simply, Warry's mistake to correct, and he hoped to do that before his own culpability was uncovered.

So he'd come to St. Giles with twenty pounds in his pocket—a vast sum that he was supposed to be setting aside in order to join the Bucknall Club—in order to pay Wilkes off and get the letter back. He only hoped twenty pounds was enough. Wilkes had been cagey in his scant communications. Warry's heart sank as he thought of the club. That was another complication, of course. Hartwell had sponsored Warry for Bucknall's, and while Warry had mistrusted the offer as much as he mistrusted the man himself, he had been desperate to join. After tonight, he would not be able to afford the membership fee. Warry's father had been happy to give him the money, of course, but it wasn't the sort of thing he could ask for twice—at least not without inventing a story about being robbed or some such.

He shivered as he passed between two buildings so tall they blocked out even the scant beams of moonlight that filtered down to the dirty streets. For a moment he was in pitch darkness, and that was when he heard a rush of footsteps and men shouting to one another and then something hard and heavy struck him across the back of the head.

His only thought as he hit the street was that he wouldn't have to lie about being robbed at all, because that was clearly what was happening.

~

Warry woke slowly in an unfamiliar bed in an unfamiliar room with an unfamiliar catalogue of aches and pains clamouring to make themselves known to him. There was, however, at least one very familiar thing about the room: Hartwell. The man was dozing in a chair by Warry's bed, his handsome profile tilted forward as his chin rested on his chest. Grey light came in through the window, and Warry's bleary gaze drank in the aristocratic lines of Hartwell's face. His usually sharp countenance was softened a little by sleep and perhaps too by the unruly curl of dark hair that tumbled down his forehead.

Of all Warry's pain, the worst seemed to be the throbbing ache in his skull. When he lifted a shaking hand to his head, he discovered it was bandaged. He groaned.

Hartwell jolted slightly and awoke.

"Warry," he said, his low voice rough with sleep.

Warry fought the urge to pull the bedcovers up, which was ludicrous because this was Hartwell. He'd fairly grown up with the man, and, besides, he was soon to be Warry's brother-in-law, if Earl Warrington was to be believed. "Where am I?"

"Hartwell House," Hartwell said, which was the residence in Grosvenor Street the Hartwells used while in Town. Warry had often been a guest there, although he had never stayed overnight. The Warringtons had their own house in St. James's Square.

Warry furrowed his brow, and immediately regretted having done so as a spike of pain lanced through his skull. He winced. "But…but how did I get here?"

A soft groan accompanied Hartwell's cat-like stretch. "Apparently you were accosted in St. Giles, had your purse taken and your skull soundly bashed, and cried out my name in your delirium. A pair of mollies brought you here."

"A pair of…" Warry's face grew hot before his aching brain seized on the greater humiliation. "I cried out your name? Balderdash!"

Hartwell regarded him witheringly. "If you can conceive of another reason you might be here, then do feel free to share it."

Warry's jaw worked, but dash it, Hartwell was right. He must have mentioned Hartwell, or how else would anyone have known to bring him there? And his skull must have been cracked like an egg because what on earth would possess him to ask for *Hartwell*? Delirium, indeed.

"I…" he said weakly. "I don't understand." His heart thudded as last night came rushing back to him. Good Lord. Wilkes! Had Wilkes been responsible for the beating last night? Had he thought to take Warry's purse and keep the letter for further extortion? Or had the robbery been an unhappy coincidence, and would Wilkes think Warry had stood him up? What if he had already made public the letter? He tried to push the covers back.

Hartwell's expression sharpened like a hawk's. He leaned

forward, bending his body toward Warry in a way that made Warry shrink back against the pillows. "Well then, that makes two of us. And I for one would very much like to know why the Viscount Warrington was wandering around the St. Giles rookery at midnight, in the company of robbers, mollies, and scoundrels, and how he managed to get his head bashed in."

Warry blinked rapidly. "I…I…How many were there?"

"I'm sorry?"

"Robbers. Did the…the mollies see? Did they see what the fellows looked like?"

"Much as I would have liked to have them to tea, they didn't linger once they'd collected a few shillings for their trouble."

Warry willed himself not to despair. So he had cried out Hartwell's name as he lay in the shit-covered street, then been dragged nearly two miles by a pair of prostitutes, and his ordeal had cost Hartwell several shillings. Not to mention how desperately he needed to make contact with Wilkes or how plain it was that Hartwell was not going to leave him alone until he offered an explanation. "I shall pay you back."

"You're more fool than I thought if you believe that's what I'm concerned about."

That put a halt to Warry's racing mind. That word—*concerned*. The echo of it was there in Hartwell's eyes. To see Hartwell looking so grave, so worried—about *him*—rendered Warry silent once again.

Hartwell stared at him sharply for a moment and then leaned back again, adopting a lazy, relaxed posture and a soft smile that Warry didn't believe for a moment. He shrugged. "Of course it's really none of my business which particular vice you were seeking last night, Warry, although I'm sure Becca will hound you relentlessly until you crumble."

"Becca?" Warry shot a hand out and gripped Hartwell's wrist. He dug his fingers in as fear clawed at him. "No, Hartwell, please! You mustn't tell her! She can't know!"

"Good Lord," Hartwell said. "What *have* you got yourself into, Warry?"

"I…" Warry swallowed, his heart squeezing as he held Hartwell's dark gaze, seeking desperately for any lie he could tell that would get him out of this house and away from Hartwell's scrutiny. Something that Hartwell and Becca might gently mock him for but not *hate* him. Because as much as Warry deserved that hatred, he wasn't sure he could bear it. And as much as he had thought he loathed Hartwell mere hours ago, in this moment, gratitude and perhaps a concussion made him long to believe he looked into the eyes of a friend. He listed his chin as the lie came to him and pushed the words out in a breathy confession. "I…I meant to go gambling."

CHAPTER 2

*H*artwell threw back his head and laughed. "That's it? That's what you nearly ripped my arm off for?" He tucked the arm in question firmly against his side and straightened his cuff. "You thought to visit a gaming hell? Why, just last week I held a Venetian breakfast. I would have invited you if I'd known you were so eager to lose your purse."

Warry's pale cheeks turned a pink that Hartwell could see even in the weak light of dawn, and his hand slipped from Hartwell's wrist. Warry might have grown into a dour figure of late, but underneath it all, the lad really hadn't changed since their childhood. Anytime Hartwell and Becca had attempted, through whispered dares and smothered giggles, to dabble in impropriety—Becca nabbing one of her father's cheroots for them to share; Hartwell blushingly taking down his drawers so that she could see how they differed under their clothes—Warry had eagerly offered to take part as well. But if they dared him—"Go on, Warry, take a suck!", the cheroot, not the other; even Hartwell wasn't so crass—he became red-faced and nearly beside himself, telling them what they were doing was wrong. That they should stop at once.

No wonder his parents had taken to employing him full-time as

Becca's chaperone. He was priggish as a schoolmarm, and it was quite pitiful to see him stammering and near to wetting himself over having so much as *thought* to indulge what was really a very common vice.

Hartwell leaned back and sighed, draping an arm over the back of the chair. The arm that Warry had gripped. Hartwell could still feel the warmth from his palm on his skin. It was startling to realise that the young man—whose hair Hartwell used to tousle and whose back Hartwell used to slap without thought—had become such a stranger that the grip on Hartwell's wrist had given him a jolt. Well. There had been that bit of fun the morning of the Gilmore rout. Those few moments where Warry had seemed himself again, and which seemed so long ago now that Hartwell refused to let himself recall them. Or perhaps it was what had transpired after that he did not wish to recall. "You do know that Becca would congratulate you if you told her you'd gone gambling?"

Warry stared at the bedcovers and didn't speak.

Hartwell softened his tone, though amusement still lingered in it. "It is all right to indulge in the lesser vices, Warry. A game of faro is hardly murder. It is not a sin to enjoy yourself."

Warry nodded ever so slightly, still refusing to meet Hartwell's gaze. While Hartwell had to keep reminding himself to stop thinking of Warry as a lad, it was near impossible not to with Warry huddled in the large bed, clutching the edge of the sheet like a child, his light-brown hair sticking in every direction, and his face…

Well, his face full of bruises, which Hartwell disliked immensely. He straightened, and his tone became clipped. "However, it was enormously bacon-brained of you to choose St. Giles for your first foray into wickedness. There are plenty of respectable hells you might have chosen that wouldn't have put you in the path of scoundrels."

"Do not scold me. I'm not a child." Warry looked up now, and Hartwell received another jolt at the blaze in his eyes.

"I will still scold you when we are old and grey, Warry," Hartwell said with attempted good humour.

Warry's face shuttered. He shifted, twisting the sheet edge around one finger. "I didn't want word to get back to my family. My father has struggled with the vice in the past, and Becca scorns him for it. I did not wish her to scorn me as well."

Hartwell's brow furrowed. "She has never said anything to me about your father's gambling."

"She doesn't tell you everything." There was a bitterness in his tone Hartwell could only wonder at.

That thought badgered him more than he liked to admit. Sometimes—usually late at night, when he couldn't sleep—it occurred to him that Becca was the only person in the world who knew him truly. His parents seemed only to appreciate the idea of him: a strong, strapping son, desired by every young lady of the *ton* and not a few young men, who could provide an heir and do proud the Hartwell line. His friend Lord Christmas Gale was good for a drink or two at Bucknall's or occasional shooting practice, but Gale was a recluse and a misanthrope. Hardly the sort of fellow you confided in. The idea that he was, on some level, alone in the world, save for Becca, was difficult to swallow. And the idea that the same might *not* be true for Becca—that she had others to confide in, including her younger brother—made him, for an instant, uncomfortable.

"Well, then. What do you intend to tell her about this?" He nodded at Warry's bruised face.

"I don't know. I...She'll ask questions."

"And hold your feet to the fire to get answers."

Warry looked up again, and Hartwell found himself absurdly eager to keep Warry's attention on him. He disliked this battered Warry who stared at bedsheets and seemed to have forgotten how to smile or laugh. A memory came to him unbidden: a spring day at the Hartwells' country home. He and Becca were outside behind a large tree, and she'd insisted they practice kissing so they would both know precisely how repulsive an act it was when they were forced to do it one day with their spouses. Warry had of course been idling nearby and eagerly piped up that he wanted to try it too.

"Well, you can't kiss me! I'm your sister," Becca had said in disgust. But then she'd grinned. "You can practice on William."

Hartwell had laughed good-naturedly and pretended to hawk great quantities of saliva into his mouth before pursing his lips and bending toward Warry. He'd assumed Warry would do what he always did—start quivering over the possibility of being caught and refuse to follow through—but to his shock, Warry had strode up to him and planted a kiss on his lips.

To Hartwell's greater shock, he'd suddenly heard his father's rough voice and been yanked away by the arm. He didn't recall what had happened after that; probably his father had blustered about impropriety and how Hartwell mustn't play games like that with other boys. He was an only son, and his focus should be on girls, girls who would grow into wives, wives who would produce heirs…

Hartwell didn't wish to recall the interaction or the kiss, which had been dry and awkward. He had never wished to disappoint his father; indeed, he'd never considered himself the sort of person who could disappoint anyone. That his hesitation to wed rendered him a source of frustration to his parents was troubling in a way he could not quite articulate.

He crossed an ankle over his knee. "I have a proposal. An arrangement that may benefit us both."

Warry leaned back against the pillows but still held himself stiff.

"You may stay here until your bruises fade, and in return, you must help me learn to court your sister."

Warry frowned. "You wish to *court* my sister?"

"Yes," Hartwell said. "There is no need to sound quite so astonished about it. If she and I are to be married, then I must know her as more than simply a friend."

"You're not going to marry her." It was said with a certainty that dug at Hartwell.

"Of course I am. It was all but decided before we were out of leading strings."

Warry wrinkled his nose. "She doesn't want to marry you."

"She said she did yesterday."

"She doesn't want to marry anyone."

"Well, she must. As must I. And so, we will marry each other. That is decided, Warry. That is not what this conversation is about."

"It is now."

This was the Warry Hartwell remembered—an obnoxious little pup, answering back over everything. Hartwell would have carried him outside and dunked him in a pond if he hadn't looked so bruised and pathetic.

"I know nothing of her romantic tastes. We've always avoided talking of such since neither of us…" He shook his head. "Well, we have both, of late, been reminded of our duty, and we have come to an arrangement, but there is no need for that duty to be unpleasant, is there?"

The furrows in Warry's brow seemed in danger of becoming permanent. "You believe I spend my days thinking on how to court my sister?"

Hartwell sighed impatiently. "No, but I know your sister has had admirers, and I'm certain you've seen her reaction to certain types of flowers or…or chocolates or sweet sayings in cards. I want you to teach me what she likes so we might present as a convincing match to Society. And more importantly, to my parents."

He marvelled at just how simple a solution it was. It was as Becca had said: they would feign courtship in front of their parents. They would marry as friends and live their own lives. She would never hold him back from anything he wanted nor he her. He only wished he hadn't been too pig-headed to see it that way in the first place.

"If you're just putting on appearances," Warry said, "surely she can pretend to like any flower."

Hartwell struggled to keep the frustration from his voice. "Well, it's not just pretend now, is it? I love your sister dearly. I wish her to feel I can be a husband to her as well as a friend."

Warry's scowl twitched into a near smile before re-etching itself firmly onto his face. "She's going to laugh at you."

Hartwell couldn't hold back a snort of amusement. "Brat." He stood, stretching, and then winced at the pop of his joints. He noted with some surprise that Warry's gaze dropped to where the tie of Hartwell's dressing gown had loosened. "Of course she will. But when she sees the lengths I have gone to in order to make myself a satisfactory suitor, she will be properly awed."

Now Warry outright snickered, and Hartwell suddenly felt he could sit there all day, trying to make little Joseph Warrington laugh. He reached out to tousle the sandy hair as he had done many times before and halted as Warry flinched away. Hartwell studied the bruises again. Perhaps that was all—Warry flinched because he ached and did not want Hartwell making him ache further.

But a niggling voice in his mind said that perhaps he and Warry had never really been chums. That his only true friend was Rebecca, that she was his sole safeguard against a lifetime of loneliness, and that he must now learn to love her as a wife, even though, in all his unformed daydreams, if he had ever imagined himself with someone by his side at all, it had been a man and not a woman.

"Do not laugh at me, Warry," he said with feigned severity, which only made Warry laugh harder. Hartwell felt a rush of warmth rise up in him, both tender and acute, and for a moment he wished…

But no.

Where on earth had that thought come from?

Even if he had ever thought of Warry as anything but Becca's younger brother, which he most certainly had not, he was an only son. And Warry was an oldest son, and wishes were for children, not for men who had a duty to their families.

CHAPTER 3

The Duke and Duchess of Ancaster, Hartwell's parents, were clearly not in residence since breakfast was held in the drawing room with both Warry and Hartwell in a state of undress. Warry wore a borrowed dressing gown in a rich burgundy brocade. He tied it snugly, a little uncomfortable to be seen in such a manner, even if it was only by Hartwell. Hartwell didn't seem similarly bothered; his dressing gown hung open, revealing his shirt underneath as well as his collarbones and a somewhat shocking glimpse of dark chest hair. Warry wasn't sure why the idea of Hartwell's chest hair was so shocking, and his head was pounding too much to think about it now.

He ate his breakfast—tea and cakes and brioche—and hoped that Hartwell wouldn't tease him any further about gambling. But then perhaps it would be better to be teased about gambling than it would for Hartwell to press him on how best to court Becca. It was ludicrous to think Warry might be in possession of some secret knowledge that Hartwell could use to pry open Becca's heart. Firstly, because Becca didn't have a secret heart at all. She wore it on her sleeve at all times for the sake of convenience. And secondly, because Warry didn't know a deuced thing about courting anyone.

And Hartwell knew Becca at least as well as Warry did. He'd even known her for longer! Warry couldn't imagine that his place as Becca's younger brother had given him any insight into her character that Hartwell didn't already possess.

He pressed his hand to his forehead, feeling the bandage that was wrapped around his skull.

Thinking about Hartwell and Becca marrying was unhappily confusing and made his head ache even more. And yet it strengthened his resolve to see this blackmail business through and to prevent the cloud of scandal from touching either of their families.

He wondered, with a stab of guilt, if he shouldn't have mentioned his father having previously wrestled with gambling debts. Not that Hartwell cared about that, but it was obvious he'd been taken aback when Warry had pointed out that Becca didn't share everything with him. In an attempt to dig himself out of a hole with his lie about seeking out a hell, Warry had unwittingly dug himself another. He'd accidentally struck a nerve when he'd told Hartwell that even Becca had her secrets, and now it seemed Hartwell was determined to know her better and to use that knowledge to court her. What a mess! Warry needed to extricate himself immediately; his life was sticky enough at the moment without adding Hartwell to the mix.

He set his teacup down, and it rattled in the saucer. "I really, um, I really ought to leave. Thank you for your offer, but I cannot continue to impose on your hospitality."

"Really?" Hartwell leaned back in his chair and crooked a brow. "And how shall you explain your bruises to your family?"

"There are other fellows I could stay with," Warry protested feebly because, apart from Lord Balfour—and Warry didn't want to humiliate himself by showing up on Balfour's doorstep looking like a battered peach—he wasn't sure that was true at all. Warry didn't have many close friends, a flaw of character he'd been hoping to correct with a membership to the Bucknall Club.

Hartwell cocked a knowing brow, and Warry wanted to strike

him. It vexed him to no end that Hartwell still had the ability to make him feel like a child. He had been treating Hartwell coldly these last weeks, he knew. Not that Hartwell had noticed. Nor did Warry believe Hartwell had a clue what had sparked Warry's animosity, though Warry recalled the incident with bitter clarity: the Gilmore rout.

The Warringtons had arrived in London two months prior, shortly after the Hartwells. Warry did not know why his family insisted on coming to the city in January. He loved the soft snowfalls that covered their country estate—nothing but white hills for miles, the sound of a branch shifting and cracking under the weight of snow, the winding trail of his own boot prints as he traversed the broad acreage. Winter in London was simply dreary. He was not charmed the way his mother and sister were by the warm lights of the shops nor the Christmas decorations that lingered after the holiday had passed. And while there was the occasional ball or rout to attend before the Season fully got underway, the scant opportunities for socialisation were not worth missing the better part of winter in the country.

Still, he had agreed to attend the Gilmore rout with his mother and sister only a few days after coming to the city. The morning of the rout, Hartwell had been in the Warringtons' drawing room with Warry and Becca, the three of them seated at the Warringtons' large French-style table, and Becca got up to use the privy. Warry's stomach dipped as it did every time he and Hartwell were alone together. He was no longer quite certain what to say around the man. A year or so ago, he would have prattled about anything that came into his head. But they were both gentlemen now, and with adulthood came a level of self-consciousness—a sense that the manners they displayed suddenly mattered more than the content of their speech. "The Clarks' goat has colic," he remarked. "They wrote me two days past. She's such a sweet thing. I would be there helping with her if I weren't here in the city. I hope she pulls through."

Hartwell shot him a look from under dark brows. "Let us hope so," he said drily. "I can imagine no greater tragedy than a dead goat. Unless of course it has sacrificed its life to provide my meat."

Warry ducked his head, chest swelling with anger. He had invited Hartwell's sarcasm as he had many times before. When would he learn? Hartwell did not care for the things he cared for.

"It is not a tragedy. Goats are only dumb animals," Warry said sharply, though it broke his heart to say it.

Hartwell glanced up from his attempt to shine the buttons of his waistcoat on his sleeve. "You do not believe that." His face bore no smile, and yet there was a gentle amusement in his eyes.

Warry shrugged. "It is true, is it not?"

"But you do not believe it."

He frowned. If he admitted he did not believe it, would Hartwell fire whatever arrow he had nocked? Taunt him mercilessly until Warry felt small and stupid?

"I do like her," Warry said softly.

Hartwell shook his head slightly and went back to his buttons.

Warry had felt foolish and resolved never to speak to Hartwell again. He resolved to remember that it was Hartwell who was only a dumb animal, and the Clarks' goat was a beautiful soul who did not deserve to suffer with colic.

Hartwell deserved to suffer with colic. Relentlessly.

"I hope she recovers." Hartwell spoke quietly.

Warry stared at him, and eventually Hartwell looked up again.

"You told me about their stomachs, once," Hartwell remarked. "Goats. They have four. Something happens in one of the stomachs that makes them belch."

Warry huffed a laugh, surprised Hartwell had remembered. "Yes. Almost as loudly as you." He surprised himself with the words, and waited apprehensively see how they'd be received.

To his delight, Hartwell laughed—that loud, cracking laugh Warry had always loved. He used to tease Hartwell without a thought. Once he'd gained enough years to hold his own against the older boy, he'd given as good as he got, and they'd often found themselves in rapid-fire verbal sparring matches that had Becca cuffing the backs of both their heads in exasperation. But he hadn't felt such camaraderie with Hartwell in some time.

"Come here." Hartwell gestured him closer, as though he wished to tell Warry a secret.

"No." Warry's lips twitched.

"Come on. I need to tell you something."

"No!"

"Why not?"

"Because I am going to lean close to you and you're going to belch in my ear."

Hartwell clapped a hand to his chest as though pained. "Warry! You wound me. I would never."

"You would, and you will."

Hartwell stood, and Warry fairly leapt to his feet. He was aware of his precarious position at the side of the table farthest from the door. If he tried to bolt around the table in either direction, Hartwell, faster than he, would likely catch him. "Hartwell…" he said warningly, gasping a laugh as Hartwell took a step to one side and Warry to the other.

"What?" Hartwell said innocently. "Warry, all I want is to tell you something very important. Won't you come here?"

"No!"

Warry hesitated for a few seconds and then bolted to his right. When Hartwell lunged, he turned and ran the opposite way. But Hartwell was ready for the move and caught his wrist as he passed, pulling Warry's back against his chest. Warry struggled so hard they knocked into the table, nearly upsetting an elegant centrepiece of pine and holly. Hartwell put his mouth to Warry's ear and let out a long, loud belch.

"Hartwell!" Warry shouted, trying ineffectually to elbow him before collapsing against the other man, breathless with laughter.

Hartwell's own laughter was in his ear, their bodies shaking against one another.

"What, precisely, is going on here?" Becca enquired mildly from the doorway.

"Your *friend*—" Warry finally wrenched free of Hartwell's grasp and staggered away. "Is a boor!"

Hartwell was fairly in tears from laughing, bracing himself on the back of a chair, and the sight caused Warry to start up again too.

"Warry brought up goat belching," Hartwell managed at last.

"I did *not*! For once, it wasn't me talking of goat belching."

Becca shook her head. "He is a boor," she agreed, going to Hartwell and jostling him lightly by the shoulder. "We are going to be late to the Gilmores' if you do not get hold of yourself. William!" At that sharp but affectionate use of his given name, Hartwell straightened abruptly, wiping beneath his eyes with his thumb. Becca took his arm. And in that moment, Warry could not have been happier. Things felt just as they used to.

"Ohhhh…" Hartwell's sigh was high-pitched with the vestiges of amusement. "That was good fun." He grinned at Warry, a huge, open grin. "Come on, pup. Your sister wants to go to the rout."

"I certainly do not!" Becca insisted. "But we must."

As Warry stared at Becca and Hartwell's linked arms, as "pup" echoed in his mind, his good spirits faded. His sister and Hartwell both looked so grown-up in their fine clothes. They touched each other with such familiarity, the two of them sparkling with confidence. Yet Warry was still "pup" to Hartwell—a term that, in the past, he'd sometimes enjoyed but that today sapped the mirth from him. He could not have back the childhood he missed. And going forward, he did not know what, precisely, he desired. He only knew there was a sudden ache in the pit of his stomach that felt like hunger, and a fear that his heart would always be wanting.

Becca and Hartwell left the room together, Becca feigning to chide Hartwell for his behaviour, while he issued overly serious apologies that he did not mean in the least. Warry stood there, watching them go.

Two hours later, he'd entered the Gilmore rout in a sour mood. It was an intimate affair held in the Gilmores' pale-blue drawing room. The food was mediocre and every conversation tepid. His mother kept nudging him toward the middle Gilmore daughter, who sat sullenly and picked at a cabbage roll and seemed to wish an end to the event with a fervour even greater than Warry's.

"She is rich, and her nose is not too large. In fact, it may rather be too small," his mother had whispered to him. His mother had quite a fascination with people's noses. He sometimes wondered idly what she thought of his own.

"This will be our Warry's second Season," his mother announced to a gaggle of women. "He was out last year but found himself a bit overwhelmed by the social whirl. He has gained a great deal of confidence this year and is ready to make a match."

It was the sort of bald-faced lie a Tattersall's auctioneer might tell about a bone-setter on the block. *He's as sound as they come! Be the name on everyone's lips as this high-stepper carries your chaise through Hyde Park.* Warry had not gained much of anything, except for a disagreeableness he was fairly certain he had not possessed last year. He did not know what was the matter with him, only that everything seemed so suddenly strange. One moment, he had been a child, playing happily in ponds and mud puddles, rolling down hills, attempting to ride the neighbour's cow, Freda. Hartwell and Becca had been right there with him, their gay laughter carried by the breeze in the summer and ringing out across the white world in the winter, as fine and lovely as the ice crystals that clung to branches. Now, all anyone seemed to talk about was making matches. Boys whom Warry had grown up around suddenly cared about the cut of their coats and what style knot to use for their cravats. Girls who had loved books and ponies now talked of nothing but their gowns. Even Becca and Hartwell, who had no interest in marriage, began rejecting his pleas to go out exploring, to play games.

Those two now spent their time talking, and Warry was bored of their conversations. With each year that had passed since Becca came out, the Warringtons had grown more fretful. "How has she not made a match yet?" he'd overheard his mother say to his father one night. "There is nothing wrong with her. She's quite handsome, has charming manners when she chooses to apply them, and her nose is so very pert."

"She has too much wit," Earl Warrington had replied. "Men do not like such wit in a woman."

"It's because she spends all her time with William Hartwell. I thought it a good thing at first, for I assumed the young man would have proposed to her by now. But he does not seem inclined to, and she seems quite content to wait."

"Let her wait."

"She is three-and-twenty!"

Half listening to his mother prattle on about how eager he was to make a match of his own as she attempted to gracefully steer the conversation away from her unmarried eldest daughter, Warry had glanced across the room. And there was Lord Balfour.

Tall, commanding, with that unnerving smoothness to both his look and his manner, he seemed a cut above everyone else at the party. Warry had thought how much easier life would be if he were such a man. Someone who could take charge of a conversation, whom others flocked to, as a group was now flocking to Balfour. Lord Balfour, it was said, had a fine sky-blue curricle pulled by a pair of matched grey horses. His waistcoats were always immaculately fitted and vivid without being garish. His shoes were as shiny as his handsome face.

There was another facet to Warry's desire beyond the need to imitate Balfour. Warry either didn't understand it at the time or was afraid that he very much did understand it, and he found himself drifting away from his mother and her audience, heading toward Balfour's crowd.

Balfour, remarking on the conformation of one of his horses, looked up and caught Warry's eye. He smiled, making his dark eyes appear kind. After holding court a bit longer, Balfour announced that he should like to go out onto the terrace. "It will be cold, yes, but there is no sight I like better than fresh snow."

Warry was the only one who volunteered to accompany him.

They stayed outside until Warry's fingers were numb and red, and there they spoke of many things. Warry was amazed at how Balfour seemed to have a solution to any perplexity of life that might discommode an English gentleman. The advice he gave, unsolicited but wholly welcome, made Warry feel that perhaps there was a future for him that wouldn't be all misery. Balfour spoke of playing the 'change, how rewarding it was, and what a generous sum a man might rake in by investing smartly. "It is our duty as gentlemen to envision what we want from life…and take it." Even the snap of Balfour's fingers impressed Warry because his own fingers were too numb to snap. "It is true, Warrington, that he who hesitates is lost." He looked Warry up and down appraisingly. "An exceedingly handsome fellow such as yourself should not be so meek."

Warry was surprised, for he had not yet heard Balfour remark on any subject but himself. Any anecdote recounted, any piece of gossip spilled, and Balfour could twist it to relate to his own life. Yet he did it in such an engaging way that Warry did not mind at all listening to his tales. Yet now Balfour's focus was entirely on him. Perhaps the only person's focus that had ever been entirely his.

And Balfour had called him handsome.

He suddenly could not feel the cold at all.

"I require no Spanish coin," he said softly.

"I pay you none. You are truest, purest gold, Joseph."

Warry turned to him, startled. He could not believe the man knew his full name. "I go by Warry."

"That is a child's name, and you are not a child."

Warry hardly dared breathe.

"Nobody ever seems to notice me," he said at last, aware of his own pitiful hope that this admission would spur Balfour to further compliments. Some part of him recalled the feel of Hartwell's arms around him hours ago, the two of them breathless with amusement. But he recalled even more sharply the way Hartwell had called him pup and left the room arm in arm with Becca.

"Isn't that a shame?" There was a tenderness in Balfour's dark eyes that Warry had not been expecting. It made him warmer still. "I can teach you to be noticed. It is not difficult. There are only a few simple tricks a man must learn in order to master those around him."

Balfour reached out and tucked a bit of Warry's hair behind his ear, letting his fingers linger for just a moment. Warry felt a surge of heat between his legs so powerful that he momentarily feared himself ill. But he was not ill. No, he had suddenly become party to the greatest secret in all the world. Were there others out there who knew what it was to be looked at the way Balfour was looking at him, or was he singularly lucky? And then he glanced to the side, through the glass in the doors, and saw Hartwell seated at a table inside, staring at him. Becca was nowhere in sight, and Hartwell's stare was so intense—brows lowered, an unbecoming twist to his mouth—Warry wondered that it didn't somehow shatter the glass that separated them.

Warry felt such pleasure then. Hartwell thought him a pup, still trailing behind the him and Becca, begging scraps of affection? Well, which of them was sitting alone, scowling, gripping his punch glass so tightly it was as if he hoped to crush it to powder, and which of them held the undivided attention of a peer of the realm? He turned back to Balfour, bowing his head slightly. "I should like to learn your secrets, my lord." He could not resist one more glance inside at Hartwell, who had turned away and was gazing at something Warry could not see, his jaw firmly set.

Later, preparing to leave, Warry found himself jostled into a group consisting of Hartwell and a few of Hartwell's chums. One of them commented on the length of time Warry had spent on the terrace with Balfour, and Warry felt grim satisfaction at the sudden colour in Hartwell's face. He wanted desperately for Hartwell to know that he was capable of making the acquaintance of a true gentleman. That he and Lord Balfour were thick as thieves now. And who did Hartwell count as friends? A handful of overgrown children, like Hartwell himself.

Hartwell cuffed him smartly on the back of his head. "What were you thinking, spending a whole afternoon outside in the freezing cold with Lord Balfour?"

Warry's satisfaction fled, replaced by the familiar beginnings of embarrassment. Hartwell was not impressed by his new acquaintance—quite the opposite.

Hartwell's friend Stevens laughed and said, "He could not hear enough about Lord Balfour's prize stallions."

Hartwell grinned. "Was that it, Warry? Were you asking Balfour about stud fees so that you might be bred to one of his stallions? You do love livestock so." It was by far the cruellest thing Hartwell had ever said to him, and Warry stopped to let the group pass around him, burning with shame and anger. Hartwell had, in the past, called him a pest, a pup, a fool. Had thrown him into ponds, had attempted to lose him in the woods after spinning tales of witches who snatched children. Had only hours ago belched in his ear. But he had never humiliated Warry so thoroughly nor so publicly.

Hartwell and his friends had gone off laughing, and Warry had stood there, unable to move, until his mother had taken his arm, still chattering, and walked out with him.

Warry shook himself back into the present, where Hartwell was staring at him oddly. "Come, Warry. Is the prospect of staying here really so awful? Let me do the chaperoning for once." He slapped the table twice with his palm. "Now. Tell me something about your sister that I don't know."

Warry choked on a piece of honey cake that had chosen that moment to lodge itself in his throat. "I...I am sure there's nothing you don't know about Becca, Hartwell."

It sounded like a lie even to his own burning ears, but perhaps he was so awkward and hopeless all the time Hartwell didn't note it. If only he could excuse himself without seeming ungrateful, then he could go and send a message to Wilkes.

Hartwell brushed a dark curl off his forehead. "Well, there must be something. I'm sure even Becca has hidden depths beyond her desire to go about putting frogs in fellows' shirts."

"You are more her friend than I," Warry said mulishly.

"She loves you a great deal," Hartwell replied with more honesty than Warry was expecting. "I believe there are things she would sooner confide to you than me."

Warry stared at his plate. Something must be wrong with the cakes, for his stomach was ailing him.

"She likes cake," he blurted.

Hartwell blinked. "Well, yes. I know that. She always has done. Who doesn't?"

Warry shook his head, searching for something that might stand a chance of surprising Hartwell and ending this wretched exchange.

"She loves books." He spoke even louder.

"Yes, I know that too."

"No, I mean...she likes a certain kind of book." Warry shifted uncomfortably. "She likes novels."

"Novels!" Hartwell looked both delighted and scandalised. "How dreadful! Your parents must be horrified."

"They don't know," Warry said. "And you mustn't tell them. Father says novels rot the brain, and women, especially, shouldn't read them. But Becca hides them under her bed."

"This is delightful!" Hartwell exclaimed. "It's exactly what I needed to know. I shall go to a bookshop and buy her as many novels as I can carry! What sort does she like? The ones where good-hearted parlour maids are seduced by evil lords of the realm and fling themselves off bridges into the Thames in paroxysms of sorrowful regret?" His brow creased. "*Is* there another sort?"

"There is…another sort. That she has…has read."

Hartwell crooked a brow again. "Go on."

"A series of books…that she likes."

"Warry, what are these books?"

"The, um." His voice dropped very low, and he spoke directly to the table. "*The Maiden Diaries.*"

"*The Maiden Diaries?*" Hartwell exclaimed. "Isn't it rumoured that a young lady can be robbed of her maidenhead simply by reading those?"

Warry squeaked. "Do not say that!"

"Forgive me, but you've just told me that Becca has read *The Maiden Diaries.*"

"I should not have said anything. She does not want anybody to know."

"Yes, well, you *did* say something."

"I know, but I should not have."

Hartwell's eyes narrowed slyly. "Have *you* read these monstrosities, Warry?"

"No!" Surely Hartwell couldn't think—"Of course not!"

"No? Never picked up a copy when she wasn't around and just…had a look?"

"I certainly have not!"

"Aha! I know you too well. You cannot lie to me." Hartwell's eyes gleamed. "Now, tell me, which was your favourite part?"

Warry opened and closed his mouth like a fish drowning on land, at once overwhelmed by images of the scene in the duchess's library where the maiden in question had a rendezvous with a dark-haired rake—in his mind, the fellow suddenly looked a lot like Hartwell—who hoisted her onto the desk and had his way with her;

a scenario which very much supported Warry's father's belief that reading novels led inevitably to moral depravity. "I would n-not...I would not *ever*!"

Hartwell was suddenly by his side, gripping his elbow firmly, and Warry realised that he had, without thinking, tried to stand, only to find his legs unwilling to support him. "Easy there." The teasing was gone from Hartwell's voice.

Warry braced himself on the table, his knees shaking. "There is something wrong with the brioche."

"Ah, is that it?" Hartwell said wryly. The other man guided him out from the table and supported him as they left the drawing room, Warry clinging to Hartwell like some swooning maiden—*no, do not think of maidens*—and terribly aware of how the weight of his body pulled Hartwell's shirt down further, exposing fully the patch of chest hair. The rest of Hartwell's chest, Warry noticed as his eyes flicked unbidden to Hartwell's torso, appeared smooth and extremely well muscled.

He endured the warmth and hardness of Hartwell's body against his as they went up the stairs. He tried once to protest that he could walk by himself, but as the corners of his vision were blackening and he was very much in danger of losing his breakfast, his words lacked conviction.

He sank onto the cool sheets gratefully, his head pounding. Hartwell pulled the bedclothes over him, pausing for a moment to eye where Warry's dressing gown fell open at the waist. Understanding seemed to dawn in his eyes as Warry received another rush of sickening shame. He did not know how to rid himself of his affliction, and now that Hartwell had seen…

"That brioche must have been rather something," Hartwell murmured, and Warry wished nothing more than to disappear from the earth. He braced himself for further teasing or perhaps condemnation, but Hartwell simply tugged the covers up until they hid his disgrace. "There now. Would tea help? Water? I am at your disposal."

Warry squeezed his eyes shut for a moment. Water might help his headache, but it could do nothing for his immortal soul. "No. I am fine. Merely overtired. I do not understand myself."

"You've had your skull bashed pretty thoroughly. Of course you are not feeling quite the thing." Hartwell patted him through the blankets and offered a slight grin, though his eyes held the same concern from earlier. "And not another word of argument against staying with me. You will remain in this bed until you are quite yourself. And you will ring if you need anything at all. Is that understood?"

Warry tried to nod, but pain ripped through his head. "Yes." Anything to get Hartwell out of the room.

"Warry…" Hartwell sounded hesitant. "Be well," he said finally. "When you are recovered, I shall take you to that gaming hell, and we shall practice sinning together."

It was, perhaps, the worst thing Hartwell could have said. But hearing the smile in the man's words, Warry was filled with a warmth that wasn't entirely shame. He did not respond, and after another moment, Hartwell drew the curtains and left the room.

He lay in bed for a while, attempting to recover his composure.

Practice sinning together.

A flash of the maiden in the library, her legs splayed, the dark-haired rake between them. He widened his own legs under the covers.

No. No, no, no, you must not. He concentrated on his breathing. The rake's shirt was open, revealing a patch of chest hair.

No, you fool.

One breath in. One breath out. He lost himself in the cool darkness of the room.

His stomach had settled somewhat, as had…the other thing. And when he felt sure he could stand, he climbed out of bed and went in search of a quill and paper.

CHAPTER 4

*H*artwell made his way to The Temple of the Muses in Finsbury Square. He wasn't sure how, precisely, one went about discretely acquiring a copy of a novel that could allegedly damn your soul within three pages, but the Temple seemed as though it must carry every book in the world.

There wasn't much that could make Hartwell blush, but the thought of paying for his purchase and waiting as it was wrapped in brown paper had his cheeks a bit hot. At least the mere existence of the book didn't send him into convulsions as it did Warry.

He didn't know when little Joseph Warrington had become such a staunch protector of moral certitude, but Hartwell did have the comfort of knowing that Warry had without a doubt at least skimmed Rebecca's copy of *The Maiden Diaries* if not actually read it. The fellow's cockstand had proved as much, Hartwell thought, fighting a smile. There was hope for the young prig yet.

He found that even when he tried to think of his house guest with annoyance, a certain amount of sympathy rose in him. He disliked seeing Warry unwell, and it enraged him to think of him being maltreated. Still, there was something a bit odd about the pup's story of wanting to gamble. If one wished to dabble in sin for the first time, one did not go straight to St. Giles. Surely one had the sense to start in a place of moderate repute.

Well, Warry had never been much for sense.

Ah, no. What a lie that was. Warry had always possessed far more sense than he himself. Which was what made the whole St. Giles business so *strange*.

He entered the shop and had to confess himself impressed by the floor-to-ceiling shelves of books. He wasn't much of a reader himself. He was only going to make an attempt at perusing *The Maiden Diaries* to better understand Becca and her desires. And yet part of him was mildly intrigued. He had listened to—and sung— his share of bawdy songs, but he had never read anything salacious. If the perking of Warry's pipe in response to a simple conversation about the book was any indication, Hartwell might wish to shut himself away in his bedroom to, ah…enjoy the fine work of literature.

"Hartwell!" A voice called out. He recognised the deep, perpetually sombre tone, and turned with a grin. His friend Lord Christmas Gale stood at a nearby shelf with a couple of volumes in hand.

Hartwell approached. "Gale! You old bastard."

"What are you doing here? I didn't know you could read."

"Aren't you amusing?"

"Rarely." Gale's world-weary countenance suggested he'd neither amused or been amused in all his five-and-twenty years. But Hartwell knew better.

Christmas Gale was a curious fellow with a dour expression that belied his merry name—probably the reason he practised it. His name, a legacy of having been born on Christmas Day, was the least odd thing about him. Gale had a knack for getting himself involved in mysteries. Whether it was a missing handkerchief or a lost child—Hartwell's opinion on which was more tragic would not endear him to any mothers—Gale could be relied upon to solve the thing before too long. It wasn't as though Gale wanted to solve mysteries, or even seemed to enjoy it, but for some reason they were drawn to him in the way cats were drawn to people who hated them.

"Are you working on a case?"

"For pity's sake, Hartwell, do not phrase it that way. I am not some brooding investigator out of a cheap novel."

"But you are investigating?"

"I am doing research."

"And that is all you will say?"

"You were missed at Bucknall's last night." Gale shifted the subject, his brow creasing in what Hartwell knew was curiosity rather than disapproval. Hartwell would have lived at Bucknall's if the club allowed.

"Yes," he said. "I had an unexpected guest."

He wondered if he ought to tell Gale about Warry's brush with danger in St. Giles, but decided that no, Warry was a mystery he would rather like to attempt to untangle himself. He stared off into the middle distance for a moment as visions of untangling Warry assailed him. Most of them involved Warry being ensnared in bedclothes. Good Lord, what had become of him? It had been too long since he'd shared his bed with anyone, clearly. He tried to think of Becca in the same way, all tangled hair and heaving bosom, but the picture wasn't as alluring. Probably because Becca would never get herself tangled in bedclothes to begin with, and if she did, she'd slap his hands away if he tried to assist. He wondered if the heroine of *The Maiden Diaries* was so damnably competent. He doubted it.

"A guest?" Gale raised a single brow in question.

"Yes," Hartwell said. "You know little Warry? The Viscount Warrington, I should say. Becca's brother. He's staying with me."

"How very risqué," Gale said, tapping his fingers over the cover of the topmost book on the pile he was holding.

"Hardly," Hartwell said airily. "I'm courting his sister, after all. Well, I shall be, all things going to plan."

"In my experience, things rarely go to plan."

"I rather think my life is infinitely less complicated than yours, my dear Gale."

Gale shrugged. "He's unmarried, though, isn't he?"

"Warry? Yes. And an oldest son, like me."

Gale nodded his understanding. While marriage between younger sons of the peerage was encouraged in many cases to curtail an excess of lesser heirs who might prove burdensome to a thinly spread inheritance, older sons were expected to wed women and continue the family line. It had been made very clear to Hartwell from the time he was a lad that he would marry a woman, and he expected Warry had been told the same. Not that there was any reason to place marriage in the same thought as Warry. Gale's intimations annoyed him. What indication had he ever given—either to Gale or to that darkened corner of his mind that kept him supplied with carnal fantasies—that he had the slightest interest in Warry?

"Well, then. Courting his sister, hmm? Congratulations on finally giving the *ton* the show they paid for."

"I'm actually here on account of Becca."

"Oh, aren't you dashedly sweet. Don't tell me she's a reader of novels? She seems like she would be."

He leaned closer to his friend. "I'm looking for one novel in particular, but it's a bit…I'm not sure where to find it."

"You might ask the seller."

"I would rather not."

Gale's surprisingly soft eyes met his with no little interest. "Oh?"

"You see, Becca has been reading"—he lowered his voice and glanced around—"*The Maiden Diaries*."

"Oh my. Naughty girl."

"Well, she's not. She's a very good-hearted girl from an excellent family, and I'll thank you not to cast judgement on my intended. But yes, it seems she is a devotee of the books."

"And you think I might know where to locate the latest volume?"

"Well...actually, I don't know if she's read the latest. I don't know how many there are or—Are there many of them? Volumes, I mean?"

"There are four thus far. With a fifth rumoured to be in the works. The author is, as you might expect, that noble friend of societies far and wide, Anonymous."

"*Four*! How does one...I mean, how much is there to say on the subject of...whatever the subject is, exactly?"

"The subject is a rake by the name of Slyfeel. His arms are as thickly muscled as a horse's hindquarters, and something else of his is comparable to a horse's as well."

"Gale. We cannot discuss this here."

"Would you like me to stop?"

"No, I must know more."

"Well, he is a cad and a bit of a scoundrel. But he is well versed in the art of pleasing the ladies. And the gentlemen. Really everyone. There is no one he has not pleased."

"You've read these books?"

"I have browsed them."

Hartwell was more flummoxed than he wished to admit. "Do you think this is what Becca desires in a husband? Strong...horse arms? And a...well versedness in pleasing?"

"Not in a husband, perhaps, but in a lover, certainly."

Hartwell felt a bit queasy. He'd rarely been the jealous type, but he suddenly wanted very much to challenge this fictional Slyfeel to a duel. One could fire a pistol just as well with regular arms as one could with horse arms, he imagined.

Gale studied him. "Do you wish me to lead you to these soul damners?"

He struggled to recover himself. "What I thought I might do was buy volume one for myself. To get a taste of it, as it were, and to perhaps better know her mind. In matters of"—he lowered his voice again—"lovemaking."

"I see."

"So do you…ah…know where I might—"

Gale sighed. "Come with me."

Twenty minutes later, Hartwell walked out of the shop with a brown paper package under his arm. He realised he was actually quite looking forward to getting home to Warry. He was nearly there when another familiar voice, far sweeter than Gale's, called out, "Halloooo! My lord!"

He stopped and turned with a smile. Becca looked lovely in pale blue, carrying a white parasol. She was accompanied by several of her cousins, a beautiful bevy of fluttering butterflies, including, or perhaps especially, Morgan Notley. Notley hadn't made his debut into Society yet, but Hartwell had heard there were already several distinguished peers counting down on their calendars until that auspicious day.

"Good day," Hartwell said, giving a practised bow.

The girl cousins twittered. Notley looked bored to death.

"Have you been in the Temple, Hartwell?" Becca asked curiously. "Good Lord, I didn't know you read."

"We all have our secrets," Hartwell said, peering at her closely in a vain attempt to discern if that was a blush turning her cheeks a pretty pink or just the bite of the cool air.

"That we do," Becca agreed and linked her arm through his.

Such a display of familiarity was hardly appropriate in the middle of the street, but Becca had never stood much on ceremony, and Hartwell supposed that they would be officially courting soon in any case.

They walked along.

Becca lowered her voice so her cousins did not hear her. "Father received a message this morning saying Warry is staying at your house. Did he really get so terribly drunk last night at Bucknall's that he can't face our parents?"

"What? No!" Hartwell gave a guilty start, remembering that he'd offered to sponsor Warry's membership at Bucknall's and had then forgotten all about it again. Clearly Warry hadn't if he'd used it as an alibi. "Why, it's nothing like that at all. You know what a dull scholar Warry is. I'm having him help to organise Father's library, that's all. It hasn't been touched in years, so it's rather an ambitious undertaking."

Becca slapped him on the wrist. "The library! But, William, I'm a far better candidate to assist than Warry!"

Not with the sort of books she liked to read, Hartwell imagined. The dry histories and collections of stale poetry in his father's library would bore her to tears. They'd always had that effect on Hartwell.

"Well," she said, without waiting for his answer, "I shall pay you both a visit after luncheon."

"No!" The word was loud enough to catch the attention of the cousins, and Becca narrowed her eyes at him suspiciously. "It's…it's a surprise," he finished lamely.

"Why would your organising the duke's library be a surprise for me?"

Hartwell unlinked his arm from hers and tried for a charming smile. "Why, if I was to tell you that, it would no longer be a surprise."

Becca narrowed her eyes. "William, if Warry is too ill after a night of drinking at Bucknall's, you could just tell me, you know. I wouldn't tease him too terribly."

Hartwell blinked. Yes, that was definitely the lie he ought to have gone with.

"I would never lie to you," he lied. He bowed again. "Good day, Lady Rebecca." And to the cousins, "Good day."

And then he fled before Becca demolished the last of his composure.

CHAPTER 5

By the end of his third day at Hartwell House, Warry was champing at the bit to get out, not least of all because he had finally received a response from Wilkes. Hartwell, upon spotting the letter on the tray, had asked if it was from his family, and Warry had been grateful for Hartwell's preoccupation with his own affairs, for Warry had only been required to murmur a noncommittal response.

Warry had made no mention of the robbery in his correspondence, offering only an apology that he had been detained on his way to their meeting and stating that he wished to set up another —*Would the Four-in-Hand do?* That was the gaming hell Hartwell had agreed to take him to. He hadn't been certain Wilkes would go for it, as Hartwell had described the Four-in-Hand as a moderately reputable establishment where Warry and his bruises were unlikely to be recognised, and Warry pictured Wilkes lurking in the shadows of the city's underbelly, unwilling to venture so far into the light. But Wilkes had agreed to the meeting time and place.

Warry was in his bedroom—well, Hartwell's guest bedroom—studying his bruises in the vanity mirror and plotting how to best lose Hartwell once they were at the hell, when there was a rap on his door.

"Yes?"

The door opened, and Hartwell stood there, looking as though he'd seen a spectre.

"Are you well?" Warry asked.

Hartwell nodded. A small jerk of his head at first and then a more extensive nod. His face was white as the curtains but for two splotches of bright red high on his cheeks. "Yes. I was just doing a bit of reading."

"I didn't know you read."

"Why does everyone keep saying that? Of course I read."

"What were you reading?"

"That is none of your concern!" Hartwell said with far more volume than Warry thought the situation called for. The man drew in a deep breath. "I was just going through some books in my father's library. Which I am organising. And you are organising. We are organising it for Becca. As a surprise."

Warry frowned. "For Becca?"

"Yes."

"I have seen your father's library. She would not like the books in it."

"Well, I suppose that's what makes it such a surprise. Why would we organise it for her if its contents are not at all to her taste? Most unexpected."

"You are acting very strangely."

"Am I?"

"I don't particularly wish to organise your father's library."

Hartwell took a few steps into the room. Warry studied their reflections in the mirror. Hartwell wore a splendid gold brocade waistcoat and a dark-blue velvet coat. His cravat was pinned with a cameo brooch. "Fortunately for you, that is only what I told Becca to keep her from coming here to visit you." He seemed about to come closer, then hesitated.

"So you…were or were not in your father's library?"

"I do not know," Hartwell said faintly, his expression many miles away.

It was unlike Hartwell to appear anything but cocksure. If he was not himself, then he had Warry's sympathy. But this could work to his advantage. "You need not accompany me tonight if you are unwell. I'm certain I shall be fine on my own."

"Of course I'm coming! I am fit as a fiddle. In fact, I came in here to bring you this." He held up a small, pearl-coloured pot. "White paint. This should hide the bruises well enough." He at last came to stand by Warry. "I could help you put it on."

Warry was unsure why he nodded, and equally unsure why Hartwell had offered. Surely Warry could apply paint to his own face? But neither of them commented on the absurdity of the exchange. Rather, Warry turned to Hartwell, who unscrewed the lid of the pot. "My mother's," Hartwell explained brusquely as he dipped his finger into the paint. "She refuses to accept that fashions are changing and insists on appearing as pale as Marie Antoinette in public." He took Warry's jaw in his other hand, and Warry promptly forgot how to breathe. "Marie Antoinette several days after death, actually."

Hartwell dabbed at his forehead. His hands smelled of bergamot, and his touch was sure. When Warry finally did draw a breath, the sound of it was unsteady.

"Does it hurt?" Hartwell frowned in concern.

"No," Warry replied softly.

"This isn't doing the job quite so well as I'd hoped." Hartwell tilted Warry's chin this way and that, studying his handiwork. Warry tried not to focus on how his stomach fluttered with each movement or how Hartwell's release of his jaw seemed a tragedy on par with the king's descent into madness.

He turned to the mirror and burst out laughing.

"Oh, come! It isn't so bad."

"Now I look like a ghost who was beaten and robbed."

"You mock my efforts, brat!" Hartwell was grinning.

Warry grew so warm inside it seemed the result of some conjurer's trick—surely one could not feel so light and alive merely through sharing a jest with a friend. *Former* friend, Warry reminded himself, though the sour thought could find no foothold amid his mirth.

He touched the white paint that had turned his spectacularly purple bruises to a pasty grey. He pressed his lips together, but another laugh escaped.

"Perhaps you need more." Hartwell dipped his finger again and cupped Warry's face, this time applying the paint using their reflections in the mirror. On an impulse, Warry turned his head to the side and made as if to bite Hartwell's finger.

"Oy!" Hartwell pulled his finger back but kept his other hand on Warry's cheek. "I'm trying to help."

"Let me do you, then we'll match." Whatever giddy impulse had got hold of Warry, he was grateful to it when Hartwell barked a loud, clear laugh. He grabbed the pot from Hartwell and rose, dipping his finger into the paint.

"I have a reputation to uphold," Hartwell protested, stepping back.

"And I do not?" Warry stepped forward and smeared a line of paint down Hartwell's nose, noting that Hartwell made no real effort to escape. He caught Warry's wrists and pushed him back gently, and they remained like that for a moment.

Hartwell exhaled softly, his thumbs pressing into Warry's wrists before his grip loosened—though he did not let go altogether. "You are such a quiet little mouse. Nobody will pay any mind to what you look like."

Warry's mood darkened at the conviction in Hartwell's tone. Hartwell may have thought to tease, but Warry knew he meant the words. With a sickening jolt, Warry recalled Hartwell's laughter as he'd mocked Warry at the Gilmore rout. If Warry were a better friend, then perhaps he would have forgiven Hartwell—

but if Hartwell were a better friend, then he should have apologised.

He tugged free of Hartwell's grip.

Hartwell wrinkled his nose theatrically, swiping at the paint. Warry's breath caught. No, perhaps Hartwell was not really a friend to him, but the ache inside Warry was such that he allowed himself to pretend, at least for the moment. He reached out and put another smear of paint across Hartwell's chiselled face, then laughed and ducked when Hartwell reached out and smacked him lightly, teasingly, on the side of the head.

"Well," Hartwell said a moment later as they stared at their twin ghostly faces in the mirror. Warry had painted Hartwell thoroughly, and in return, Hartwell had added another layer over Warry's bruised skin. "If the idea is not to attract attention, I'd say we've certainly destroyed any hope of that."

Warry couldn't help his smile. "Aren't we handsome, though?"

"Well, you know, I suppose we are."

Their shoulders touched. Warry quite liked them being that close. As a child, he'd often imagined what it would be like to have Hartwell's full attention, and for a reason other than to be teased or scolded by the older boy. Now, he could feel how sharp the air was between them, crackling with warmth. If this was pretending, then what joys must true friendship hold?

Hartwell glanced at him. "Our cravats should match as well. It will complete the vision. Let me get you a pin."

He squeezed Warry's shoulder lightly before leaving the room. Warry gave a long sigh. Grinned at his reflection in the glass. So very recently he'd been the sullen, awkward Viscount Warrington, good for nothing but following along behind bolder, handsomer peers. Now here he was, about to enter his first gaming hell and meet the blackmailer who sought to ruin his family. He feared scandal above anything, to be sure, but perhaps with Hartwell by his side, this night would take on an air of adventure. And he would not be quite so frightened when it came time to do the difficult part.

∽

*A*s promised, the Four-in-Hand was neither ostentatious nor shabby. Its patrons were deeply engrossed in their various card games, and most spared not a glance for Warry and Hartwell and their unnatural pallor.

Warry hesitated, reminding himself that to enter a gambling establishment was not an immediate stumble on the slippery embankment leading down to hell. As Hartwell had pointed out, people gambled all the time. And if he was here to try to save his sister, then surely that mitigated the circumstance somewhat.

Hartwell hummed as he gazed around the room. "What shall we play?" he asked, nudging Warry. "What do you fancy? Piquet? Whist? Casino? Faro?"

Warry was terribly out of his depth. "I don't know how to play."

"Which ones?"

"All of them," Warry said, embarrassed. Hartwell took him by the elbow and steered him toward a table.

"We shall start with faro then." Hartwell sat and tugged Warry down into the seat next to him.

Warry's sense of misery deepened as Hartwell pulled out his purse and exchanged much of the contents for coloured betting discs, all the while making conversation with their fellow gamblers at the table. Their fellows were a mix of men and women, some dressed quite soberly, and others covered from top to toe in frippery and finery. Warry could barely keep from staring at one woman who seemed in danger of her bosom tumbling from the scant bodice of her evening gown every time she moved and wore a turban, trailing ribbons, in a shade of pink that was almost violent. The man seated next to her, in contrast, was dressed in plain, rough clothes, that although they were neatly worn suggested that he was a labourer or costermonger of some sort. Warry could not imagine any other circumstances under which two such very different people would be sharing a table. As the conversation flowed around him, loud and jovial, he heard accents that belonged to all parts of London, from the House of Lords all the way down to the Billingsgate Fish Market.

Hartwell peered inside his purse, and then shrugged and handed it over to Warry. "Watch for a few turns, then you buy in."

"I…" The purse might have weighed a hundred pounds for the way it lay so heavily on Warry's conscience.

Hartwell leaned toward him and spoke quietly in his ear. "It's a gift, Warry, or a loan if you prefer."

Warry nodded dumbly, tightening his grip on the purse. "I…I shall do as you say then and watch a little first."

He wondered if Wilkes was already there and if perhaps there was enough money in Hartwell's gift to buy the scoundrel's silence for a little longer until Warry could make some arrangement to secure the principal elsewhere. Twenty pounds was perhaps no small amount to Hartwell, or to the woman in the startlingly pink turban, but for most people in this room it would be more money than they earned in a year.

His mind racing, he tried to concentrate on what was happening as the players each placed their tokens on one of the thirteen cards the dealer had laid out. The dealer then turned over two cards from the deck, a winning card and a losing card. Those around the table who had chosen the winning card were paid a token; those that had chosen the losing card gave theirs up to the dealer. That seemed simple enough, but Warry quickly got confused when it came to betting on the high card or betting on the losing card or betting on which order the final cards were dealt. Nobody else seemed at all consternated; conversation around the table continued as cheerily as ever as bets were made and changed rapidly with each new play. If Hartwell had meant to start him out on faro because it was simple, perhaps gambling wasn't for Warry at all.

Warry watched the game for as long as it took Hartwell to become interested in the play, and then stood, murmuring, "Excuse me for a moment."

Hartwell didn't even notice as he slipped away into the crowd, and Warry was glad of it, although that didn't explain the strange pang inside him as he glanced back at the table and saw Hartwell engrossed in the cards.

CHAPTER 6

Hartwell was halfway through his first stack of gambling chips and his second port when he discovered Warry was no longer sitting beside him. The fellow was often as quiet as a churchyard mouse, though he had a few teeth when he was prodded well enough, so Hartwell didn't feel too guilty. He was concerned, though, as no doubt Warry could get himself up to all sorts of trouble on his first visit to a hell. He regretfully rose from the table and scanned the crowd, hoping to catch a glimpse of Warry's wheat-gold hair and unnaturally white face. They would have looked a pair of fools in polite society, but nobody in the Four-in-Hand paid them any mind at all. Where else but the Four-in-Hand could a minister rub elbows with a molly and neither of them be offended by the contact?

He wandered through the crowd, moving from table to table in an attempt to locate Warry, and thought of how he'd applied the white paint to Warry's face, and how his fingertips had tingled with sensation as he'd drawn them gently across Warry's bruises. He thought also of how Warry's eyes had been wide, their blue-grey depths full of some indefinable emotion that made Hartwell's stomach lurch, and how his mouth, hanging slightly open at

Hartwell's audacity, had appeared so lush and plump. In truth, he looked much like Becca, but Hartwell had never felt his blood heat from being so close to her, and neither had he felt a tingling throughout him as though his body was filled with champagne bubbles. The sudden stand in his trousers, well, Hartwell was no stranger to those, but usually they weren't accompanied by such an array of other odd sensations like the buzzing in his skull or the tightness in his chest.

Warry was damned confounding.

And a damned magician, apparently.

Where could he have disappeared to?

He made his way toward the back of the hell, toward a small, dark alcove known as the Grand Ballroom, which was anything but. The only dancing done there was whatever fancy footwork the dealer engaged in to avoid being caught with cards up his sleeve. God help him if Warry had found his way in there.

A figure appeared suddenly in his path—a man in a green velvet coat that had seen better days, wisps of greying hair clinging to the edges of a shiny bald pate. "Ah, Hartwell! I thought that was you. My old eyes aren't what they were."

"Lord Grayson." Hartwell gave a polite nod. "It has been some time."

Grayson had served as a hunting companion to Hartwell's father for many years, until his "old eyes" rendered him more a danger to fellow hunters than he was to game. The fellow held up his near-empty glass. "Will you join me for another?"

"I'm actually trying to find—"

"Ah, Hartwell, it is good to see you." Grayson took his elbow, leading him toward a particularly rowdy table. "Come, come. I want to hear how you've been. No hard feelings between you and your father, I hope. I told him he was being too harsh. I myself didn't marry until my eyes started to go. I still don't know whether my wife is a whey-faced blowse or a diamond of the first water, but she keeps me from running into walls, so I suppose it matters not."

"What's this?" Hartwell shook free of the old man's grasp. "What is it you told my father that he was being too harsh about?"

Grayson laughed good-naturedly. "Why, about cutting the purse strings if you don't hurry it along and get married. 'What's the rush?' I asked him. 'Let the boy enjoy his stag days.' Lady Rebecca Warrington is young and healthy. Whenever you two do get around to it, she'll produce fine heirs."

It was as though a veil had been draped over Hartwell's surroundings. Faces blurred, and voices echoed. His throat was dry, and he had the sense of being outside his body. "My father is going to force me to marry?"

He was able to focus on Grayson enough to catch the startlement in the man's rheumy eyes. "Not force! He certainly can't force you."

"Cut the purse strings, you said?"

"He hasn't told you?"

"No. No, he has neglected to mention it."

Grayson dropped his gaze to his shoes. "Well, far be it from me to stick my old nose where it doesn't—"

"You've already stuck it. Now tell me precisely what my father said."

Hartwell was reeling. He and his father had always got along fine. His mother said she found the pair of them pig-headed and hard to reason with, but both of his parents had always seemed proud to have a tall, strapping, sought-after son. He knew they wished him to marry, and he knew they had been a bit cross when he'd spent his first Season, and each one since, snickering in corners with Becca, dancing with other young ladies only when courtesy demanded it. But he'd never felt himself to be the sort of disappointment a father might cast away in despair.

Grayson tried to clap his back but got mostly air. "Hartwell, I'd best not—I'm sure your father will bring it up when he's ready. I must return to my...ah...they'll be waiting for me to deal...in." He stumbled off toward the raucous table.

Hartwell stood very still, breathing hard.

His father was plotting to force his hand. And without a word to him! The man would lament to Grayson before he'd sit down with his own son and have a conversation.

He ran a hand through his hair. He needed to find Warry. Now. Damn it, where was the pup? He stumbled into a woman in a high-collared gown. For a moment, her eyes looked like Becca's. He apologised and hurried on, letting out a roar of frustration that was lost in the din of the hell. When he found Warry, he'd skin him alive.

～

Wilkes had the same impossibly small, pointy face and over-large eyes that Warry remembered. Those eyes immediately found Warry's bruises beneath the white paint, though Warry could read neither satisfaction nor surprise in the fellow's expression.

"Do you have the letter?" Warry demanded as soon as they were ensconced in a corner of the Grand Ballroom.

"Read for yourself, sir." Wilkes slipped Warry a folded sheet of paper.

Warry thought about bolting with the letter, but he doubted he'd get far. He glanced about him, wondering if Wilkes had brought his cohorts. He unfolded the page and squinted at the words. The handwriting was familiar, and the more he read, the more his stomach twisted. It seemed somehow more terrible than he had remembered, and yet the relief of finally holding it in his hands again was profound. He finished and looked up. "You had no right to take this."

Wilkes sniffed, twitched, and coolly snagged the letter from Warry's grasp, tucking it back into his own coat. "Your father dismissed me without my pay. I had to leave with *something*."

Warry passed his tongue over his teeth, deciding not to remind

Wilkes that he had been dismissed for stealing a silver candlestick and a box of snuff. He took Hartwell's money from his pocket. "Well? What do you want for it?"

"I already got what I want." Wilkes's gaze passed once more over Warry's battered face. "And I'm only the messenger."

"What do you mean?"

"Joseph!" boomed a voice. Warry whirled to see Lord Balfour approaching.

His stomach seemed to drop clean to his shoes as shock and horror battled within him. Good Lord, Balfour could not be allowed to know what he was here for. Warry shifted instinctively as though intending to hide Wilkes from sight with his own body.

Everything about Balfour was polished to a fine sheen. His hair was perfectly straight and seemed to be made of the same patent leather as his shoes. His cane and his teeth glinted. He was handsome, yes, but he seemed at first glance like something one ought not to touch, an item intended for display only. Yet as Warry had got to know him, he'd found that the man was not all polish. He could be amusing—even crude—and had a competence that drew Warry hesitantly into its shelter. There was nothing Lord Balfour did not know. He knew the steps to every dance. He knew precisely what a gentleman should be drinking in every location and circumstance. He knew how to flip his hat in the air and have it land on the end of his cane. And he knew even more than Warry about the stomachs of cows.

Warry's horror turned to relief as he realised that Balfour might even know what to do about Wilkes.

"What on earth is on your face?" Balfour asked, reaching out to smudge the white paint with his thumb. His gaze held an intensity too intimate to be brought before Wilkes.

"Oh, um…" Warry was so nervous, he could think of no lie. "Hartwell and I did it. For a lark."

"You should wipe it off at once. It does you no favours. And I do so enjoy your lovely features." He brushed his thumb along Warry's cheek.

Warry's heart seemed to pour fire into his veins. Balfour made a habit of these quiet, subtle touches that unspooled like ribbons of pleasure and inevitably tangled into a knot of shame. Worse still, the shame often became exciting in ways that Warry could not articulate. Becca might mock his friendship with Balfour—"Oh, he's teaching you to be a man, is he? Keep in mind, Warry, I wouldn't dance with a 'man' like that even for the satisfaction of stepping on his toes"—but Warry *felt* stronger around him. Balfour made navigating the social whirl seem easy. He made Warry believe he deserved to be seen and admired. If Balfour could look at him with such naked desire, then surely others might too.

Warry met his gaze uncertainly as Balfour used his finger to tilt his chin up.

Had Wilkes not been watching, Warry might have closed his eyes and made a soft sigh. Frightened as he was in the moment, some part of him knew only gladness at being near Balfour.

Then Balfour said, "You have seen the letter?"

"The letter?" Warry repeated, confused.

Balfour hedged him in with his large body, cutting off Warry's line of sight to the rest of the room. Warry's stomach twisted again, and he stepped back. Something about this was not right. How had Balfour managed to appear at Warry's precise moment of need?

"Do not play dumb, Joseph," Balfour said mildly. "Naturally though it seems to come to you." He turned to Wilkes, sliding the letter out of the man's pocket with surprising delicacy. "Thank you, Wilkes. We have no further need of you here."

Oh, this was very bad indeed.

Warry licked his lips as Wilkes slunk off into the shadows. Balfour smiled with no feeling at all behind it. "An old associate of mine," he said with a nod in the direction Wilkes had gone. "He does not hold your family in high esteem. As you are no doubt aware." He snapped the folded letter through the air, then tucked it into his pocket.

Warry watched it disappear with the sense of a trap slamming shut on him. Wilkes and Balfour…How was it possible?

"Your sister," Balfour continued, "is full of surprises."

Warry tried with everything in him to banish the details contained in that horrid slip of paper. The words Becca had written to Miss Lilley, words that belonged in *The Maiden Diaries*. Words he himself had read after taking that letter from her bedchamber. God, he had never meant to leave it where it might be—*had been*—discovered. Yet for a moment, he aimed his anger at Becca rather than himself. How could she have been so foolish to put those thoughts to paper? It was one thing to harbour desires that would not yield an heir, but to harbour desires for a *servant*…Becca was the daughter of an earl, and Miss Lilley was a commoner—now that was indeed a scandal. Not only to harbour had those desires, but to have described them so…*vividly*…

This would ruin her. It would ruin their family. Their younger siblings' marital prospects would be dashed, and they would be driven from balls, routs, and concerts by wagging tongues and dagger-sharp glares. Not to mention what it would do to their father. Earl Warrington doted on Becca, thought her the sweetest, purest, most beautiful young woman in the world. He took the sharp side of her and blunted it in conversation by calling it "spirit" or "vivacity." If he became aware of what she had so vivaciously done with the younger children's former governess…

Warry must not let it happen. He had to get the letter back.

He opened his purse and attempted to keep his tone flat as he said, "Name your price."

Balfour covered Warry's hand with his own. "Do not be in such haste to give your money away. Wilkes was the one who required a monetary fee. What I require will not cost you a penny."

"What is it you want?" Warry wondered why he had not yet jerked his hand free of Balfour's.

One side of Balfour's mouth twitched up, and he released Warry. "It seems I am being undeservedly condemned to that most hideous of fates—marriage. Without boring you with details you have little hope of comprehending, let me just say that I have recently experienced a spot of trouble with my investments. There is a rather sizable inheritance I may claim following my grandmother's imminent death, provided that I am wed by the time that happy day comes to pass."

Warry understood the words but not what they signified.

"I shall admit, I at first had my eye on your sister."

"My sister!" He felt sure he had bellowed it loudly enough to stop all conversation in the room, but on went the laughter, the howls of defeat, the clinking of glasses, and the rattle of chips.

"Yes. She is pretty enough and finely bred. Then, at the end of last Season, I noticed you at the garden party at Curlew House, though you did not see me watching. And I knew you were the Warrington I wanted. When your family returned to the country, I would sometimes pay Wilkes a coin or two to search about your room and send me word of what he learned of your habits and personality."

Once again, horror mixed with a strange, sick wonder inside Warry. He could recall days when the usually sullen Wilkes was more animated, and he could recall his own embarrassingly hopeful reaction to his valet's attentiveness. Even his servant's attentions had been a lie—a plot to glean information for Balfour. And yet...Balfour had noticed him. Not only noticed him but been so taken with him that he had set Wilkes to spy on him. It was a level of attention Warry had never suspected he could command. He had held a peer of the realm in thrall without knowing it.

Oh God, what sort of pathetic mongrel was he to take that scrap and make a meal of it? The man was blackmailing him for Christ's sake!

"One day, Wilkes came to me with the most *intriguing* letter. He had found it in your bureau."

Warry forced his expression to remain neutral, though from the glint in Balfour's eyes, he was far from successful.

"I at first thought you had written it, and please, do imagine my surprise. But it quickly became apparent that these were your sister's ramblings. Very detailed, don't you think? The part where she describes—"

"Stop!" Warry hissed. "Do not say another word about my sister. She'll never have you."

"You're quite right. She shall not. That was merely the initial draft of my plan—to use the letter to secure her hand. She has a sizable dowry, after all. But it was not she I wanted, even as a prize to trot forth before my ailing grandmother. Then you came to me that day, Joseph, at the Gilmore rout. It truly seemed God's doing. You were so enchanting, even in your naivete, and I wished to"—his gaze slipped down Warry's body before returning to meet Warry's eyes—"guide you. As it matters not to my grandmother whether I wed a woman or a man, my path forward became clear."

Warry could not speak. He knew now what was coming, but he could only watch this new dreadfulness unfold as though from a great distance.

Balfour's next words were spoken quietly enough but seemed to rise above the din of the hell. "Joseph, in exchange for my silence on the matter of your sister's virtue, I should like to ask you to marry me."

Warry closed his eyes. Rage set fire to his very bones, and then shame doused him like ice-cold water until he was but a shivering, miserable creature. How could he not have seen what Balfour was before this moment? How could he have leaned into touches the way he had, basked in Balfour's admiring gaze? How could he have cherished each moment the man spent lavishing attention on him, teaching him, *guiding* him?

The man was a monster. Warry wouldn't wed him for all the riches in England.

And yet...what would be worse: the ruin of the entire

Warrington family or a loveless marriage? People entered loveless marriages all the time. Becca was currently considering one with Hartwell—though they at least were friends. What Balfour was proposing seemed more terrible than that because it was clear now that Balfour was his enemy and had been throughout the whole of their acquaintance.

Balfour smiled and leaned in, and it was all Warry could do not to flinch back. "If you don't agree, then I am afraid I shall have no choice but to make the contents of this letter public."

"I..." Warry swallowed. "Why would you want me?"

"Fishing for compliments, dear?" Balfour asked, his smile thinning. "Because, Warry, I have already married once for duty, and I am inclined to do it this time for pleasure." He rubbed his thumb along Warry's cheek again. "And I expect that you, my dear boy, will prove quite pleasurable."

Warry's head swam. "But blackmail? You were my friend, sir! Or at least I thought so. And...and my parents will not..." He shook his head. "I am my father's heir."

"Yes," Balfour said. He dragged his thumb along Warry's bottom lip, gaze sharpening. "There's the rub. It is your burden as heir that your father will expect sons from you, and it isn't in your nature to disappoint him, is it? Not without the right incentive, at least. And so here it is, the right incentive: Do as I say, or I shall ruin your family."

Warry, blinking rapidly, remembered that Balfour already had a son and heir, though he rarely mentioned him. It was Warry's understanding the boy was being raised on Balfour's estate in Suffolk by an army of governesses and tutors. Warry wondered if, once he was married to Balfour, he'd be hidden away in the countryside as well.

"A week, Joseph," Balfour said. "In a week, we shall make public our engagement. Your enthusiasm for our match will, I have no doubt, convince Earl Warrington to give us his blessing."

Enthusiasm? Warry felt faint.

"That stricken look is counter to our purpose." Balfour *tsk*ed disapprovingly. "I shall expect you to partake in a very public courtship and to appear delighted through every moment of it. I do not like to make threats, especially not to you, my dear, but I hope I am understood."

"Yes," Warry rasped, his throat dry.

"Yes?"

Warry nodded. He had a duty. To protect Becca. Protect his family. Face the consequences of his own terrible actions. That letter…it could not be made public. "I will do my best to see you have my father's blessing." He pulled back from Balfour at last as though his agreement had broken some spell between them and no part of him remained in the man's thrall. And yet, wasn't every part of him now Balfour's? The thought made him ill.

"Very good. And one day, I shall require you to tell me how your sister's vulgar *billet-doux* ended up in your bureau. I gathered that you two were close, but really, Joseph…"

Warry made a strangled sound of protest, and Balfour laughed. "The letter. You will not—"

"The letter, my dear boy," Balfour said, "shall be my wedding gift to you."

He reached out and took Warry's hand without permission and raised it to his mouth. He pressed his lips to it, his dark eyes glittering, and lingered there as though he was trying to parse every warring expression that must have shown on Warry's face.

"Warry!" someone called.

Warry jerked back, pulling his hand free, both grateful and horrified to have been discovered.

It was Hartwell, striding toward them with a face like thunder.

"What the devil is going on here?" he demanded, glaring at Warry, then at Balfour and back to Warry again.

Warry resisted the urge to wipe the back of his hand on his trousers. "I…"

"Hartwell," Balfour said with a purr. "What a pleasure."

"Balfour." Hartwell cut the name off sharply. "I believe I asked what was going on here?"

Warry blinked at him, unable to think of a single word to say, except for those he could not, under any circumstances, utter, such as *Please help me, Hartwell*. He gasped when Hartwell reached out and grasped him by the wrist, tugging him close to his side as he glared at Balfour.

"We're leaving," Hartwell said. "Now."

Balfour chuckled and waved them off. "I shall speak to you again soon, dear Joseph."

Warry felt like a recalcitrant child dragged along by a nursemaid as Hartwell tugged him through the crowded hell, weaving their way between the tables toward the exit. And then suddenly they were outside on the street, in the sharp bite of the cold, and Hartwell released Warry and stood with his back to him as he pulled on his gloves.

"Good Lord, Warry," he said, sounding somehow uncaring and annoyed at once. "I lose you for five minutes, and suddenly you're getting cosy with Balfour in a dark alcove. Do you think nothing of your reputation?"

He strode out into the street to whistle down a cab.

Warry waited silently on the footpath, staring down at his shoes and trying uselessly to blink away the stinging in his eyes, sick in the knowledge that, had he truly cared nothing for his reputation, tonight would have gone very differently indeed.

CHAPTER 7

Hartwell lay in bed well into the early morning hours, trying not to think of Warry in the room down the hall. Warry had not spoken a word to him on the ride home, and Hartwell had not attempted conversation. The Four-in-Hand might have been a hell, but it was frequented by enough of the *ton* that there was every chance Warry might have been spotted in a compromising position with Balfour. Hartwell had no doubt that what he'd seen had been a seduction in progress. His stomach turned as he remembered the way Balfour had kissed Warry's hand, while Warry, no doubt frozen with shock because he really was an utter naïf, had simply stared at him wide-eyed like some trembling little fawn.

Yet he could not hold onto any sort of frustration with Warry, for it only turned to shame and confusion at his own behaviour. He still felt, after all these years, as though he ought to be looking after Warry. And, just as when they'd been children, he felt the weight of his own failure in that regard. The reason he did not know how to be a husband to Becca, or a proper friend to Warry, was that he had always been so very assured of his place in the world: at its centre. Every other person was merely a side player in the Story of William

Hartwell. He supposed it was like that for everyone, to some degree. But he had always found it enough to simply *be* William Hartwell, Marquess of Danbury. He might behave like an idiot; his mood of late might be a bit disagreeable, but overall, people had always liked him. Tutors, school mates, his parents, other people's parents…they'd all generally considered him good-natured, endearing. Crass, at times, but forgivably so.

Now, with things changing so suddenly, he feared that being William Hartwell was no longer enough. If his own father could consider disinheriting him, well, then love was not so stable a thing as he'd thought. And wasn't it now just a matter of who he would fail most gravely? His parents. Becca. *Warry.* The harder it became to waltz through life, the more tenaciously he clung to the notion that it was still easy, and the less he wanted to bear witness to the struggles of those around him, lest they prove somehow contagious. Pure cowardice. The same cowardice that'd seen him dragging Warry from the Four-in-Hand, chiding his indiscretion rather than speaking to him as a friend. The same cowardice with which he'd curtailed their interactions after that childhood kiss, so that he hesitated to throw his arm around Warry with affection, or clapped him on the back, or embraced him. Because he could not let his father see that Warry meant anything to him.

Yet he recalled the morning before the Gilmore rout when he'd held a laughing Warry in his grasp. When things had suddenly felt better between them than they had in years. It had echoed, he thought now, a day long ago when they'd been playing soldiers. He and Becca had been twelve, Warry eight. It had started with Becca and Hartwell as English officers, chasing Warry, a French spy, around the Warringtons' vast country estate. But Warry's manoeuvres had been clever, and as Hartwell had crept toward the shrub he was certain hid Warry, the lad had shocked him by pelting him with fruit from the highest branches of a pear tree. Hartwell had scrambled up the tree, laughing with abandon and dodging a whole hail of pears, swearing that when he caught

Warry, Warry would regret it. Warry's answering laugh was pure delight and suggested he did not take Hartwell's threat seriously in the least.

Hartwell could only make it halfway up to where Warry was perched. They had negotiated from their separate positions, Warry assuring him that he knew a way to lure Becca into trap, if Hartwell would join forces with him. Hartwell, who would usually have quailed to even think of betraying Becca in any matter, had agreed.

And so they had laid their trap for Becca, with Hartwell calling her name, pretending to be bleeding from at least a dozen bullet wounds made by that dastardly Frenchman. Yet when the moment had come for Hartwell to spring up and join with Warry in capturing Becca, he found himself instead being dragged across the grass to their makeshift gaol—one of his arms held by Warry, the other by Becca.

"I apologise," Warry said, not sounding sorry in the least. "I had already persuaded Becca to the French cause before you attempted to negotiate with me."

Hartwell had begun laughing in disbelief. The little wretch!

"Stay quiet if you know what's good for you," Becca told him.

Hartwell swore on the grave of Curtis, the old family cat, that he would come quietly. But naturally he broke away at first opportunity, rounding on Warry with a cry of "traitor!" Warry shrieked and took off running, Hartwell in pursuit. Hartwell caught him easily, wrapping his arms around Warry's waist, Warry laughing too hard to make any practical effort to free himself.

"Becca, what should I do with him?" he'd called. His chest felt light at the sensation of Warry shaking with laughter in his arms.

"You could try admitting that we bested you," she called back.

He'd leaned down to Warry's ear to ask, "And what is so funny about making a fool of me, hmm?"

But he could not stop his own laughter. Nor could he make himself let Warry go. Warry could have twisted from his grasp easily at that point, but he did not. Instead he seemed to lean back against Hartwell, and Hartwell's stomach fluttered madly. Warry's hair smelled as sweet as the pear tree he'd so recently climbed.

"It is not so difficult," Warry replied, gasping. "You do much of the work yourself."

Hartwell squeezed him, digging his fingers into Warry's ribs and producing a yelp that became another peal of helpless laughter.

"Let me go!" Warry demanded when he could draw breath. "Or else."

"Or else what, you treasonous wretch?"

Warry strained half-heartedly against Hartwell's encircling arms. "Or else I shall tell you all I know of donkey bladders until you are so bored you release me."

"*Donkey* bladders?" Hartwell tightened his arms around his captive. "I am all ears."

Becca came to stand before them, her hands on her hips. "Oh William, you will not last half a minute."

"No, I'm ready to learn." He leaned close to Warry's ear again. "Come. Tell me about donkey bladders."

"Well, they are very…bladder-like."

Hartwell jostled him, prompting another bout of snickering. "Is that all you've got for me?"

"A donkey urinates for an average of twenty-one seconds."

"Do you hear this, Becca? What are your parents paying for his education? Whatever the sum, it is too much." To Warry he said, "And?"

"Umm…"

"You do not really know anything about donkey bladders at all, do you?" He caught Warry's wrists and pulled them behind Warry's back. "You have made an empty threat. Now you shall have to stay here until you tell me something truly interesting about donkey bladders."

Warry struggled for a moment, then gave up with a sigh that sounded equal parts amused and indignant. "They are as large as a human head!"

Hartwell scoffed. "That could not possibly be true." Could it? He supposed donkeys were reasonably large. And human heads fairly small, when one really looked at them.

"Well, probably not so large as *your* head," Warry conceded.

"You little…" He released Warry's wrists to dig his fingers into his sides. Warry squealed and stumbled forward, but Hartwell caught him again and they both fell to the ground, Hartwell on top of Warry.

Warry stared up at him, the picture of wide-eyed innocence. "But truly, how is it that your head is so big when there is so little to fill it?"

"That's it." Hartwell straddled him, taking his wrists and pinning them to the grass on either side of his head, both of them laughing too hard to breathe.

"William!" Becca said sternly. "Stop sitting on my brother."

Miss Lilley, the Warringtons' governess, had come out onto the lawn and scolded Hartwell and Warry for playing so roughly, then scolded Becca for allowing it. And my, hadn't Becca's spine snapped straight at that, and hadn't she demanded in a voice like a military commander's that Hartwell get off Warry at once.

He found himself smiling in the darkness. Where was that Joseph Warrington? Who was this fellow who wished to gamble—both in the hells and with his reputation?

He started at the sound of a door creaking down the hall. Then soft footsteps heading for the stairs. His heart thumped. Now, he supposed, was a chance to shrug off his cowardice. To attempt to have a conversation with Warry. He got out of bed and slunk to the door, pulling it open silently. Down the stairs he went, following the wobbling light of Warry's lamp past the drawing room, the sitting room, and at last, to his father's library.

He did not follow Warry into the library right away. He was uncertain how to announce his presence in a way that would not startle the other man. At last he stepped into the doorway and gave a soft knock on the frame. "Warry?"

Warry swung round, nearly dropping the lamp. "Hartwell!" he whispered.

Even in the dim light, Hartwell could see that Warry looked wretched. He appeared to have washed the white paint off, and now his fading bruises showed dark in the lamplight. The expression in his eyes was flat and hopeless. His body was tense, one arm curled around his stomach as though he was about to be sick. "I—I could not sleep. I thought perhaps a book…"

Hartwell stepped forward. "You do not look well."

"I'm fine," Warry said tersely.

"Is it what I said to you earlier, as we left the hell? I truly am sorry. It really isn't such a disaster, what transpired between you and Balfour. Many gentlemen have done worse. *I* have done worse."

Warry appeared frozen for an instant. Then he muttered, "Please. I don't wish to discuss it any further."

Hartwell studied him, and Warry turned his head so that most of his face was in shadow.

"I'm sorry," Warry said after a moment. "I only meant to borrow a book and then return to bed." He held up the lamp and scanned the shelves.

"I don't know that we have any books on donkey bladders."

Warry turned sharply to him. Hartwell's lips quirked.

Then, to his surprise, Warry's did too. His expression lost its weary hopelessness, and he looked less like he might eject the contents of his stomach. "You think there is any book on the subject I've not yet read?"

Hartwell chuckled. "Are they really as big as a human head? Donkey bladders?"

"Of course not."

"I knew it!"

Warry actually laughed. "At the *time*, I did not have much information about donkey bladders. But I have since studied the subject."

"Of course you have."

As suddenly as he had opened up, Warry seemed to shut down again. His lips pressed together and he drew Hartwell's dressing gown tighter around him. Hartwell could have shouted in exasperation. What *was* it that plagued Warry? The lamp fell briefly on the backgammon set on a small round table near the window. He crossed to the table. "Do you play?"

It seemed to take Warry a moment to comprehend what he was asking. "Oh. Becca tried to teach me once. I was not very good."

"Fancy a game?"

"I'm a bit tired."

"Will you be able to concentrate on your book, if you return to bed?"

The answer, Hartwell was fairly certain, was no. And sure enough, Warry shook his head. "I cannot concentrate on much of anything at the moment."

Hartwell began to set up the board. "This will help pass the time. And when at last you grow weary of losing to me, perhaps then you will feel like sleeping off the pain of your defeat." He offered a tentative smile and was absurdly relieved when Warry snorted.

"Come," Hartwell said softly. "You seem as though you've had a dreadful night. I'm sorry to have contributed to that."

Warry jolted visibly. Tugged at the edge of the dressing gown. "I apologise as well. I realise that, with your pending engagement to Becca, I reflect poorly on your family when I reflect poorly on mine."

Hartwell shook his head and rolled his eyes. "Yes, because that's what I'm concerned about. Sit down, will you?"

Warry walked over and set the lamp on the windowsill next to them. Took a seat.

Hartwell watched the play of shadows over Warry's face. "Does it still hurt?" he asked, gazing at Warry's bruised forehead.

"What?"

"Your head?"

Warry leaned back in the chair. "I hardly feel it anymore."

Hartwell arranged checkers on the thirteen point. In a way, he envied Warry the risk he'd taken with Balfour. Warry evidently desired the man and was not holding himself back. Innocent little Warry, stammering at the very mention of *The Maiden Diaries*, was perhaps finding some hidden bit of spine he had not known he possessed. But Balfour was precisely the sort of peer who could mould Warry into something he was not. Who cared only about status, and would never care which direction the hooves of cows grew if you did not trim them properly. Not that Hartwell had ever been much concerned with cow's hooves. But to hear Warry speak on the subject was more of a treat than Hartwell had ever been able to admit to himself. He often wished he were half so passionate or knowledgeable about any subject. And Balfour would never appreciate it, just as he would never appreciate goat belches or donkey bladders.

They began to play, and Warry quickly gained the upper hand.

"What were you on about, 'Becca tried to teach me once?'" Hartwell demanded. "You're quite good."

Warry shrugged. "It's just luck."

"I could have used your luck at the faro table tonight."

Hartwell noticed Warry's hand shook on his next turn.

It hit Hartwell then: What if Warry did *not* desire Lord Balfour? That seemed rather difficult to believe, given that Warry and Balfour had spent the entire afternoon together at the Gilmore rout. He recalled that awful moment he had witnessed between the two of them through the terrace doors, Balfour stroking Warry's hair and Warry shooting Hartwell such a self-complacent look through the glass. And Warry and Balfour had spent weeks in each other's intermittent company since then! But what if…

"There's always brandy," he offered. "If you still can't sleep after this."

Warry placed his hands under the table. "I'm sure I'll be fine."

Hartwell sighed. To hell with it. "Warry, if he—Balfour—was attempting to do anything you did not wish—"

"Stop!" Warry's voice rose with a rather frantic-sounding anger. "Hartwell, what are you suggesting?"

"I only—"

"He did nothing that I did not also want. It was as you said. I was careless with my reputation." He studied the gameboard.

"I see." Hartwell did not see. And so he went on, despite the tension radiating from his companion. "Becca says you have not been yourself of late."

Warry's head snapped up, and he glared at Hartwell as though daring him to say something further. Hartwell thought of all he would like to say, but decided upon: "And I must agree."

Warry's eyes narrowed just a little, the gold of the lamp creating twin points of light in his pupils. His gaze dropped again.

"You are far above Balfour."

Warry shifted, knocking the table with his knee, making the checkers slide. "Don't be absurd. You think me quite below everyone."

"Is that truly what you believe?" Hartwell asked softly.

Warry looked up. "Don't you?"

"No," Hartwell whispered, quite horrified that Warry could think it. "That's not the truth of it at all."

The lamp cast such strange shadows on Warry's face, Hartwell could not be quite sure what he was seeing. But it seemed that something hard and sharp inside Warry was dislodged, and his eyes were suddenly pleading in a way that made Hartwell desperate to mend whatever was wrong between them.

"I don't like to see you hurt."

Warry's expression shifted. There was something dazed about it. Then uncertain. And then, quite possibly, angry. And after that, he seemed determined to appear as though he felt nothing at all.

Then he grinned suddenly, though it was a shadow of the smile Hartwell could remember seeing on him years ago. He moved a checker, winning the game. "You are easy to distract," he said triumphantly.

Hartwell stared at the board, tongue pressed between his front teeth, fighting a grin of his own even though he had a feeling *this* was the real distraction—a change of focus, luring Hartwell away from the subject of Balfour. Still, he played along. "You false little beggar."

"I should think you'd have learned after all these years not to trust me."

Hartwell thought again of holding a laughing Warry in his arms, the lad triumphant after the deception he had pulled off with Becca. He ached somewhere so deep within himself, he had not a clue how to heal it. "It is not my fault you use those lovely, innocent eyes to manipulate me."

"Lovely? How much did you have to drink tonight?"

Hartwell cracked out a laugh that sounded like a gunshot in the quiet room, leaning back in his chair. "Not nearly enough."

"I wish you would simply admit that I am your superior."

"I shall speak no such falsehood." Except that it was the truth, Hartwell realised. It had always been the truth.

Warry rose, leaning over the table, shadows shifting and turning the pale skin of his throat red-gold. Hartwell momentarily stopped breathing. Oh, fuck. Fuck. Whatever he was feeling, it could not possibly bode well for his future. Warry tilted his head. "Do you wish to play again, or would you find it too humiliating?"

Hartwell rose too. "I wish, brat, that you would come just a step closer."

Warry laughed and pulled back. "You are threatened by my prowess at backgammoning."

Hartwell's brows lifted, and they both stared at each other for a moment. Warry looked a bit shocked at himself, but soon he was snickering again, biting his lip to contain his amusement. Hartwell smiled briefly, looking down at the checkers. "I shall damn myself any way I choose to respond to that."

The silence returned between them, and with it, a tension that filled the room.

"What is it?" Hartwell whispered, not sure what he hoped Warry would say. That he did not care for Balfour at all? That he would like to backgammon Hartwell right here in the Duke of Ancaster's library? That he wished for Hartwell to lie with him and hold him until he slept? God, Hartwell would have done it. Anything to keep them from sliding back into the coldness that had existed between them these last few weeks.

"Nothing. I have made fool enough of myself tonight."

Hartwell's brow furrowed. "I rather thought we were enjoying ourselves."

"Not now. At the hell." Warry braced his hands on either side of the game board, gazing down at the evidence of his victory without seeming to see anything at all.

Hartwell finally said, "Warry, if this is about money...If that is what draws you to Balfour..."

Warry shook his head as though trying to throw off the very suggestion. "Stop."

"Well what is it then?" Hartwell's voice rose.

Warry's expression grew as angry as Hartwell had ever seen it. "'What is it then?' You think I owe you an explanation for the company I keep? You think I am so greedy, so shallow as to want his money? You don't believe me capable of making my own decisions, for my own reasons, about who I...wish to spend time with?"

"That is not what I said and you well know it," Hartwell protested.

"Yes, it is. And it is what you believe. If you wish to know what I see in Lord Balfour, perhaps it is the fact that he listened to me that day at the Gilmores', instead of humiliating me." Warry's voice was alive with hurt. Hartwell tried to recall precisely what he'd said that afternoon. Closed his eyes briefly, shame bolting through him. He'd been casually cruel to Warry, and now he could not think for the life of him why. Because he had seen Warry and Balfour gazing at each other with such intensity, and that had hurt for reasons he had not understood but was very afraid he was beginning to understand now.

He stepped around the table and held out his arm, unthinking. Warry raised his own arm as though to fend him off, and then somehow ended up stumbling into him. Hartwell placed his arm around him. Rubbed his shoulder, then pulled him into a full embrace, moving his hand slowly up and down Warry's rigid back.

Gradually, Warry's shoulders dropped. He shook slightly. "If you don't like to see me hurt, then why did you say that to me?" He whispered into Hartwell's dressing gown.

"Quite right," Hartwell murmured. "You're quite right." *Because I am a coward. And a jealous fool. And I cannot say the things I want to say to you, for I must say them to your sister.* "I should not have. And I am very sorry."

"Let me go," Warry begged softly.

Hartwell obeyed with some reluctance.

Warry scrubbed his face with his hand. His eyes were dry, but his breathing was shallow. "It doesn't matter."

"Of course it does."

Warry stepped away from Hartwell. "Balfour respects me. He sees me as a man. He does not mock me for my interests, nor question every decision I make. You could learn much from him, I think." He snatched up the lamp. "I'm going to bed."

He strode from the room without so much as a glance at Hartwell, closing the library door firmly behind him.

Hartwell's head pounded. Was it true? Had he, with his casual cruelty, pushed Warry into the arms of a man who made Hartwell's stomach turn?

Did the man only make Hartwell's stomach turn because he had held Warry's hand tonight and kissed it?

You could learn much from him. Shame was too hard to sit with, and so he let it give way to frustration. Warry was the one who could not be honest with himself. Who did not quite believe that he was no longer a child, that he was a man, beautiful and intelligent and worthy of someone far superior to Balfour. Perhaps not Hartwell, for Hartwell did not deserve him either. And why was Hartwell even thinking it when he was going to marry Becca?

His annoyance grew. Let Warry make his foolish mistake then. Maybe he would learn something from it. Warry's words came back to him: *"...nor question every decision I make."*

Hartwell was damn well going to question this one. Not out loud; he'd learned his lesson there. But fucking hell, he had a right to his thoughts about Warry and Balfour. Balfour, respect Warry? Lord Balfour respected Lord Balfour and no one else.

He slapped the table. Not particularly hard, but with just enough force to make the backgammon pieces jump. Then he rose and went to bed.

～

Warry didn't join Hartwell for breakfast the next morning, and Hartwell poked petulantly at his Scotch egg until he'd rather ruined it. He set it aside and ate his seedcake instead. It was dry and tasteless. A note had come for Warry an hour ago; he'd had his valet take it up to him, trying not to care that the seal bore a large, swirling B. He was vexed by the way he'd left things with Warry last night. And yet the memory of Warry's smile yesterday as they'd fooled about with the paint, as Warry had declared victory at the backgammon table, was on his mind like a brand. It now seemed a waste to spend his life doing anything other than coaxing that smile again.

Perhaps he had pushed too hard last night. There was certainly nothing stopping Warry from spending time with Balfour if he so chose. What Hartwell needed to do was focus his efforts on courting Becca. If his father had not the decency to talk to him before making threats behind his back, Hartwell could play that game as well. By the time his parents returned, he and Becca would be prepared to announce their engagement. And it would be a decision entirely of their own making, uninfluenced by the elder Hartwell's meddling, the matter settled before the awful ultimatum could be delivered.

Hartwell had devoured a significant portion of *The Maiden Diaries* yesterday, but it had brought him no closer to knowing how to prove himself a husband to Becca. It had only served to make him feel ravenously desirous, ashamed of said desirousness, and deeply confused as to whether this fellow Slyfeel was truly what women wanted.

So he had decided to go with cake for now as a means of winning Becca's favour. He'd had Cook create a confection of strawberries and cream and pack it up for him along with a picnic lunch. Then he had written to Becca, informing her of his intent to call at noon. They would take his carriage for a drive through the park and stop to picnic.

He started at the sound of footsteps. Warry entered the room, fully dressed, and for a moment Hartwell's breath caught. He looked worse than he had three nights past when he'd been dragged, unconscious, to Hartwell's doorstep. Worse than he had when Hartwell had first caught him in the library. But there was a determined placidity about his expression that let Hartwell know he could not expect a straight answer were he to ask how he was.

Unbidden, the image of Balfour kissing Warry's hand flared in him like fever, and he had not the stomach to dwell on it.

"You're late," he said coolly. "But there is still enough here to make a meal of."

"I'm going out. Balfour is taking me for a drive in his curricle. After which, I will have him drop me at Warrington House."

That hit Hartwell quite like a blow, but he made no reply.

"I thank you for your graciousness in allowing me to recover here, but I shan't take further advantage of your hospitality."

Hartwell leaned back, tapping his fingers on the table. "So you and Balfour are courting, then?"

Warry nodded, his movements stiff. "Yes. He has been paying me attention for some time, and he has sent word this morning that he should like to strengthen our acquaintance." He paused. "I know that I am not well versed in courtship. To you I must seem awkward and ignorant. But I do care for him."

"Well, isn't that lovely." There was nothing to be done about the ice in Hartwell's tone. Curse it, he had sworn last night that he would make no further remark on the subject of Warry and Balfour. Yet he could not stop himself. "So that was why you wished to go to the gaming hell? I thought it perhaps a chance for us to spend time together, but you thought only of whether you might arrange a meeting with Balfour there."

Warry's eyes widened in what looked like mingled shock and regret, but he quickly mastered himself. "I appreciate your taking me. It was…I had fun. But yes, I arranged to see Balfour as soon as I knew where we were going." He paused, his teeth tugging his lower lip. "This feeling I have…I cannot cease thinking of him. I suppose at first I was afraid of Society knowing my true feelings, but I am no longer afraid."

That was a bald-faced lie if Hartwell had ever heard one. "You still have your bruises to explain to Becca."

"They're not so noticeable anymore. When I wear a hat, it covers most of them."

All right, you little fool, Hartwell wished to say. *Go and have your curricle ride with Balfour. Leave me in peace.*

Instead, he said, with an indifferent chill he hoped would linger with Warry for the rest of the brat's miserable life, "The pleasure was all mine, Lord Warrington."

Warry flinched slightly but nodded. "Good day, Lord Hartwell."

And then the little whelp, whom Hartwell should have drowned in the frog pond all those years ago, walked away.

CHAPTER 8

*B*ecca seemed in low spirits on their ride, which was perhaps convenient as Hartwell was shrouded in bleakness himself and did not wish to be cheered.

Still, as their carriage bumped along, the sun and the familiar company seemed to shake loose some of his bile, and he found himself instead vexed by the lack of conversation.

"You are quiet today," he pointed out unnecessarily.

"I suppose I've been doing a lot of thinking in the past few days." Her hands were clasped in her lap with a demureness that did not suit her.

"Ah." He nodded. "Thinking." He could come up with nothing more to say, which vexed him further. Not wishing to feel like a stranger in the presence of his dearest friend but not certain how to treat her now that she was his future wife, he condemned them both to a lingering and awkward silence. After which point, he picked up the box he had stored under the carriage seat.

"This is for you. It is cake."

"Cake?" She took the box. "What is the occasion?"

"Need there be an occasion? It is cake."

"This is most generous." She opened the box and peeked inside. "It involves strawberries."

"I thought it would go well with our picnic in the park." He cleared his throat. "I also wrote you a poem."

"A poem?" She looked as though she did not know whether to laugh or open the carriage door and leap out.

"Yes. I know poetry is not where my skill lies, but I thought to do something special for you." He pulled a piece of paper from his breast pocket and started to hand it to her, then drew it back. "I suppose it works best if I read it to you. Isn't that how these things are done?" He unfolded it and began to read.

"Becca, your eyes as the sun do light, each blessed day and darkest night. Your hands are pale, your arms are long. When you speak, it seems an angel's s—"

"William," she interrupted gently. "What is this about?"

"Hmm?" He glanced up. "It is about your arms and voice and eyes."

"No." Her gesture encompassed the cake, the poem, the carriage. "This. Are you trying to frighten me off marrying you?"

He started. "No! No, quite the opposite."

A smile tugged her lips. "Then it is as I feared. You are trying to court me."

Hartwell supposed it was a very bad sign indeed if she did not know whether he was attempting to woo her or frighten her away. What would the rake Slyfeel do? It was the wrong question to ask himself, for Slyfeel would inevitably put his head under her skirts right there in the carriage and create a situation in which she took the Lord's name in vain. Multiple times.

"I do not wish you to fear marrying me." He spoke honestly. "I know this is not what either of us wanted, but I would like you to feel as though I can be a true husband to you. And I do not wish to see you cheated of being wooed. You deserve that part of it too."

She laughed, but it was a sound of pure joy—no mockery in it at all. "I don't think you realise how sweet you can be," she said to him fondly. "But I do not desire a suitor. I want my friend by my side. I want us to make the life we want. Whatever that ends up meaning."

"And we will," he promised.

"I will, however, not protest if you wish to give me cake."

He laughed, but the sound faded quickly as he gazed at her. She was extraordinary. She always had been. And though he feared he could not love her in all the ways husbands ought to love their wives, there was a sense in which his love for her ran deeper than any vow made before a priest. "Yes," he murmured.

"You need not trouble yourself with writing poems or praising my arms, which are apparently of a length so significant you felt compelled to mention them in your poem, or organising your father's library to surprise me. Let us announce our intention to wed when your parents return. And let us forever be friends who share a home. And cake."

He nodded, too struck by the reassurance she offered to speak.

After another moment, she asked, "Is that where Warry is? Did you leave him to finish the library? I've had a letter from him, but I can't tell you how strange it is that he has sequestered himself in Hartwell House for days to help you arrange books."

She was fishing, he knew. His story had been far from convincing, and he could not fault her concern. "He is returning to you today. He was very…generous in his assistance."

Her eyes narrowed, and while her lips were curved slightly in amusement, she was far from satisfied. "What are you keeping from me?"

Hartwell sighed. This was not his tale to tell, and yet he desperately wished to tell it. "Warry and Balfour are courting."

Becca's eyes widened. "*What?*"

"He says Balfour has paid him attention for some time, and while he knows himself to be inexperienced in courtship, he does care for the man."

"No. No, we must put a stop to this," Becca insisted. "That man is…not right for my brother."

"We've treated him as a child for too long, Becca." Hartwell knew he was arguing the point to himself rather than her. "We must let the decision be his."

"But you do not approve."

"No," Hartwell admitted quietly. "I do not."

She glanced out the window. Her hands were once more folded in her lap, but now she was clasping them tightly enough that the knuckles whitened.

Hartwell continued, "I do not understand how the boy who followed us around, chattering about anything and everything, has become so withdrawn and unsure. I sometimes think I should give my fortune to listen to him tell me one more time about a goat's four stomachs. If Balfour gives him back some confidence, makes him happy, then I suppose we must respect that."

"He was not so withdrawn until he met Balfour," Becca said firmly. "Even last Season, you remember, there was joy in him."

Hartwell did remember. And it gave him some measure of hope to know Becca felt Balfour was wrong for Warry too.

I hope Warry sees in time how wrong he is. I hope he regrets this horribly.

And in nearly the same beat of his heart, he wished Warry was still tucked into the guest bed at Hartwell House where Hartwell could keep an eye on him. Make him smile. Keep him safe.

∼

*H*yde Park was lovely. It being March, the ride was cool, and Warry wished he'd worn a scarf. The winter had not been a bad one, although the tail end of it was proving to linger, the pattern of generally bright and sunlit days marred occasionally by chilly, drizzly ones such as this. It had been several years since Town had seen what Warry's father called a 'real' winter; winters these days seemed damper and more miserable rather than sharp and cold. Warry could remember visiting the frost fair several years ago, amazed at the story of an elephant being led over the frozen Thames, even if he hadn't witnessed it himself. He'd bought hot chocolate and he and Becca had gone skating. Their parents had declared the other children too young, which had led to Charlotte wailing all the way home, but not even that had ruined Warry's good spirits. He'd promised to take Charlotte to the next frost fair, but every winter since then had been too mild for the river to freeze over.

There wasn't much traffic on Rotten Row when Balfour drove the curricle over to that end of the Park so that they might watch the riders. A pair of gentlemen raced half-heartedly, though neither they nor their horses seemed much inclined to break a sweat. Warry feigned more interest than he felt, mostly to avoid looking at Balfour. Balfour had been polite and chivalrous from the moment Warry had climbed up into the curricle beside him, which seemed like nothing more than a cruel trick now that Warry had glimpsed the man's true nature. A part of him would have preferred that Balfour acted like the monster he was.

Instead, Balfour chatted about the weather, the latest news from the Continent, and the slow start to the Season that year. Although people had been coming to Town since just after Christmas, the Season had yet to really warm up. Why, there hadn't even been any scandals as yet. Warry's skin prickled when Balfour said that with a sly smile, because they both knew Balfour held the power to uncover one.

"I do believe our match will be widely talked about," Balfour remarked.

"I suppose so," Warry said carefully, uncertain of the man's meaning.

"Marriage can either be a very beautiful thing or a very ugly one."

Warry's throat tightened with the implications of that statement.

Balfour went on. "My father was courted by a Lord Bainbridge, many years ago. To hear him speak of it, Bainbridge was his one great love. He cares not at all for my mother. She destroyed his happiness, you see. She did it bit by bit, day by day. They had no other children. There was no other option available to me but to endure that household in all its misery. Such terrible things she would say to him. To me."

Warry gazed out at the people promenading. He did not want to feel anything for Balfour—the pain of the man's betrayal was still too raw—but in spite of himself, he spared a moment's pity for a small boy in a loveless household. His own upbringing had been full of kindness and indulgence, and he supposed it was unjust that some were granted such blessings and some were not—in the way he'd often thought it unjust that his mother adored him but seemed to find Becca wanting in everything but looks.

"For years, it made me hard and bitter." Balfour rapped on the curricle's side as though to jerk himself from his reverie. He turned his gaze toward Warry, his grin false and strange. "But I have come to enjoy a rich social life and the symbols of status that come from being my own man rather than my father's puppet or my mother's target practice. I have even begun to believe once more in love. I'm no romantic, you understand, but I should very much like to have what my father had with Bainbridge. And Joseph—" he paused. "I have known since that first afternoon we spent together that you are capable of both feeling and giving this love."

Warry chewed his lip, wishing that Balfour's flattery had no power over him. Wishing he did not sit there wondering if it was true. Did he have a rare and admirable capacity for love, and would there be others, if he could only get free of Balfour, who would see it?

Perhaps I would have given it freely to you had you not trapped me, he wanted to say.

People were broken in all sorts of ways. They sometimes use disagreeable methods to achieve their ends, but didn't they all want essentially the same thing? To be loved? Could that brief flash of pity he'd felt for Balfour grow into forgiveness, and might they have a marriage that was at least civil? "My parents sometimes seem strangers to each other." He didn't know what else to say. "That is certainly not what I want for myself."

"Then I'm glad we've made this promise to one another." Balfour smiled with sincere warmth as though that promise they had made to one another was not born of sickness on Balfour's part and terror on Warry's.

Warry was wrung out with the effort of maintaining his composure by the time Balfour took him home to St. James's Square. He entered the house, glad that Balfour hadn't insisted on coming inside with him, and tried to make for his bedroom unseen.

"Joseph?" his father's voice rumbled as he crept down the passageway toward the stairs. "Is that you, my boy?"

Warry backtracked to the doorway of his father's library. It was a modest room, and nothing as grand at all as the library at Graythorpe, the family estate in Norfolk. His father, small and round, sat behind his desk and peered at Warry over the top of his spectacles.

"It *is* you!" he said and rose to his feet. "Where on earth have you been?"

"I was staying with Hartwell," Warry said, glad of his father's predilection for keeping the curtains closed, even on sunny days, and working by lamplight. He hoped the comfortable dimness of the room would hide his bruises.

His father rounded the desk and approached him, staring up at him. He only came up to Warry's shoulder. Becca always said how glad she was that she and Warry had inherited their looks from their mother's side because their mother was tall and willowy, whereas their father bore an uncanny resemblance to the frogs that Becca liked to shove down fellows' shirts. It was a terrible thing to say but wholly true, although Warry couldn't help but think that if they'd both been a little shorter and a lot rounder, then perhaps neither of them would have caught

Balfour's eye. Being frog shaped seemed a small price to pay for that privilege.

Earl Warrington peered up at him. "Are you wearing white paint?"

"I…" Warry must not have washed his face as thoroughly as he'd thought.

"I don't understand fashion," he said, and *hmph*ed. "Lot of nonsense if you ask me. I expect it's the done thing, is it? Did Morgan put you up to it? That boy has more frills than Beau Brummell's cravat collection." He pushed his spectacles further up his nose. "And look what happened to him!"

"To Morgan?" Warry asked, thinking worriedly of his younger cousin. Morgan was a ludicrously beautiful young man, whose greatest ambition in life was to haunt the tailors' shops in Jermyn Street and spend his entire fortune on hats. Warry was very fond of him despite all his silliness. "What's happened to Morgan?"

"No, to Brummell." Earl Warrington snorted. "Though Morgan did visit earlier and talked my ear off about buttons." He gave Warry a dark look. "*Buttons.* I had to foist him on your sisters in order to get any peace at all."

"Oh," said Warry faintly.

Earl Warrington returned to his desk and picked up a letter to peruse. "So, what were you doing staying at Hartwell's? Becca said something about a library?"

"Yes. Hartwell wanted some help in organising it."

"Ah!" His father set the letter aside and peered at Warry again. "And what do you think about this idea of Hartwell and Becca?"

Warry's heart skipped a beat. "It's a good match."

"Yes," Earl Warrington said. He paused suddenly, his brows drawing together. "Though I always thought…" He jolted. "Never mind."

"You always thought what?" Warry felt suddenly hot in the dim little room.

His father waved the question away. "No, no. It's of no importance. And what about you, my boy? Have you met any young ladies you like the look of? Or are you going to be like your sister and spend ages dithering around?"

"I..." Warry swallowed again, screwing his courage. "No young ladies, no."

His father's expression sharpened.

"But my friend..." How that word stung now! "My friend, Lord Balfour, has indicated a certain fondness for me that he believes would only grow stronger if we were to...to marry."

Earl Warrington sat back heavily into his chair. "Oh, Joseph..."

Warry held his chin up with difficulty.

Earl Warrington sighed and removed his spectacles and rubbed them against the cuff of his shirt. "Far be it for me to be as intractable as George—"

George Hartwell, Warry realised, Duke of Ancaster and Hartwell's father.

"—but I must own to a little disappointment. You are a firstborn son. You will be Earl Warrington someday. It pains me to think that if you choose a marriage that is by design childless, you will have no son to pass the title on to."

"No. But it shall go to Thomas, and if not to him, then to Clarence."

Thomas and Clarence were his younger brothers. Thomas was fourteen. Everyone had assumed there would be no more children after Thomas, but Clarence had been rather a surprise. He was three now, a stubborn fat little dumpling with a bellow on him as loud as any costermonger's.

His father sighed again. "This Lord Balfour, does he...does he make you happy?"

Warry's composure nearly broke. He'd expected his father's disapproval, not concern. He'd expected his father to be angry with him or at least annoyed, and it was a task of Herculean proportions to force out an answer in the face of what he knew to be his father's love.

"Yes," he lied, trying to keep his voice from wavering. "He makes me happy."

~

Warry would have preferred to spend the rest of his life closeted away in his bedroom undisturbed, but it was not to be. It was the Season, after all, and the whole point of coming to London was to see and be seen. He had wondered, months ago in Graythorpe, if perhaps this Season he might find a spouse. He'd certainly never suspected the circumstances in which it would happen, though. He'd had vague and unformed ideas about catching someone's gaze at a ball and discovering perhaps that they were as clumsy at dancing as he was and would much rather talk about botany, poetry, or the agricultural benefits of four-field crop rotation. He'd had fantasies of discussing these things late into the night at the Bucknall Club, drinking port with Hartwell perhaps, who would look at him with a spark of admiration in his eyes, having undergone some sort of miraculous transformation where he suddenly realised Warry wasn't boring at all. Warry wasn't sure what would have precipitated that transformation, but it was a fantasy, so it didn't matter.

He lay on his bed, not caring about wrinkling his clothes, and thought back to that time he'd kissed Hartwell. They'd been children still, and the kiss—prompted by Becca's teasing and ended by the Duke of Ancaster's outrage—had no right to still be seared into his memory the way it was. Although he had nothing else to judge it by, Warry was quite certain the kiss had been terrible, clumsy and awkward in its execution, but it caused a flutter in his belly just the same—both then and now—because he'd wanted it so very much.

Thinking of doing the same with Balfour transformed that flutter into nausea.

He sat up quickly as his door was rudely pushed open, and

Becca sailed inside. She was still undoing her bonnet, the ribbons trailing.

"What's all this nonsense about you and Balfour?" she asked, her eyes flashing.

"He…" Warry felt like a cornered animal. "He has expressed his interest."

"Of course he has," Becca said. "You're not terribly ugly in the right light." The quirk of her mouth told him she was teasing, but then her expression grew serious again, full of concern. "But why on earth have you expressed it back?"

Warry had no answer for her, but fortunately, Becca didn't require one.

"It's the Marchlands' ball tonight," she said, and then, off his look, "Of course you forgot! But you must go. This is only your second Season, Warry. I'm sure you'll find a paramour who isn't as…" She hesitated for a moment, which was very unlike her. "Well, someone who will make a better companion for you."

"I will go," he muttered. Balfour had made him promise he would.

Becca sat on the edge of the bed, placing the bonnet beside her, and studied him. She seemed prepared to say something biting again, but then her gaze grew unbearably gentle. He would have turned away but for the fact that he had not seen that expression since he was a boy and had got battered in some scuffle or other with larger, stronger lads.

She spoke softly. "I have not seen your smile since we arrived in London, save for the hour before the Gilmore rout. I have watched the light I have always sought in your eyes fade to nothing. You are my brother, and yet you suddenly seem a stranger. And worse, you have come to treat me as a stranger. That is not how we ought to be, Warry."

Now he did turn away, fearful of the tightness in his chest and throat. "You're being overly dramatic."

"No," she said simply. "I am not."

He forced his gaze back to hers, his body so tense now that pain seared from his chest to his jaw.

He did love her dearly. She had seemed many things to him over the years: a second mother, a confidante, a mild bully, a friend. Never a stranger.

Perhaps if he told her about the letter…

No.

Yet, she would know what to do. She always did.

But then why was she marrying Hartwell? If she truly knew her way out of any tight corner, then she would not be succumbing to their parents' pressure to marry. She would not be laying claim to a man like Hartwell, whom she could not even love properly, when he belonged with someone like…

Oh Lord, no.

He stared into her bright blue eyes which were filled with confusion and disappointment. How would he even begin? The very word 'letter' felt dirty on his tongue, having seen the things she had written to Miss Lilley, the desire she had expressed so boldly and in such detail. Could he ever express such a desire to someone? It would be like letting a tiger loose from its cage to wreak havoc upon Society. He tried to imagine telling Hartwell which part of *The Maiden Diaries* he had liked best—for he had read all the volumes, in their entireties, more than once. His favourite was the scene in volume one, chapter twenty-one, where Lady Blossom asks Slyfeel to tup her and her stableboy both at once. The three of them tumble in the straw of an empty box stall. Slyfeel touches the stableboy in a place Warry had never thought one could ask another human to touch. There are pages describing the stableboy's breathless whimpers, his pleas to continue. The pleasure that racks his body under Slyfeel's sure touch.

Just thinking about it set a desperate hunger racing through him, and just as quickly, shame ran ice cold through his veins, quelling that fire. He did not know if he envied Becca her boldness or despised her for her lack of propriety. She had always been so unconcerned with decorum. When he was a boy, a group of lads had taunted him for his interest in the types of sediment found in a nearby rock ledge. They'd pulled at him, slapped him, and one had thrown stones at him. When Becca saw this, she had raced toward them, picking up the largest branch she could find along the way and then using it as a sword in combat against the other boys, who had all tucked tail and run. He had been so grateful to her in that moment. He had felt such love.

She reached out now, and her cool hand brushed back the hair from his forehead, revealing what he knew were the yellowing vestiges of his largest bruise. In a panic, he sat up, forcing her hand away. She seemed about to speak and then with a soft exhale, dropped her hand back to her lap.

She would do anything for him. And he for her. Which was precisely why he could not tell her. He did not require his older sister to fight his battles for him anymore. He was responsible for this mess—*he*, and not she, despite her recklessness in putting such thoughts to paper—and he would rescue her from it.

He straightened his rumpled clothes so that he might perhaps look slightly less like a boy in need of mothering. "If you cannot be happy for me," he said coldly, "at least leave me alone. I wish to rest before the Marchland ball."

The hurt in her gaze gave him a rush of guilt and power in equal measures. She stood, her eyes narrowing ever so slightly, and offered the most economical of nods. "Whenever you are ready to tell me what pains you," she said softly, "know that I will still love you."

Then she turned and left.

CHAPTER 9

"You look as if you've a plot to murder the paper hangings."

The voice was Gale's, and Hartwell turned to face his friend.

Gale's countenance was weary as ever as he continued. "Please don't. I have enough on my plate without another dastardly deed the *ton* will wish me to provide motive for."

"This is awful," Hartwell growled. He gestured angrily to the great assembly room, decorated all in gauzy white so pristine one feared to retrieve a glass of punch, lest one spill it on some snowy drape or rug. "This place looks as though the cherubim were sick all over it. What is the meaning of this decoration?"

"Well, according to the invitation, the theme is last days of winter. I don't believe it was chosen with the express purpose of offending you, though I'm certain that is a bonus to the Marchlands, considering how you neglected to dance with their eldest daughter even once last Season."

Hartwell sighed.

"Could it be," Gale wondered aloud, "that it is not the decor which offends you but rather watching the Warrington boy nestled cosily in an alcove with that pompous, animate wax statue?"

Hartwell did not even wish to look where he knew Gale was looking. He had glanced in that direction too many times this evening already. Across the room was indeed a little alcove, its curved walls decorated with enough white wreaths to resemble a loosely disguised ritual for summoning Beelzebub. A white brocade settee had been placed with its back to a broad, arched window. On that settee, Balfour and Warry had been engaged in conversation for some half an hour.

About what, Hartwell could not imagine. The only topics he had ever heard Balfour speak on were creatures he had killed hunting, sherries he possessed that were finer than all other sherries, horses he sought to purchase but never would because their fetlocks were all dysfunctional, and the shortcomings of other members of the *ton*.

But perhaps to someone as dull as Warry, these topics were of interest.

"I care not what he does," Hartwell said. "I am offended only by the number of wreaths."

"Well," Gale said. "I am in theory here escorting my sister—"

"Clarissa?" Hartwell inquired, seeking any change in topic.

"No, I believe it is one of the others. Mary, perhaps?"

"You do not have a sister Mary."

"It is so difficult to keep track. Do I have an Annabelle?"

"You have an Anne-Marie."

"That must be who I am thinking of. Yes, well, she has made a new friend, and they appear to be hitting it off quite nicely and are currently under the watchful eye of the friend's mama. I do believe I could get away with a few turns about the garden, should you require…air."

Hartwell shook his head slowly. "I shall stay here. I must ask Rebecca to dance."

"Ah, yes of course." Gale sounded highly ironic, which irritated Hartwell further. "Is a date set to announce the engagement?"

"My parents are only just returned to Town. I thought I would give them another day or two of believing I am hopeless before showing what a good and worthy son I am and announcing my intention to marry."

Gale studied him with what seemed like mild curiosity and complete disinterest both at once. "From your tone, it sounds as though it will be a joyous occasion indeed." He gazed across the room yet again. "I do not know which of you looks more as though he has just been told he will be stoned to death at first light—you or young Warrington."

Despite himself, Hartwell aimed another glance in that direction—just as Warry tipped his head back and laughed at something Balfour had said. "He's laughing," he told Gale, his jaw clenched.

"Mmm. So convincingly," Gale murmured, still watching the scene in the alcove.

Hartwell was in no mood for whatever Gale thought he knew about the whole of humanity. "If I can, I will find you later. Right now, I wish to get punch." He stalked off toward the punch bowl, aware that he had until quite recently fancied himself above such childish storming and muttering. He had only just convinced himself not to dash his newly poured glass of punch across the infuriating whiteness of the nearest wall when he saw Balfour lead Warry to the dance floor.

This was too much. He knocked the entire glass of punch back in one gulp.

"Why, hello. You look like just the sort of brooding gentleman with homicide in his heart with whom I cannot resist the prospect of a dance."

He closed his eyes at the sound of Becca's voice.

"Come," she said softly, taking his arm. "I have been watching too. I am just as sick at heart as you. But let us go dance as though we are not insufferable mother hens who would cluck at a grown man for waltzing with whomever he wishes."

Out to the dance floor they went. Hartwell's body knew the steps well enough, which was a blessing, for his mind could focus on nothing but the sight of Warry and Balfour, Balfour's broad hand between the slightness of Warry's shoulders. Waltzing! Why, just last Season, Lord Richfield had asked Becca for a waltz at the Haverfords' rout, and her mother had nearly set fire to the drawing room with the heat of her silent disapproval. She may have wished a match for Becca above all other things, but the impropriety of waltzing with a man one barely knew trumped even her desire to see her daughter wed.

As they turned about the floor, Hartwell caught glimpses of Warry's besotted expression.

What had Gale meant by Warry laughing "so convincingly"? Warry looked happier than Hartwell had seen him in months. He attempted to focus on Becca, who was ravishing in a gown of deep burgundy, her hair pinned up and set with garnets. She had said it was all right that they remain simply friends. That he need not ever act any other way toward her. But what sort of arrangement was that for her? She was so beautiful, so funny, so wonderfully alive. She ought to be waltzing with somebody who could love her in all the ways one person might love another.

When they turned again, Balfour had one waxy hand cupping Warry's face, and was gazing down at him with the look of a man who had just got all he wanted in the world.

Hartwell stumbled. Becca yanked him back in step. A moment later, he stumbled again. "Hartwell," Becca said firmly, releasing him in midstep without a thought, it seemed, for the other merry couples who still turned around them. "Go outside and take a few breaths. Come back in when you are ready to play your part again."

He stared at her numbly. That was all it was, wasn't it? A part to play. Everyone there was to some extent a player in a vast drama that was never quite true to who people really were or what they truly desired.

He nodded wordlessly, grateful to hear the music winding down just as he began what seemed an interminable trek to the back garden. Maybe his retreat would not seem so out of place.

The garden was, thankfully, empty. Anyone who had been outside taking the air had hurried in again when the waltz started up. He paced back and forth amid the hedges, which were draped in white muslin apparently intended to resemble snow. He paused before a monstrous tree in a vast stone pot. If he stood on the far side of it, he was blocked from view of the house. He leaned against the pot, which was nearly as tall as he, feeling the prick of the bottommost evergreen branches through his hair, the cool smoothness of the stone lip against the back of his neck.

It was spring. A time of love and joy, he thought bitterly. Why on earth did the Marchlands wish to make it winter again?

Spring was for frogs and flowers. For games of chase about the garden. For hiding behind trees to tell secrets.

For...

A memory flashed through his mind—his father's hand striking his cheek, sending him reeling across the library into a shelf of stuffy old books.

"I do not care that it is 'acceptable.' It is not acceptable for my only son, my only hope for an heir."

The pain in his cheek had been dull compared to the lingering burn of Warry's lips on his.

No.

Hartwell fairly shook himself like a wet dog. That was not how things had transpired the day he'd been caught kissing Warry. He and his father were always quite amiable. That moment with Warry in the back garden was but a silly peccadillo to be left behind in the haze of childhood. He and his father had laughed about it. He had told his father that very day that his true love was for Becca. That he would marry her one day.

No, that wasn't right either. He raked a hand furiously through his hair. He had certainly not been the one to plant the ridiculous idea of marrying Becca in his parents' minds.

Another flash of memory: He was pleading with his father, promising that he *would* one day marry Becca. Anything to persuade his father that his desires urged him toward a wife who would provide heirs and not a husband who, even if Hartwell loved him more dearly than life itself, never could. No. No, his mind was making more of that day than there had been to it, taking his father's disappointment and stretching it out like the growing shadows of a nightmare into something much larger and darker than it was. It wasn't his father who hated some hidden part of him, it was himself. His father's faint suspicion and cautious disapproval didn't run so deep or so violently. Yet he was, to a degree, deeply afraid that it could if only those suspicions were proven.

He looked round at the sound of footsteps, angry and relieved at once to have his thoughts interrupted.

His relief dissipated when he realised the footsteps were Warry's.

Warry appeared equally startled to see him. "I needed some air," Warry said defensively.

Hartwell stared.

It seemed that light shimmered all around the other man, though the garden held only the glow of the moon and the weak flickering of candles from inside the house. Barely enough for the two men to identify each other.

Warry was not meant to kiss him that day. He was meant to be too frightened of putting a foot wrong. He was meant to flee at the merest whiff of indecency. The Viscount Warrington was like the Marchlands' assembly room—so pure and snow-white that he began to seem wicked through sheer excess of virtue.

It is you, Warry, you false thing. You are the reason for my present condition. You are the reason I will announce my engagement to Becca in three days' time. Why are you out here? What more could you possibly want from me?

"Breathless with the giddiness of new love?" Hartwell asked dully.

The moonlight caught Warry's eyes, which were so still as to be unnerving. "I suppose you would know nothing of it," he replied.

"I know better than any when it is a lie. A show put on for those barking spectators whose tongues will wag if you so much as let your smile slip whilst you waltz."

"If you are speaking of your own interrupted waltz with Becca, yes, you made quite a spectacle of yourself. Tongues were already wagging as I left." Warry's tone was hard and cold, echoing the false winter around them.

"Did you come out here to badger me?"

"No. As surprising as you will find this, not everyone arranges their lives based on your movements."

"I did not imply that everyone does. Merely you. I have allowed you to dog my steps since nearly your first breath, and you have given me nothing in return but hours of vexation and tedium."

"I shall go back inside to Balfour, then. He seems far from bored with me."

Anger welled in Hartwell's chest. Shocking that such heat could engulf his heart so thoroughly in a fraction of an instant. As Warry turned to go, Hartwell grabbed his arm, tugging him back behind the stone pot.

"Tell me the truth," Hartwell demanded as Warry fell against him with the force of the pull. "That is all I ask."

"The truth of what?" Warry growled, shoving Hartwell off and then whirling them both in a circle that ended with Hartwell's back slammed against the massive stone planter, Warry somehow gripping his wrists, pinning them against the stone surface. Even Warry looked shocked.

Hartwell was dizzied with feeling: desire, frustration, a sorrow that seemed to reach back through all the years he and Warry had known each other. A longing so deep he might drown in it. How could a mere pup break him like this? Because Warry was far from a mere pup. And that was what made Hartwell's heart pound.

They were both breathing hard. The moon shone directly down on them, outlining Warry's lips in silver. The whites of his eyes gleamed. Hartwell had to wet his own lips just to be able to speak. He started to shift his arms, a tentative experiment, and Warry shoved his wrists harder against the stone. The force of it sent an unexpectedly pleasurable jolt through Hartwell.

"What is it you plan to do to me?" Hartwell attempted a rakish smile. Had a feeling he failed.

Warry didn't answer. Just held Hartwell there, staring at him.

Slowly, Hartwell moved again, and this time Warry let him lower his arms. Warry didn't let go of Hartwell's wrists, but Hartwell took hold of Warry's as well and rather politely walked them both in a circle so that now Warry's back was against the planter. Hartwell did not push or pin him, simply backed him up until Warry could, perhaps, feel the coolness of the stone through his coat and shirt.

"Tell me you feel nothing for me," Hartwell said. "Tell me you feel nothing in this moment, and I will leave you be. Tonight and forever. I will never speak to you again if that is what you wish. I merely ask that you do not lie to me." The softness of his tone belied the force of feeling within him. He tried not to shiver at the way his thumb had slipped under the cuff of Warry's coat and was now pressed upon the pulse of his wrist.

The warmth of Warry's breath and body cut through the chill of the evening as the other man panted hard, his head tipped back against the planter. His wrists still in Hartwell's grasp, he nonetheless shoved out with such force that he caught Hartwell in the chest, his palms connecting with the front of Hartwell's coat with a *womp*.

Hartwell gripped him a little tighter. Warry shoved him again, this time forcing Hartwell back a step. "You know nothing of me.

You know nothing of my life!" His voice was low, but so raw with anger that it hurt Hartwell's own throat to hear it. "You spent the whole of our childhood treating me as though I were weak, and—and completely unnecessary. You do not now get to stare at me from across the room as though I belong to you. I *never have*."

He tried to shove Hartwell again, but Hartwell lifted his wrists and held them over his head against the stone. Not hard. Warry could escape easily if he wished.

Warry gasped, looking up at Hartwell with an expression Hartwell recognised as fear, even in the dark. He loosened his grip further, a numb horror winding through him. Never in all his life, not even now, half sick with jealousy and quite furious with himself for it, would he have wanted Joseph Warrington to look at him in fear.

Yet Warry's next gasp, which ended in a shuddering exhale through parted lips, was far from fearful. And that was even worse.

He released Warry altogether. His and Warry's harsh, shallow breaths were drawn in unison for a moment before Hartwell spoke. "Then go. If I do not belong to you in any small way, if there is no part of the last nineteen years you would keep, then go." He had wanted it to sound benevolent, dignified. *Go with my blessing*. Instead he sounded hurt and bewildered.

Warry held his wrists in front of him, almost as if imploring Hartwell to take them again. Hartwell knew that was wishful thinking. "I did not say you do not belong to me. I said I do not belong to you."

Hartwell had not realised his misspeak. "Is there any difference?" he asked hoarsely.

Warry's eyes were so wide they seemed replicas of the moon. And in the darkness at their centres was a need that was unmistakable as it echoed Hartwell's own.

The next moment, it was Warry who had Hartwell's wrists again and was kissing him madly. His mouth was warm and soft and forced against Hartwell's as though he had been starving for such contact for a long, long time.

Hartwell got a hold of himself and slipped his hands from Warry's grasp to cup his face. With every ounce of strength inside him, he gentled the kiss, using his hands to lessen the pressure, to draw the moment into something long and tender.

This was peace.

This was a dip in time, silent and delicate as a doe placing her hoof in fresh snow, where they no longer existed in reality. Where Hartwell could simply have *this*.

With a deep inhale that drew Warry's breath along with his own, he pressed his body the whole length of Warry's, his knee sliding between the other man's legs. The whimper Warry made held both shock and need in it, and oh, the thought of having Warry somewhere he could properly undo him made every muscle in Hartwell's body tense with desire.

He pulled back suddenly. *Good God.* To have lectured Warry about his reputation the other night, and to now have…

Oh no. Oh God.

"We cannot," Hartwell said curtly. Oh, for Christ's sake, he had not meant to say it like that. But fear was rapidly overtaking even desire. If his father found out, or Becca, or Balfour, or *anyone*…

Then came a moment longer than any before, in which the haze in Warry's eyes cleared to allow in recognition—and then a betrayal that seemed to hone the moon's silver light to a blade.

"Go back to him." Hartwell spoke quietly. "Since you care for him so."

Warry stared at him with such hurt and fury that Hartwell could not help but feel a brief sense of satisfaction. *Now you know what it is to watch you waltz with Balfour.*

It did not last. There could be no satisfaction so long as he saw hurt in those blue eyes.

Warry tore himself from Hartwell, folding his arms against his midsection as though Hartwell's very touch might have poisoned him. "I should have known," he muttered. He stood there, hunched over, anger in every line of his body. Then he strode toward the house. Hartwell leaned back against the stone, breathing hard, and after a moment peered over his shoulder, watching Warry step back into the light.

CHAPTER 10

"An engagement!"

Warry straightened from where he'd been slumped on the chaise longue as his mother swept into the drawing room.

"Isn't it wonderful!"

He struggled to respond, afraid, in his confusion, that she spoke of the arrangement between himself and Balfour. Then he recalled the news that had been imparted to him in last evening's haze.

"Yes, yes, wonderful indeed!" his mother went on, picking up one of the cakes Warry had left on the tea set and taking a bite. She swiped crumbs from the corner of her lip with her pinkie. "I don't know when I've been so happy! Your sister is finally engaged. She and Hartwell certainly kept us waiting long enough. I had begun to fear it would never happen."

Warry let his head flop back against the cushion.

"We've decided to formally announce it at Lord Balfour's ball next week, which is the first true event of the Season." By true, of course, she meant important, by whatever metric it was these things were measured by the *ton*. "Warry, dear, I'll need your word that you will be there."

Warry's insides turned to ice. He would be there of course. Balfour would insist on it. But the day of Balfour's ball also marked the end of the week that Balfour had given their courtship before he turned up at the Warringtons' to declare his intentions to the earl. Would the Warringtons have two engagements to announce that night?

Warry wrinkled his nose and strove to keep his tone sullen rather than panicked. "Of course I will. Though nobody will even notice me with Becca and Hartwell to gush over."

"Nonsense, darling." Lady Warrington sat beside him on the chaise longue, smoothing the fall of her dress with a delicate, practiced hand. "Getting your oldest child engaged is like finally pulling the stuck cork out of a bottle. It pops free, and all the contents come rushing out!" Her brow creased, and she reached over to pat him gently on the knee. "Did I just compare my darlings to a bottle of wine? Perhaps, but no matter—now that the cork is popped and Becca is engaged, you will start to receive plenty of interest. As will Charlotte, though she's only seventeen!"

Warry nodded warily. Obviously his father hadn't yet spoken to her of Warry's interest in his "friend" Lord Balfour. Or maybe he had, and this was her way of reminding him that he still had plenty of prospects to choose from, and perhaps he should be looking elsewhere. Warry doubted it though; his mother had never been one for keeping her feelings on a subject to herself, especially when the subject was her children. She was direct to the point of shocking bluntness on occasion, a sin gladly forgiven by her large circle of friends because she was beautiful, rich, and tangentially related to the House of Hanover. Warry loved her desperately and wished he had inherited her same forthrightness instead of the awkward timidity he'd got from...well, he wasn't entirely sure where it had come from. Perhaps he was just the useless runt of his parents' otherwise robust litter.

And speak of the devil.

A small figure barrelled through the doorway, his leading

strings trailing from his frock. At three, Clarence was almost old enough for a skeleton suit and probably far too old for leading strings, but he was something of an escapee and had never seen a doorway—or a window—he didn't try to rush through in search of new adventure.

He glared at Warry and his mother, and then made a beeline for Warry's leftover cake.

"Oh, where are your manners?" Lady Warrington chided as Clarence smashed a fistful of cake in his face as though she hadn't just done the same thing, albeit with more delicacy. "You could choke, darling!"

"We can only hope," Warry said sardonically. He personally thought that, when it came to swallowing cake, Clarence could unhinge his jaw like a snake's.

His mother didn't seem to notice. She clapped her hands together like a young girl. "Oh, isn't it just wonderful? I have invited the Hartwells to tea this afternoon to celebrate the soon-to-be joining of our families."

Warry's stomach dropped. If this day could get any worse, he wasn't sure how. "Please stop saying 'isn't it wonderful,'" he muttered.

"When it stops being so wonderful, I shall stop saying it is so." She frowned at him, tugging his unknotted cravat lightly. "You really should change before tea. You look frightfully discomposed."

Warry glanced at his trousers. Passed a hand through his mussed and dirty hair. "I shall not come to tea."

"Don't be absurd. We must have the whole family assembled. Even the little ones." She glanced fondly at Clarence, who had crumbs all over his plump, sticky face.

"Ah yes, that makes me so much more inclined to attend."

His mother shot him a glare of warning. "Stop being difficult."

"Top berng difficuwt!" Clarence echoed through his mouthful of cake.

"I have a headache." Warry hoped he sounded reasonable, despite the childish whine trying to creep into his voice.

"Oh, pooh. Some fresh air will do you good. It's a lovely day. We will serve tea in the garden."

"I said I do not wish to be in attendance!" he snapped.

His mother stared at him, her shock evident. Warry felt a flash of guilt, but it was quickly replaced by anger. He fairly launched himself upright and stalked out of the room, slapping the doorframe as he exited—a gesture that was both less satisfying and more painful than he'd expected. He pounded up the stairs, shutting his bedroom door so firmly behind him that it echoed through the house.

~

An hour later, he was seated at the garden table in fresh clothes. Becca sat to his right and Hartwell across the table from her. Warry snuck occasional glances at Hartwell, who looked well in a gold waistcoat with a crisp white shirt underneath. Hartwell studiously avoided looking at him, which was just as well.

Warry was still smarting from the chiding his mother had given him through his bedroom door. But the mood at the table was every bit as horrid as he had been imagining. His mother chattered gaily, his father offering a grunt of agreement every now and then around a finger sandwich. The Duke of Ancaster kept laughing heartily as though every word out of Lady Warrington's mouth were a witticism while the duchess, Hartwell's mother, remarked repeatedly on the excellent quality of the tea. The only saving grace was that Warry's Clarence had made such a fuss that he'd been sent from the table in the company of the governess.

Becca kept a placid smile on her face throughout but seemed a million miles away. Hartwell put far too much effort into appearing glad of his engagement, even taking Becca's hand at one point, which turned her serene smile to a look of confusion before she seemed to realise she should be pleased at the display of affection. Charlotte had a series of questions for Becca about how Hartwell had proposed, and it was clear from Becca's vague answers that the proposal story was not one worth sharing. Warry imagined it had been made in haste—and in anger—by a pathetic, selfish man who could not make up his mind what he wanted.

Or was it he who had strung Hartwell along? he wondered guiltily. His head pounded such that he could no longer recall who had begun whatever strange game they were playing. He only knew that he was miserably ashamed of himself, for many reasons.

And that Hartwell had embraced him that night in Ancaster's library. Had fairly begged him to say what was on his mind.

I do not like to see you hurt.

Warry had been the one to walk away.

Hartwell had returned Warry's kiss. He had returned it with such passion and tenderness, with such undeniable need. But then, instead of saying aloud that he desired Warry, instead of praising Warry's beauty or murmuring sweet words to him, he had pushed him away. As though Warry were once more the annoying younger brother following along on an adventure. *Go home, Warry. You are not needed here.*

"Go back to him. Since you care for him so."

Warry had already spent most of the Marchlands' party in forced conversation with Balfour about the man's many fine possessions, tensing each time Balfour let slip hints about what he might like to do with Warry once they were wed. He had made himself smile. Made himself laugh, made himself dance. Made himself recall that he deserved this for putting Becca in danger. To kiss Hartwell after all that had felt like salvation, however briefly. To be pushed away and ordered back to Balfour had been…

He ought not to think of it.

All he knew was that he would rather spend another evening on a settee with Balfour, attempting to appear bright and animated through a one-sided conversation about Balfour's sherry collection than spend another moment in the garden.

He drained the last of his tea and stood. "If you'll excuse me—" he began.

"Oh, Warry!" His mother waved him back down. She addressed the table. "I fear our Warry is a bit envious to see his sister so happily engaged."

The blood drained from his face.

She went on. "I told him not to fret. Rebecca having been spoken for—with the Season scarcely underway, I might add—he will see an outpouring of attention. He will make a match of his own in no time!"

The blood flooded back to his face in hot streaks as the Duke of Ancaster laughed and agreed.

"I am not envious," he said, trying hard to keep the fury from his tone. "I merely wish to rest."

Charlotte tugged Warry's sleeve. "Oh, Warry, do stay. I never see you anymore."

He was aware of the message behind the words: *Sit down. Smile. Act as though everything is marvellous, or mother will have a fit later.*

Warry, coward that he was and always had been, discounting one brief and ill-fated moment last night, sat. All eyes were on him —except for Hartwell's, which were determinedly on his plate.

"Perhaps Warry does not desire a match," Becca said suddenly, loudly. "Some people do not, you know."

Their mother's smile faltered. "Yes, well. Some may believe it is not what they want, but marriage is one of life's great joys." She turned to her husband as though for affirmation.

"Hmm?" Earl Warrington glanced up, his mouth full of seed-cake, which he promptly swallowed. "Oh, yes. Yes, it's…something." He coughed. "To be cherished," he added hastily.

"I wasn't even sure I wanted to marry George at first," the

Duchess of Ancaster confessed, placing her fingers over her lips as though to belatedly stifle the small squeak of laughter she let out.

The duke laughed uproariously. "I only had to ask her three times!"

There was general laughter, including a peal of giggles from Charlotte, who looked back and forth between members of the table as though she was uncertain what, precisely, they were all laughing at.

Then Hartwell's voice boomed out, cutting through the near-manic gaiety. "Well, of course Warry wants a match. One need only note the happiness in his eyes when he looks upon Lord Balfour."

Silence fell. Warry felt something inside him wrench painfully, but he was far too shocked to speak.

Hartwell chewed the last of his seedcake, glancing around the table. "I'm so sorry," he said in unconvincing penitence, his gaze meeting Warry's for a mere second. "I assumed it was common knowledge that Warry and Balfour are courting."

Warry stared at Hartwell, hoping upon hope that the force of his anger might be enough to drop the fellow dead. It was not, alas— nor was the vicious kick Becca dealt Hartwell under the table—and the marquess remained very much alive. He met Warry's eye and held his gaze this time, speaking deliberately. "You *did* say you were no longer afraid for Society to know how much you cared for him. Forgive me."

Lady Warrington had initially made a small, sharp gasp at the news, and now she said tentatively, "Lord Balfour?"

Earl Warrington cleared his throat. "I was not sure when Warry wished to make it public, but I suppose congratulations are in order on that end too." He raised his teacup as though it were a champagne flute and knocked his tea back with such haste it seemed his throat would be scalded.

"You knew?" Lady Warrington demanded.

Ancaster seemed to have run out of things to laugh at. He

addressed the earl seriously. "You would allow your eldest son, your best hope for an heir, to court a…a man?"

Earl Warrington's eyes narrowed slightly. There was tension between his father and the duke that Warry had not noticed before. "I wish for my son to do what makes him happy."

"Well, Balfour certainly makes him happy," Hartwell said, taking a page out of Earl Warrington's book and throwing back his tea as though it were a stiff belt of whiskey.

"If only anyone gave a single thought as to what might make me happy," Becca said archly.

"Whatever do you mean?" Hartwell's reply fairly dripped sarcasm. "Surely we are the happiest couple in London right now?"

Charlotte was glancing up and down the table once more. "I'm confused. Is everybody…not really happy?"

"You know"—Ancaster suddenly placed both palms firmly on the table—"I could do with a bit of exercise. William has told me you have a wonderful archery range on the other side of those trees." He gestured at the copse.

"Ooh!" Charlotte squealed. "Yes, let us have an archery practice!"

Even Becca seemed genuinely cheered by the prospect. "Oh, might we?"

Hartwell clearly struggled to smile. "An excellent idea. I should like to know who the better shot is between my future wife and me." He glanced across the table. "Warry? What do you say we fire a few arrows?"

~

Ancaster went first and proved himself a respectable shot. His son followed and did abysmally, managing to land one arrow of three on the outer edge of the target. The others were lost somewhere upon the grass.

Becca went to retrieve the arrows and then returned to the line, panting and fanning herself. "I ought not to have changed into my archer's jacket," she said breathlessly, laughing. "It may give my arms more freedom, but I am sweating like a hog."

"Becca," her mother hissed. "Ladies do not speak of sweat. Or hogs."

"Or freedom," Becca muttered. She took her place before the target, nocking her first arrow. "Come, watch how it is done, William!" Everyone's mood seemed to have improved significantly, except for Warry's. He would have bargained with the devil to get the day to end.

Becca sank her first arrow into the centre of the target. Then her second, then her third.

She crowed in triumph; the sound echoed by Charlotte. Hartwell whistled and hurried to fetch the arrows.

"See that you don't ever get on the wrong side of your future wife, William!" Ancaster called jovially.

"My turn!" Charlotte cried.

"Be careful," Becca chided her. "Do not kill anyone."

"It was one time," Charlotte protested. "And I didn't *kill* Lord Thickbeard. Merely frightened him."

"Charlotte!" their mother hissed. "We do not name gentlemen according to the thickness of their facial hair."

Becca rolled her eyes, taking an arrow from Hartwell and passing it to Charlotte. "It was closer than was at all comfortable."

Two of Charlotte's arrows missed the target entirely, but the third landed near the bullseye. Charlotte was ecstatic. "Warry, your turn!" She passed him the bow.

Warry stepped up to the line, making a desperate deal with God that if he shot one round, God would send him a thunderstorm or a flood or a rain of brimstone; anything that would put an end to the horrible afternoon and, preferably, wipe Hartwell from the face of the earth. To think he had felt sympathy for the man, wondered if the mess they were in was his own fault. Yes, Hartwell had comforted him in the library and kissed him tenderly in the Marchland's garden and suggested, on both occasions, that they belonged to each other in some way neither of them seemed able to define. But he had also pushed Warry away last night, announced Warry's courtship of Balfour to both of their families, humiliated him once more.

"Perhaps Warry will be so kind as to shoot wide and make me feel better about my fiancée showing me up," the man in question remarked from behind him.

Swiftly, calmly, as though his mind were divorced from his body, Warry fired three arrows, one after the other, directly into the bullseye.

Silence greeted his triumph where cheers had greeted Becca's, but then he realised he had somehow filtered out all sound that was not Hartwell's voice, which murmured, "No, I suppose not," without a trace of its previous good humour.

Becca clapped and bounced on her toes. "I can't believe my younger brother is beginning to match me in skill! Look sharp, William. You are by far the poorest shot of the group."

Warry turned and found himself staring directly at Hartwell. "If only you knew what you were aiming for," he said icily, "perhaps you would not fire so blindly."

"You fired so many arrows so rapidly. Was it not enough to sink just one?"

"You might tell me." Warry's gaze flicked to Becca.

"I'll try again," Hartwell said without looking away from Warry. "I feel quite warmed up now."

Becca fanned lightly under her arms. "I'm afraid I cannot make the trek to the target again. Warry, be a dear and fetch the arrows but leave one in the centre. I wish to try to split it after William has had his turn, and I know *he* won't plant any in the bullseye."

Seething, Warry headed for the target, glancing up at the sky to see if God had any intention of making good on their deal. The sky remained a vivid blue with soft white clouds and a bright sun.

He heard Hartwell say, "Where is that extra arrow? Ah, Charlotte, might you show me how you nock it?"

Warry reached the target and pulled several arrows out, leaving one in the bullseye. He started back toward the line, then hesitated, looking back at the holes in the target and remembering a day long ago spent fetching arrows for Becca and Hartwell as they practised. Hartwell had been a poor shot then too.

As he turned round to continue forward, there were gasps, and a shriek—and in the same instant an arrow buried itself in the ground, inches from his feet.

He looked up, not quite sure what had happened. He saw Hartwell standing at the line, holding the bow. Charlotte was beside him, her hands clapped over her mouth.

"I am sorry," Hartwell said, looking to the others but not at Warry. He sounded rather stunned. "I meant only to practise my form. I did not mean to loose the arrow."

Becca looked angry enough to tear out her intended's eyes. "You could have killed him!"

Warry glanced down at the feathered shaft sticking up from the grass, then back at Hartwell.

Yes, he could have. Last night, certainly. If Hartwell had kept going, if he hadn't pushed Warry away, Warry might have died in bliss. No fewer than a dozen times over the past years, Hartwell could have slain him with a look, a word, a touch, and Warry would have welcomed it.

Ancaster tried to laugh. "Perhaps Lady Rebecca would be so kind as to help my son adjust his form. He seems quite hopeless."

"Nonsense." Becca also made an attempt to laugh lightly. "I'm too sweaty to stand that close to William. He would call off the engagement at once. Warry should do it. That shall be William's punishment for his carelessness. To learn from a man four years his junior and ten times his better how to fire an arrow."

It seemed Warry would never convince his feet to move. He stood on the grass between the target and the others, wishing for a blinding instant that they would all take up bows and fire into him, for that seemed the only proper way for the nightmare to end.

There was Balfour's voice in his ear, telling him he would prove a pleasure. Balfour's hand at his back, steering him about the floor in a waltz. And there was Hartwell's breathless sound of need as his mouth closed over Warry's. The deliberate certainty with which he had announced to everyone that Warry was happy with Balfour.

He met Hartwell's gaze again and saw in it the same tortured longing from last night. The bow hung at Hartwell's side, and he looked completely lost. Helpless.

Warry knew at once what he must do. It would be the simplest, most perfect revenge—and a most deserved punishment for himself as well. Silently, he closed the distance between them and took up a place at Hartwell's side, dropping all but one arrow onto the grass. He lifted Hartwell's arm and positioned the bow for him. Heard the hitch in Hartwell's breathing and felt the brief seizure of the other man's muscles before he surrendered and allowed Warry to guide him.

Warry pressed his body against Hartwell's, wrapping his arms around the man so they were both holding the bow. He nocked the arrow expertly, resting his chin briefly on Hartwell's shoulder. The shudder that passed through Hartwell nearly produced an answering one in him. He held his breath as Hartwell tipped his head ever so slightly back, as though he suddenly ached everywhere, just as Warry did, and was simply too exhausted to fight anymore. Warry let go of the bow with one hand so Hartwell now held the arrow in place. He placed his other palm against the small of Hartwell's back, and revelled in the force of Hartwell's jolt.

The bow was shaking so badly, Warry feared there was no chance of the arrow hitting the target. But he waited, letting the heat of his body seep into Hartwell's. No one in the world existed but the two of them right then, and Hartwell seemed to know it too. He lowered his bow arm, letting the arrow droop downward and the tension slip from the string, but Warry nudged him. And waited, his hand on the back of Hartwell's waistcoat, noting how slim, almost delicate, the nip of the man's waist was. At long last,

Hartwell lifted and steadied the bow, pulling back the string. His breathing was still quite audible and ragged. Warry very subtly adjusted Hartwell's aim so the arrow was positioned perfectly for the target's centre.

Then he turned his head slightly and whispered in Hartwell's ear, "Go on then. Fire."

CHAPTER 11

"I cannot believe I didn't see it before." Becca was near to wearing a furrow in the lawn with her pacing.

Hartwell was not entirely sure how they had got to this small, relatively sheltered patch of lawn, far from any windows and potentially prying eyes. The rest of the group had retired indoors after archery, but Becca had held him back and asked that her maid be sent out so that she might have a "conversation" with Hartwell. Hartwell was also not entirely sure what Becca had said to Annie to convince the young woman to stand a discreet few yards away— Hartwell hoped out of earshot, but given how loudly Becca was speaking and the way the girl was glancing furtively at them every few seconds, most likely not.

"This explains a great deal. A *great* deal."

"What are you talking about?" Hartwell tried to keep his tone cool, but after what had unfolded on the archery green, that seemed an impossible task.

She whirled on him. "Do not play the innocent with me. You have kept enough from me already. You love my brother. I suppose I suspected it—yes, I'm sure I did—but I did not truly see it until now."

"What?" He did not even have to feign his shock because her words were so patently absurd. *Love* Warry? Certainly, Hartwell had admired the lad on occasion. Anybody with eyes could see how attractive he was. And yes, he had kissed Warry last night, and yes Warry's lips had been sweet indeed...but it had been a mistake. A terrible one that he had rectified by pushing Warry off and sending him trotting back to Balfour like a good pup before Warry ruined his prospects with Balfour and the *ton* began whispering that Hartwell could not get enough Warringtons to suit him.

What had got into Becca? She was usually a sensible woman. Not one to throw around words like *love*, the way some girls did.

"William, I'm going to need you to catch up with me. You look at my brother the way I look at cake, and when he is not attempting to glare the entire world into submission, that is how he looks at you too. Is that why you went out to the garden last night at precisely the same moment he also needed air?"

Hartwell couldn't speak. That was all the answer Becca needed.

She heaved a sigh of frustration that made Annie glance around again. "William Hartwell! Did you propose to me because you are angry that my brother is courting Lord Balfour?"

"Of course not! I proposed to you because we agreed that to marry for convenience would benefit us both."

"You proposed to me last night, after you had been out in the back garden, with all the finesse of a losing faro player throwing his cards onto the table in disgust. Did you do it merely to hurt him?"

"How could you think that of me?" he asked with a surge of righteous anger. "We needed to get engaged, and so we got engaged. Your brother may do whatever he likes with Lord Balfour. I care not. It is possible that I have looked at him once or twice and thought him attractive, but I imagine you of all people would understand if my desires do not run solely in the direction of women."

"You think that is what I care about? William..." She closed her eyes briefly, then opened them again with resolve. "I do not care who you share your bed with. I myself am—have been—entangled with women. With one woman in particular."

Hartwell stared at her, not shocked, but hurt. "You never told me."

"Yes, well. Society heaps enough shame on women without us advertising our indiscretions. I have always thought you one of the more understanding and compassionate men I knew, and yet…this was not a woman I could ever marry, you understand. Our dalliance had to be a secret, and I tell you this now with the understanding that you will repeat it to no one."

He wanted to say of course—that all her secrets always had been and always would be safe with him. He wanted to take her in his arms and embrace her and revel in the knowledge that they were alike. That their marriage would prove a success simply because they understood each other so well. But he could think of nothing except his confusion and humiliation as Warry had pressed their bodies together and guided his arrow on the green.

He had hit the bullseye. That was the funny thing.

He shook his head. "You and your brother both," he spat. "No thought for your reputations at all. I thought you had more sense than he, but clearly I was mistaken."

Her eyes flashed the deepest hurt he could ever recall seeing in them—God, she looked just as Warry had last night when Hartwell had ended the kiss—and then that hurt transformed to pure fury. "Why do you speak of my brother's reputation?"

"You should have seen the spectacle he made of himself at the Four-in-Hand the other night. I found him in a darkened corner, Balfour kissing his hand most lasciviously—nearly salivating as he did so—and Warry adoring every second of it."

"The Four-in-Hand? What on earth was Warry doing at a gaming hell?"

"Perhaps he takes after your father."

Becca looked as though he had slapped her. "My father's habits are none of your concern."

"Aren't they? We are to be family soon. The Warringtons' reputation will be very much my concern."

Becca drew herself up, fire sparking in her gaze. "The engagement is off. I will spell it out for you, as you are too thick-skulled to see, what you did to Warry today—revealing his courtship with Balfour before the whole table—the way you have just spoken about my brother and about me…I would not marry you for all the world."

Hartwell started in alarm. "You cannot do that."

"Can I not? I believe I just did."

"Becca, if I do not get married, and soon, my father will cut me off. I will lose my fortune."

She laughed, the sound high-pitched and furious. "Oh, well then, so long as you are playing with my brother's heart and my future happiness for a reason so excellent as money."

"*Me*, play with your brother's heart? Oh, that is rich. If you could see the way he has played me, all the while clinging to Balfour—"

"Somehow I doubt that is the whole of the story."

"This is entirely your fault, you know. You mother him incessantly, and it has driven him right into Balfour's arms."

"Would you care to stop speaking?" Her eyes blazed. "For you have gone from inexcusable to the very border of unforgivable."

Hartwell stepped back, startled at her vehemence. Unforgivable? He and Becca were the closest of friends. There should have been nothing between them that was unforgivable. They'd fought in the past as fiercely as cats and dogs, and yet Hartwell had never doubted that sooner or later one of them would make amends and they would go on as before. But now? Becca's gaze was fiery, but her expression was cold, and Hartwell knew that she was not lying or exaggerating. She truly meant it.

"Your *brother*…" he began, and then had no idea how to continue.

Your brother torments *me.*

And oh, it would have been a much easier torment to withstand if only Hartwell didn't *want* the damn boy, and if only it didn't make him feel sick to his very soul to imagine Warry in Balfour's bed—and not just because of the piercing jealousy that image caused—but because Hartwell wanted, in some part of him that was pure and free of taintedness, for Warry to be *happy*. He knew, with no shadow of a doubt, that if Warry bound himself to Balfour through marriage, nobody would ever see his shy, hard-won smiles again. It infuriated him that whatever stupid game Warry was playing, he was willing to marry a man like Balfour and sentence himself to a lifetime of suffering the man's attentions instead of just admitting Hartwell was right, and he was making a terrible mistake.

Damn Warry and his pride.

Damn all the Warringtons and their pride, in fact.

"Don't marry me, then," he said, lifting his chin. "See if I care a whit. And when you're an old maid because there is no one worthy of your attention, and Warry is buried in misery because there's no one beneath his, we'll see who is happy, shall we?"

Becca slapped him.

Hartwell's head went back fast, in shock more than in pain.

"How dare you," Becca said. Her face was pale. "Get out. I don't want to see your face again. We are no longer friends."

Hartwell let his mouth curl up into a sneer as he bowed. "As you wish, Lady Rebecca. Good day."

~

"Balfour, hmm?" the Duke of Ancaster said in the carriage on the way home. "Good God."

"It's not a terrible match, I suppose." The duchess tapped her gloved fingers on her knee. "If one cares not for heirs. Perhaps the earl favours the younger boys over Warry, do you think? Warry's always been a little…" She pursed her lips and stared at nothing for a moment, her brow creasing. "Odd. Yes, odd. Do you remember when they came to stay with us, and nobody could find him, and he was out with one of the farmers helping with the lambing?"

Hartwell remembered. Becca had thought it amusing, and everyone else had considered it terribly gauche, but Hartwell had thought it strangely charming. Not the fact that Warry had eventually been discovered covered in blood and sheep's afterbirth, but the way he'd lit up when talking about holding a newborn lamb, his eyes bright and his expression joyful.

"Still," the duchess continued thoughtfully, her gaze finding Hartwell, "you really oughtn't have shot at him."

"It was an accident, Mother." Hartwell's sour mood was not improved by being trapped in a carriage with his parents.

"Yes, dear, just like the time my embroidery needle slipped and gouged your father," she said drily. "I wonder, though, if Warry's oddness is not precisely what makes the match work. Balfour is quite odd himself."

Hartwell was glad someone agreed with him on that point.

"He keeps fine horses," the duke noted.

"Yes, but surely you recall the rumours about his association with the Warringtons' former valet. The one who stole their silver? Well, they did not admit he stole the silver, but certainly the silver went missing at the time he was dismissed, and the earl refused to write him any letters of recommendation."

Hartwell pricked his ears at that. This was not a story he'd heard before.

"And we all know," his mother continued, "what that means. The valet was Joseph's too, I believe."

"Ah, yes." The duke nodded. "But I keep telling you, my dear, a man may rub elbows with a low-life in a gaming hell and have it count not at all against his reputation. And speaking of gaming hells, I would not doubt that the fortune Balfour is set to inherit factors into the earl's decision to allow the match. Warrington's gambling debts are greater than he'd like to admit, and Balfour does something rather baffling and mysterious with stocks I believe."

"Stock?" the duchess asked. "Do you mean horses?"

"No, my dear. The markets, you know? The exchange." The duke shrugged. "While I can't ever approve of a first son marrying a man, I do understand if the earl is hoping to join his household with Balfour's estate."

Hartwell barely felt the jab, so bewildered was he by this new information. Balfour was an associate of Warry's former valet?

The duchess shifted in her seat. "I suppose. But Earl Warrington was livid when he dismissed that servant. You'd think it would disturb him to see his son matched with a man who hobnobs with the fellow who stole from his household."

"We don't know that he hobnobs."

The discussion descended into familiar, airy bickering. Hartwell reached for his father's walking stick and used it to rap on the ceiling. "The Bucknall Club!"

"Oh, really," his mother murmured.

His father grunted.

Hartwell escaped the carriage when it drew to a stop outside the club, bidding his parents a good day. The doorman welcomed him politely, holding the door open so Hartwell could sweep inside, and once in the lobby, a boy divested him of his hat and gloves.

The club was a series of sumptuous rooms where a gentleman might drink, converse, gamble, read, dine, or even escape the day by taking a nap in one of the gloriously comfortable wingback chairs. It was still early, so Hartwell wasn't expecting any of his friends to be there yet—they were mostly night owls—but he spied Stratford, as shy and meek as a country parson, poring over a broadsheet. He nodded a hello and continued on into the next room where he was pleased to see Gale glaring at a glass of port while being genially accosted.

"But how on earth did you know the letter in question was hidden inside the cover of the old book?" a young man with alarmingly golden curls asked.

Gale took a swig of his port. "Well, it was obvious! Tiresomely obvious!"

Hartwell moved forward and shooed Gale's admirers away. "Has there been another story about you in the newspapers?"

"*The Morning Post*." Gale sighed and slouched deeper into his seat. "I must flee to the Continent or to some uncivilised part of the world where nobody can read. America, perhaps."

Hartwell sat. "That seems drastic. Especially as you must still conclude your current case."

"Dammit, Hartwell, I have asked you not to call it a case."

"Just tell me who your lead suspect is."

"Wouldn't you like to know?"

"Is it murder or something duller?"

"If I tell you it is a financial crime, will you talk of something else?"

"Not a chance. But perhaps if you tell me what the *Post* said about you…"

"You may find that out easily enough."

"You know I don't read."

Gale barked a laugh. "So, you do not know what happens in chapter twenty-one of that dirty little novel you picked up?"

Hartwell felt himself colour up. "Well…"

"Just as I thought. You will be asking me to find you volume two tomorrow." Gale tilted his glass and stared after the golden-haired fellow. "Why won't people just let me be? I don't like them, and there's no reason they ought to like me."

"Don't be peevish," Hartwell said peevishly.

Gale narrowed his eyes, a dangerous expression indeed coming from him. "I was going to say congratulations on the engagement, but of course she's already broken it off, hasn't she?"

"How can you possibly know that?"

"The cuff of your sleeve," Gale said, gesturing vaguely. "Archery accident? And, if I'm not mistaken, one of your cheeks is a little more pink than the other. Combined with your countenance, well, it's—it barely even matters how I know, actually. I'm right though, aren't I? Of course I am."

"Of course you are," Hartwell muttered. A waiter appeared with a drink, and he took it, almost pouring it over his lap as he attempted to study his cuffs. There was a faint mark on one where the string of the bow had snagged during Hartwell's earlier misfire, but damned if he knew how Gale had put it all together. The man had the knack of taking seemingly random pieces of information and putting them together to make a whole. "Yes, I accidentally almost shot Becca's—"

"Brother," Gale said, nodding. "Warry, not the younger ones."

"How can—"

"Because she wouldn't have slapped you over any of the others," Gale said, swirling his Port in his glass. "But *Warry*." He narrowed his eyes again. "Accident or no, Lady Rebecca is far too clever to not see some greater significance in it."

"I shall go and sit in the other room with Stratford if you're not silent on this matter at once."

Gale shrugged and took another swig of his port. "Then we shall consider the subject closed." He set his glass aside and tapped his fingers on his knee. His eyes gleamed, and Hartwell knew there was no respite coming. Gale was an awful, awful man. "Tell me, then, what were your thoughts on chapter twenty-one?"

CHAPTER 12

From his room, Warry heard Rebecca come back inside. He could also hear that she was sobbing as she thumped up the stairs and into her own room, shutting the door with conviction. If any decency existed within him, he would go to her and try to discern the cause of her distress.

But he was not a good person, no matter how hard he had tried to be. He had put Becca in the path of harm. He had taken her private property and read her darkest secrets. And now, because of his wickedness, she stood to be ruined.

He lay on the bed, his hands clasped over his belly as he stared up at the ceiling. The scent of the outdoors still clung faintly to him —as did, unless he imagined it, a faint trace of Hartwell. He retained only a hollow echo of the rage he had felt at tea. It was as though his subtle humiliation of Hartwell had cooled something within him that had been burning for some time.

He recalled the day he had discovered the damning letter. He and Becca had been fighting over something silly, and he was angry enough to want to give her a scare. He had searched her trunk while she was out, rummaging beneath her spare bedclothes, knowing she kept her diary there. He did not intend to read it, only to hide it until she realised it was gone and panicked.

But when he picked up the diary, a note slid out from its pages, half-finished, in Becca's elegant, flowing script. A letter to Miss Lilley. He should not have read it, or once he had begun to, he should have stopped after a couple of sentences when he comprehended the extremely personal nature of the missive. But the things Becca described in the letter…He had not even known two women could do such things together. And then he had understood, with a flood of fear and hope, that if two women could engage in such acts, then it was not mere fantasy to imagine he might one day do similar things with another man.

This was before he'd discovered *The Maiden Diaries*, and he'd possessed no resources save that letter on coupling with a member of the same sex. Had not quite put shape to his own desires until that very moment. The fact that he and his sister were alike in that way made the shame slightly more bearable. He had fled with the letter, unable to bear the thought of being discovered with it in Becca's room and equally unable to prevent himself from reading it all the way through. Sitting on the floor of his own bedroom with his back against the closed door, he had devoured every word.

After that, getting revenge on Becca suddenly seemed a small thing in comparison to his realisation that she had loved their governess. For the letter was not merely about the physical act of love; it held tenderness as well. Were he to have such tender feelings for another man, perhaps it would not be so terrible because Becca was the same. And Becca was good, so it could not be wrong to be like her.

He knew that men sometimes married men, of course, and women sometimes married women. But his parents had only ever spoken of Warry's future wife, and he'd always understood that, whatever the law might say, for men to marry women was the natural way of things.

He should have put the letter back, but something had

distracted him. His mother calling him for tea perhaps. Warry had slid the letter into his bureau drawer, intending to replace it, never guessing Wilkes would steal it first.

And now, without ever intending it, Warry was again responsible for Becca's misery.

Her sobs made him nervous. Was it possible she had seen his gesture on the archery green for what it was—a wordless declaration that, as much as he despised Hartwell, he also desired the man? Was she furious with him?

A knock on the door startled him. A servant entered, bearing a note. "This came for you, sir."

Warry took it, heart sinking as he recognized the handwriting on the envelope and pulled out the card. It simply read, *You will join me at the theatre tonight in Drury Lane at 8:00. B.*

And if he did not? Warry thought in a blaze of fury. He was not Balfour's whelp to be called to heel.

"No reply," he informed the servant, who bowed and left. Warry closed his eyes and let himself drift.

If he could not have Hartwell—and to be clear, he loathed Hartwell and only wanted the man in the most purely physical sense—yes, there, he had admitted it—then perhaps he should begin preparing himself to share a bed with Balfour.

He did not know why the idea unnerved him so. Balfour was handsome, though he lacked much of Hartwell's natural beauty. It was frightening to think of engaging in the act with someone as morally destitute as Balfour—and yet, wasn't Warry every bit as bereft of morals? And wasn't it, in some odd way, even more frightening to imagine engaging in the act with someone he cared for? Balfour, above all else, possessed confidence. He would be able to instruct Warry as Warry remained uncertain what would be expected of him on his wedding night.

He let one hand slip lower on his belly, then crooked his finger to drag along the exposed skin where his shirt had come untucked from his trousers.

It was madness to allow himself the indulgence, but he imagined his own hand was Hartwell's. Imagined Hartwell's ragged, hushed breathing as he gazed at Warry with an expression of exhausted longing. He tipped his chin up, imagining he was looking up at Hartwell, eyes wide, breathless and uncertain but trusting the other man to guide him.

He moved his hand to the front of his trousers. Closed his eyes and exhaled. He spread his legs slightly, an offering to his imagined companion, whose lips twitched upward and whose eyes grew soft and hazy with lust.

He caressed himself again, but finding the contact not quite sufficient, he slid his hand down the front of his trousers. His excitement was humiliatingly evident, even as he reminded himself there was nobody to witness his humiliation. Nobody except his phantom, who delighted in the sight of his arousal, who was guiding his hand in slow movements up and down the front of his drawers, dampening the fabric. He had done this only a few times before, always inhibited by shame and never with a fantasy so vivid to spur him on.

He stayed his hand and panted out a few desperate breaths. Then he reached into his drawers, caressing the full length of his hardness, and imagined Hartwell's parted lips as he gazed down at Warry, wonder in his eyes. With his other hand, he dragged his nails along his inner thigh. The sensation made him gasp and twist.

He should not continue. He risked madness, blindness, and myriad other pollutions if he saw the foul act to its completion. Yet the softness of Hartwell's gaze before him made it seem as though nothing about it was wrong.

Warry stroked faster, increasing the pressure. His breathing was harsh, and he closed his throat in an effort to stifle it lest it be heard through the walls. But Hartwell wanted to hear him. Wanted to witness every moment of his pleasure and his torment.

That thought was fire in his veins.

He threw his head back and gasped once more as his core

contracted, his hand suddenly webbed with stickiness. He remained there for a moment, every muscle tensed and trembling, his eyes squeezed shut, his panting seeming to roar in his ears. Slowly, he flattened his arched spine against the mattress and stared at the ceiling.

He felt more alone now than ever. Through the walls, Becca's muffled sobs echoed. Late afternoon had darkened to evening, casting strange shadows about his room.

He did not go down to dinner, but when the time came, he summoned his valet, changed out of his soiled drawers and his trousers, and put on evening dress. Then he went downstairs and called the carriage round to take him to the theatre.

※

He arrived late and did not know the location of Balfour's box, but he need not have worried. The man waited for him in the lobby, his gaze cold.

"You're late," Balfour said unnecessarily.

Warry did not know anybody who arrived on time for the theatre. He hardly thought slipping into a box late was cause for concern and said as much.

"I do not care what time the performance begins or what anyone else does. I asked you to meet me here at eight o'clock."

"I was otherwise occupied."

Balfour's mouth tightened. "Perhaps you forget that you are promised to me." He took Warry's arm.

Warry pulled away. "Perhaps you forget that does not make me your servant."

Balfour gazed at him for a long time, expression unreadable. "We shall announce our happy news at my little gathering in two days' time. I rather think it best for us to hasten this marriage along."

Warry's heart pounded. "What about asking my father?" That

had been his last hope—that perhaps his father would refuse. Balfour had tasked him with convincing his father, yes, but if the earl opposed the match vehemently enough…

Balfour gave him a cold, flat smile. "Won't he be surprised?"

He was stonily silent as they made their way to his box, and Warry followed, numb with fear.

He had no hope of concentrating on the performance, and when an intermission arrived, he was most relieved. "I require some air," he said, hoping Balfour would not follow.

A vain hope. He walked out the front doors with Balfour on his heels and stood in the chilly night, surveying streets that suddenly seemed strange and overly dark. Was this to be the rest of his life? Having Balfour snap his fingers and tell him where to be and when? Standing in cold and darkness outside this rout or that performance with no conversation between them? Hartwell might be loathsome, but there was an easiness to being with him—well, except when the man was deliberately being difficult.

His memory of Hartwell's smile was so vivid it was jarring to suddenly hear a familiar voice coming from a little way down the street.

"Oh, they came to see a *show*, did they?"

Warry looked around.

Light from a gas lamp caught a tall figure wobbling like a skittle as he balanced precariously on the back of a flower-seller's cart. The man's hat was askew, and his arms were flung wide, but it was unmistakably Hartwell. Warry's heart sailed in relief before he recalled just how little he wanted to see the man.

Gale stood below his friend, stretching out an arm in an effort to get Hartwell to lower his. "All right, old chap, let's get you down from there, shall we?"

Hartwell spun in a circle. "Well, here is a show for you all!" His words were slurred, and he stumbled as he finished his rotation. Gale barely caught him. "The engagement is off. Ladies and gentlemen, she says the engagement is *off*, so you may all go home."

"My friend." Gale's voice rose in temper. "This is not the show anyone came to see."

"But it is my very favourite show!" Hartwell proclaimed. A crowd was gathering, and a nearby constable skirted it, seemingly unsure whether to intervene. "The tragedy of Lord Hartwell, Marquess of Danbury."

Warry heard Balfour say something but ignored him, slipping closer to where Hartwell stood.

"You're going to get yourself arrested," Gale said firmly, attempting to keep hold of his companion's knee. "Come, we must leave now."

Hartwell gave Gale a firm kick, which caught Gale off guard such that he stumbled a few paces away.

Warry saw what was going to happen before it did.

Hartwell tipped back on his heels, waving his arms for balance. His hat tumbled off into the street, and an instant later, he began to fall backward too.

Warry did not know how or why he did what he did next. He only knew that a moment later, Hartwell was lying flat on his back in the street, and Warry had somehow caught him in time to prevent him from cracking his head open on the cobblestones but not, he realised, in time to prevent him from landing in a pile of manure left by the flower-seller's horse.

He got more applause and laughter from the appreciative crowd than the actors inside the theatre were getting.

"Help me," Warry ground out as Gale appeared by his side, and together the two of them hauled Hartwell to his feet.

Everyone was talking at once, and the constable remained uncertain of what to do. Warry climbed to his feet, dusting pebbles and filth out of his palms, then turned to the constable. "It is all right," he said. "I will see him home."

Hartwell was sputtering beside him, lifting one manure-stained leg and then the other as though in disbelief.

Warry realised Gale was studying him with interest. The man

leaned closer to Warry and spoke in a low voice. "I keep a private room off Russell Street. Number thirty-three. I suggest you take him there. His parents would be most displeased to see him in this state." He slipped Warry a key.

Warry turned to whistle for a hack.

A hand on his shoulder spun him around, and Balfour glowered down at him. "What do you think you are doing?"

"He requires assistance. I am going to take him somewhere he can rest."

"If you accompany that filthy drunk anywhere," Balfour said with icy precision, "you will regret it. Get back in the theatre."

Warry noticed that Balfour's gaze had dropped, and he followed it to find his own hand still clutching Hartwell's elbow.

"Think where your loyalty lies." Balfour's tone was deadly.

Hartwell blew air through his lips like a horse. "Quite a third act, I must say. Where is my walking stick?"

"Come," Warry said, leading him away from the crowd and from Balfour. He had no doubt he would pay for this when next he found himself in Balfour's company. He must only hope that he alone would bear the brunt of Balfour's displeasure; that Balfour would not seek to compromise Becca in retaliation.

Hartwell could barely stand up straight, and his breath reeked of port. Warry urged him hastily into a hack, wishing to spare him further embarrassment.

The ride was tense and silent. Hartwell stared down at his filthy shoes and breeches. There were a million things Warry wanted to say—to wound Hartwell, to reassure him, to make him laugh so that they might be friends again. But he remained silent until they arrived at number thirty-three.

Warry dragged Hartwell from the carriage, turning his head at the combined stench of Hartwell's breath and the manure on his clothes.

He sighed when he entered the building and found himself facing a staircase.

"Come," he muttered. "You must try to walk."

"I am trying," Hartwell mumbled. "You are the one who must walk."

Warry gritted his teeth and began the arduous process of carrying a grown man up a set of stairs.

He groaned in relief as he kicked the door shut behind them. Hartwell sank to his knees on the floor, and Warry let him go. Warry could scarcely see to light a candle. He finally managed it and carried the candle over to the bedside table. There was a decorative vessel there. Or perhaps it was not decorative, but rather, intended for just the purpose Warry had in mind.

He brought it to where Hartwell knelt and set it before him.

"You will feel better once you've been sick." Warry knew this only from his father, having never been in his cups himself.

"I don't think I shall ever feel better," Hartwell said pensively. Then he leaned forward and vomited, both into and down the side of the vessel.

"Look away," Hartwell ordered too late. "I don't want you to see this."

"I have been sick before, Hartwell."

Hartwell nodded thoughtfully, the candlelight casting a golden glow on the tips of his eyelashes.

Warry took out his handkerchief, and, determined to remain as matter-of-fact as possible, dabbed at the corners of Hartwell's mouth. Hartwell screwed up his face like a child and tried to twist away.

"Stop it," Warry said. "I'm trying to help you."

"I do not need your help. I need another glass of po-oooort." He sang the last word as though he were performing in an opera.

"That is the very last thing you need."

"Then you have not heard my engagement is off."

"Half of London heard, not thirty minutes ago."

"You have no sympathy."

"You make it difficult to."

"When will the good doggie trot back to Master Balfour?"

Warry barely stopped himself from planting Hartwell a facer. "I am not with Balfour right now. I am here with you. Not that you will appreciate it."

"I...appruh..." Hartwell trailed off, swaying.

"Are you finished being sick?" A foolish question, and not one Hartwell would be able to answer with any sort of accuracy.

"Oh, I am *done*."

"Then stand up." Warry pulled him mercilessly to his feet. Hartwell stumbled into him and then adjusted his balance. Warry led him over to the bed. Hartwell started to collapse, but Warry held him up with an arm around his waist and began unbuttoning his waistcoat. His coat had already been unbuttoned at some point in the evening and hung open.

"Little Joseph Warrington. This is not at all proper."

"You cannot sleep in these filthy clothes. And now you have vomit on your coat."

This silenced Hartwell long enough for Warry to strip him of his coat and waistcoat. His shirt was more or less clean, so Warry allowed him the modesty of keeping it on. He very determinedly averted his eyes from where the shirt hung open, revealing that patch of chest hair, and began to work on Hartwell's breeches.

"Most improper," Hartwell repeated so softly that it came across more as a sigh than words.

"You'll thank me later," Warry muttered, wondering how the man could be half-naked and in utter disgrace and still render Warry the one embarrassed.

"I thank you now," he said quietly as Warry helped him remove his shoes and step out of his breeches.

Warry guided him down onto the bed and stripped off the soiled stockings, his knuckles brushing against the dark, curly hair of Hartwell's calves.

"Warry?" Hartwell's voice was so strained, the word sounded like the prelude to a deathbed request.

"What is it?"

"I have to piss."

With another sigh, Warry fetched the vomit-covered jug, careful not to touch the soiled parts of it. Hartwell got gracelessly to his feet, supporting himself on the night table. With his other hand, he fumbled in his drawers. Warry set the jug on the floor and turned away. It sounded as though Hartwell more or less hit his mark. Warry poured a glass of water from the washstand and attempted to get Hartwell to rinse his mouth and then spit into the jug. He took the vessel and the dirty clothes and deposited them outside the door, where the smell would not be so overwhelming.

When he returned, Hartwell was sprawled on the bed once more, one arm dangling over the edge.

"I fell into horseshit," he solemnly informed the ceiling.

"Yes, you did."

"I am humiliated."

"You certainly are."

Hartwell tilted his head toward Warry. Warry knew he should blow out the candle, that he was being wasteful, but the glow it cast on Hartwell's handsome face was mesmerizing. "You saved me."

"I only wished to avoid a further scene. Someone needed to stop you before you did something even more foolish."

"Would you have helped me even if I had?" Hartwell's seriousness gave him a paradoxically childlike air.

"I doubt it. Most likely I would have allowed the constable to drag you out and then cart you off."

Hartwell laughed, but the sound was anxious. "Thank you." He spoke sincerely. "I know I have disgraced myself tonight. I know you are supposed to be at the theatre with Balfour. I am sorry you are here instead."

"I'm not," Warry said honestly but without kindness.

Hartwell swallowed hard, then swallowed again. Warry did not wish to see him afflicted with the sorrow that often accompanied drunkenness in his father, so he searched about for a topic of conversation.

"You helped me in a similar situation once," he said. "Back when we were children."

"What are you on about?"

"When I fell into the frog pond. I was freezing afterward. You pulled me out. You boxed my ears, but then you…looked after me."

The memory was coming back in more detail than he could bear. He recalled the child he had been, shivering, keeping his arms stiff at his sides and making no move even to hug himself for warmth. Hartwell had wrapped him in his coat and had ushered him inside the house and into his bedroom.

"I probably pushed you in," Hartwell murmured. "I was always doing that."

"Not this time. This time I fell. Took too much water into my lungs. I was terrified, thrashing about."

Hartwell nearly closed his eyes. "I remember. I was sss—so frightened of what my parents—and your parents—would say if they knew Becca and I hadn't been w-watching you properly."

"You pulled the blankets up to my chin. You told Becca to go have Cook make me some soup."

He had stayed in Warry's bedchamber until Warry was fed and warm and drifting off to sleep.

"I wasn't helping you." Hartwell spoke brusquely, no longer slurring as much. "I didn't want to face our parents' wrath was all. I was supposed to watch you, and I failed. It was as simple as that."

Warry studied the line of his throat, the small bump of his Adam's apple. "I don't believe you."

Hartwell swallowed yet again. "I was scared…something would…I was afraid you were…hurt."

"I know."

Hartwell tore his gaze from the ceiling to meet Warry's, candlelight flickering in his eyes. "I remember when we played soldiers. And you betrayed me."

Warry laughed. "One of my great triumphs."

"She says she does not even wish to be friends anymore. She said I was unf—unforgiveable."

"There is little you could do that Becca would find unforgivable."

"I have done it."

"You will speak to her again when you both have had some time to think."

Hartwell opened his mouth, but no words came out. Finally, he grimaced, and his focus returned to the ceiling. "Shouldn't you be going?"

"I should."

"You are not getting up."

"No," Warry agreed.

Hartwell crossed his bare ankles. "I am quite cold now. Though I know it is my own fault."

Warry reached out and tugged at the covers. Hartwell tried his best to lift his hips, and together they got his legs stuffed under the blankets.

And then Warry stood, stripping down to his shirt and drawers.

Madness, certainly. Brought on by his earlier act of self-pollution, perhaps. But he climbed into the bed beside Hartwell and lay there, stiff and afraid to shift in the slightest lest their bodies touch. But he could feel the warmth coming off Hartwell despite the man's assertion that he was cold.

Hartwell did not speak. Seemed scarcely to breathe. Then he gingerly rolled onto his side, facing away from Warry.

"Relax, my lord," Warry said drily. "We are merely going to sleep."

"Very well," Hartwell whispered.

Warry turned onto his side, and, after a moment's hesitation, placed his arms securely around Hartwell's middle.

Hartwell's breath hitched.

"You will feel warmer soon."

"I do already."

"Sleep."

"I…"

"I said sleep."

Hartwell murmured something Warry could not make out, and Warry longed to ask him to repeat it. But in another moment, Hartwell had placed his hands over Warry's, and his breathing had slowed. Warry lay awake a long while still, wondering if perhaps madness was not quite so bad as people made it out to be.

CHAPTER 13

Hartwell woke to a pounding head and a vague sense of regret for things he could not quite remember. He blinked his eyes open. Surely his regret could not have been for the lovely young man lying on his side next to him, his shirt clinging to the smooth line of his spine. Hartwell couldn't ever imagine finding himself regretful to wake like this. He reached out and placed his fingers gently on the curve of the young man's hip, pinching the fabric of his shirt and drawing it up. A sliver of pale skin came into view, and the young man mumbled something petulant and sleepy, turning slightly as though he meant to burrow face-first into the pillows.

Hartwell stroked that skin meditatively, and his brain awoke, as was its custom, a lot more slowly than his body. He was in Gale's room off Russell Street, a pleasant enough little place, and one Gale retreated to in order to escape his horde of sisters, whose names he pretended never to remember. At least Hartwell presumed it was a pretence. For a man who could recall every detail of a newspaper article he'd read six years ago, right down to the punctuation, he'd often wondered if Gale's vagueness when it came to his sisters was an affectation. Or perhaps Gale's brain was as singularly peculiar as those same newspapers proclaimed, so fixated on minutiae that he really couldn't tell Clarissa from Anne-Marie from Cordelia from Eugenie. The point was, Gale kept a room where his family could not find him, and Hartwell had been the beneficiary of it on more than one occasion in the past when he'd drunk rather too much. And on more than one occasion when he'd wanted to take a pretty young fellow into bed with him without risking either of their reputations. Gale's landlady was rather fierce in her guarding of his privacy. So whatever Hartwell'd got up to last night, it couldn't have been all bad if it had led to that.

He rubbed a hand over his jaw as he yawned and was immediately assaulted by the stench of his own breath. Good Lord, his poor companion. Hopefully he'd been as drunk as Hartwell and hadn't noticed.

He stretched a languid arm to the bedside table where Gale kept a dish of comfits. He grabbed a handful and tossed them into his mouth, crunching softly.

Hartwell traced his fingertip down to the dip of the young man's spine, following it for the few scant uncovered inches that he could before it vanished inside his drawers. The young man mumbled again and shifted backward on the mattress, bringing his delicious arse into contact with Hartwell's prick, which was standing proudly. Hartwell rocked his hips forward, a moment of glorious contact that had him shivering with delight, and wakened his companion.

The young man flopped over onto his belly, sadly not in invitation, and then turned his head to squint at Hartwell.

"Warry!" Hartwell exclaimed, aghast, sitting bolt upright in a way that made his aching head throb even harder. "What the deuce are you doing here? Do you mean to be undone?"

"Wha...?" Warry blinked again, and then awareness seemed to crash over him as suddenly and sharply as a bucket of cold water. He scrambled off the bed, ending up on his knees on the floor, and stared at Hartwell balefully from behind a curtain of messy wheat-gold hair. "No! I am not undone! There was no undoing! And besides, why should I be the one assumed to be undone? You're the one with the...the..."

Hartwell drew the blanket over the evidence of his arousal. "Because you're younger, and of a lower rank, and courting another man!"

"And you're engaged to my *sister*!"

"No," Hartwell said, drawing a hand across his eyes. "I am not."

Warry's gaze was suspicious. "You say that, and yet I thoroughly suspect you and she will make up."

"No," Hartwell said again, "The engagement is well and truly done. And so it is your reputation that will suffer most if it is discovered we were abed together, you fool."

He had a flash of memory, both terrible and wonderful, of lying on his side last night with Warry's arms wrapped around him from behind, Warry's breath tickling the hair on his nape, and how, addled with drink and still shaken with his tumble into horseshit, he'd dozed off feeling impossibly light and warm.

Daylight, it seemed, had shattered last night's strange closeness because here they were again, at each other's throats like a pair of dogs, growling and snapping.

Wouldn't it be something to rise and lift Warry by the arms, to manhandle him back onto the mattress, and for them to screw like a pair of dogs? Hartwell's mouth closing sharply on the side of Warry's neck, on the crook of his shoulder. Each time he would gentle the bite after savouring Warry's cry; he'd keep his teeth anchored softly in the skin and flick the sore spot with his tongue. He'd kiss and lick at the flexing muscles of Warry's shoulders as he pounded into him from behind.

Wouldn't it be something to truly undo him?

Warry was staring at him as though he might be in possession of similar thoughts. For one moment, Hartwell thought about commanding him back to bed. Begging quietly, through kisses, for another chance. He wouldn't push Warry away this time. He had neither the strength nor the desire to resist the young man before him.

"You're such a coward," Warry said simply.

Hartwell would have thought himself inured to any further hurt from Warry. Yet Warry had shown himself last night to be by far the more grown-up of the two of them, and the words pierced him almost as deeply as Rebecca's had.

Warry continued. "I cannot make up my mind whether I am more vexed with you for not going at once to put things right with my sister or for sitting there"—his voice began shaking, though not with fear—"staring at me as though you have never wanted anything more in the world and yet remaining silent."

"Warry. It is my duty—"

"Fuck…your duty." Warry put a long pause after the word *fuck* as though he needed a moment to be sure he had actually said it.

"Then come back up here," Hartwell said crisply.

Warry's eyes widened nearly imperceptibly.

"Come on then. I'm not the one cowering on the floor. Come back up here and learn what it means to be undone." There. The gauntlet was down. Let Warry show himself to be all bluster.

Warry hesitated. His shoulders lifted as he drew in a long, uneven breath. His gaze dropped to the floorboards.

"I see I am not the only coward here." All the coldness Hartwell attempted to infuse into his tone was undercut by a ruefulness he could not mask.

Then Warry rose, and it was Hartwell's turn to sink back slightly. Warry climbed onto the bed, knees digging painfully into Hartwell's shins through the bedclothes until he was straddling him, and they were face to face. Hartwell dug the remains of the comfits from the grooves of his teeth with his tongue, then swallowed hard.

"Well." There was no hope of keeping his tone light. His throat was rough with the vestiges of sleep, with the force of his desire. "Here we are."

"Shut up."

Hartwell's prick stiffened further.

Warry reached out and felt Hartwell's cheek with the tips of his fingers. Hartwell knew he'd have a shadow about his jaw—his beard grew as fast as the mythical beanstalk—and he imagined holding Warry from behind, burying his face in the man's neck, feeling Warry tense at the rasp of Hartwell's rough cheek against his smooth skin.

Hartwell held his gaze, letting him explore. Warry's fingers curled in toward his palm, and his thumb moved across Hartwell's lower lip.

God, my God, I'm not going to last long enough to undo him.

Warry's thumb moved to his upper lip, and Hartwell waited until it had nearly completed its circuit before nipping suddenly.

Warry jerked his hand back, then laughed, the sound a release of tension for them both.

Hartwell grinned.

"Do not!" Warry commanded on a snicker.

Hartwell reached for his wrist and guided Warry's hand back to his mouth, then he slid his lips around Warry's first finger, sucking gently.

Warry's breathing grew rapid. He squirmed on Hartwell, the movement shifting the fabric of his drawers so that it beautifully outlined his hardening prick.

Hartwell ran his tongue across the pad of Warry's finger, then sucked harder.

"Hartwell," Warry whispered, not so much in plea as in wonder, as if he were trying to reassure himself that Hartwell was real, that this was truly happening.

Hartwell could have used such reassurance himself.

He flicked Warry's finger several times with the tip of his tongue, then withdrew. He slid his thumb to the pulse on Warry's wrist and pressed lightly, then leaned forward and kissed Warry's palm.

Warry's voice was low. "If this is what it is to be undone...I cannot say I mind it."

"This," Hartwell growled, "is merely a prelude."

He gripped Warry's hips, fingers slipping down the waistband of his drawers to trace his hip bones, which produced a startled moan and a lovely contraction of Warry's stomach muscles. He hoisted Warry closer to him. Kissed him fiercely while his hands found their way under Warry's shirt, pushing the fabric up and exposing his slender waist. The sight of all that bare, smooth skin could drive a man mad.

He hooked an arm around Warry, cupping the back of his neck in order to kiss him more thoroughly. Then he moved his hand south, sliding it down the back of Warry's drawers.

Warry's moan was deeper now, and he leaned forward, sticking his perfect arse out so that Hartwell might have better access. Hartwell palmed one firm, muscular cheek, and caught Warry's tongue between his lips, sucking hard as he squeezed Warry's arse.

Warry's hands were planted on the mattress on either side of Hartwell's hips now, and his arse was lifted so he was nearly on all fours. Hartwell fumbled for the string of Warry's drawers, smiling against Warry's mouth as he found one end. He tugged, the knot came undone, and the drawers slid off Warry's hips. Hartwell undid his own drawers and shifted upward, lifting Warry with him. Now they were both kneeling, drawers pooled around their knees, and Hartwell jolted, gasping like he'd been punched as Warry's prick brushed his own.

Warry whimpered desperately and pushed his hips against Hartwell's.

Hartwell had been deeply, deeply wrong about which of them was to be undone. As the hot length of Warry's prick rubbed against him, he called upon every reserve of strength he had to maintain control. He gripped Warry's arse and held him as hard as he could against his own body, kissing the side of Warry's neck as his fingers dug into firm muscle. Those whimpers—of shock as much as pleasure—were absolute music. The way his head tipped back in surrender as Hartwell licked the salt of sweat from his neck and then tugged the skin in his teeth.

"Hartwell." The name was the softest exhale but held as much desperation as if Warry had shouted it. Warry's hands were under Hartwell's shirt now, sweeping across his chest, and Hartwell paused just long enough to remove the garment entirely, tossing it to the floor and then kissing Warry once more as he tugged Warry's shirt up and off. The cuffs caught on Warry's hands, and Hartwell seized the opportunity, winding the fabric around Warry's wrists and giving him a light shove so he fell back on the mattress, his new bonds pulling tight.

Warry stared up at Hartwell, his eyes glazed over with lust. His bare chest moved in and out with shallow breaths that sounded almost painful. There was a vivid welt at his throat where Hartwell had bitten and sucked.

My mark, Hartwell thought with satisfaction, thinking smugly of Balfour looking upon it.

His desire waned.

Balfour. Balfour couldn't be permitted to see the mark. Warry would be…God.

It was just as Warry said. He was a coward. At once too craven to claim Warry as he wished and too weak to resist him either, even when it was clearly best for everyone that they avoid each other.

Need seared his body. He wanted to place a thousand marks like that all over Warry's skin—each one a brand, each a warning to Balfour and a promise to Warry.

"What is it?" Warry whispered anxiously.

Hartwell smiled. "What a lucky man I am," he replied, voice low and roughened by an unexpected surge of emotion he did not care to examine too thoroughly. He trailed two fingers down Warry's belly, nearly to the base of his prick.

Warry's back arched as he made an attempt to pull free of the shirt, one tail of which was still twisted in Hartwell's grip. Hartwell growled a warning at him, which set him panting hard, a challenge in his eyes as he seemed to debate whether to obey and lie still. Hartwell had not thought his prick could get any stiffer, but Warry's desperate squirming, the need in his gaze, the sight of him half-bound and helpless beneath Hartwell all conspired to bring Hartwell to a nearly unbearable level of arousal. And then Warry's parted lips curved up, ever so slightly, as his harsh breaths came and went, and Hartwell lost all sense of reason.

The whole world be damned; he had come too far to stop now. He lowered himself over Warry until their bodies nearly touched. Warry's prick was rigid against his taut belly, and with his hands caught above his head, he could do nothing as Hartwell lowered himself further still so their cocks pressed together. He let go of the shirt and slid one arm beneath Warry, supporting himself with the other, then began rocking slowly. Warry gasped and shuddered. The poor fellow started to bring his bound hands down but stopped himself, instead giving a sweet, shuddering sigh of surrender. That was precisely the sound Hartwell had longed to hear, and it was even more beautiful in reality than in any of his fantasies. Hartwell kissed the very edge of Warry's underarm, a spot that proved just as sensitive as he'd hoped—especially when Hartwell rasped his unshaven cheek against it. This drew another whimper from Warry, who arched again, then wrapped his legs around Hartwell and crossed his ankles over Hartwell's backside.

Oh, this man. This beautiful, breath-stealing man. There weren't enough hours in the day to take him apart as slowly and thoroughly as he deserved. Hartwell would need weeks, maybe months to learn every inch of soft skin, every moan and whimper and cry that could be drawn from that elegant throat. Yet as glorious as it was to imagine taking all that time, his desire was urgent. He was not certain he could bear the pleasure of teasing Warry's perfect, lithe body a second longer, not when his own body was fairly trembling with need.

Somehow he survived the act of kissing the swell of Warry's

chest, just above his nipple, and then laying his lips, butterfly-soft, between each of his ribs. Warry turned his head to press his mouth first into his own shoulder, then Hartwell's, in an effort to stifle his cries. There was stickiness between them, and Warry's body suddenly fell slack. Hartwell finished an instant later, surprised by the force of it. He slid his arm gently out from beneath Warry and braced his elbows on the bed, his hips still pressed to Warry's. His arms shook so hard he nearly collapsed onto his companion. Instead, he let his head drop, his dark hair hanging before his eyes, a vision of absolute beauty beneath him. He pressed a kiss to Warry's chest, which glistened with sweat. Then another on each of his collarbones. Warry's gasp this time was softer, the sort of sound one made at the edge of sleep—though his dazed eyes roved the ceiling, and his next inhale was enormous, like the first breath of a half-drowned man after the water had cleared from his lungs. Hartwell shushed him gently. Warry's narrowed eyes found his, his brow wrinkled, and a whimper squeezed from his throat as he sighed out. Hartwell rested his chin, with its prickly stubble of whiskers, in the hollow of Warry's navel just to watch the lad squirm—which he did, to Hartwell's delight.

At last, Hartwell shifted to lie alongside him.

Warry turned to gaze at him. He still appeared stunned and breathless. *Undone.* And yet there was now an affection in his gaze as pure as a dog's. Hartwell had not been prepared for that. How artless Warry could seem. How adoring.

Guilt pushed away the warmth in Hartwell's belly. In a few more moments, Warry would lose that awestruck look, and the truth of what they had done would hit him. The truth of it was just now hitting Hartwell. He couldn't bear to witness that shift in Warry, to see adoration turn to wariness then contempt. He reached out and stroked Warry's cheek, understanding that it would likely be the last time. From now on he would well and truly stay away from Joseph Warrington. He did nothing but harm when he was near him.

But instead of horror dawning on Warry's handsome face, he smiled slowly. Then he tilted his head and nipped gently in the direction of Hartwell's thumb, an echo of Hartwell's earlier gesture.

Hartwell's stomach plummeted gracelessly.

"What happens now?" Warry whispered.

Panic seized Hartwell. Warry was looking to him for an explanation, a solution. How could they have done this, and how could they ensure Warry's reputation remained intact? Hartwell's mind raced. They must leave the building at different times, for a start. Perhaps there was a back entrance—

But then Warry said, "Might we try this again sometime? Do you think Gale would allow—"

"Again?" Hartwell echoed sharply. His shock was genuine. *Might we try this again sometime? Might I casually risk my entire future so that we, two unwed gentlemen, may continue to swive in your friend's apartment?* Was Warry serious?

It took Hartwell several seconds to find his voice again. "What happens *now* is that I will go and make things right with Becca, you will return home, and we will never speak of this again."

Warry's brows knit together. And then horror did dawn. "Was it not…Was I not…?"

"Oh, stop it," Hartwell said in exasperation. "Do not tie yourself in knots thinking on this. It was a bit of fun is all. Do not spoil it by making it something bigger than it is. You are courting Balfour, are you not? Then there is nothing to be done except to return to our lives."

He was already climbing out of bed, not wishing to see Warry's expression. *Protect him. The way you have failed to do again and again these last days. Perform this one last cruelty so that you might finally keep him safe.*

Warry was beside him in an instant, gripping his elbow. "No. You will not do this to me again. I know your feelings for me, and I feel the same for you. You and Becca were already planning to allow each other your freedoms. And if I am discreet, Balfour need never—"

Hartwell threw off his hand. "Enough!" he roared. "That is enough. Do you hear yourself?" He laughed, the sound high pitched and nearly hysterical. "Our feelings? What use are feelings? Think! For once, Warry, use that head of yours. Think of your—"

"If you say my reputation, there is a jug of vomit and piss just outside the door that I shall crack over your head."

Hartwell had not realised there was a jug of vomit and piss just outside the door, but it did not take a man of much learning to imagine how that had come to be. He had no doubt Warry meant the threat.

Warry went on, as furious as Hartwell had ever seen him, with that break in his voice that Hartwell remembered well from childhood when Warry would get so angry at Hartwell and Becca's teasing that it would bring him to the brink of tears. "You're always going on about my reputation. But I am not the one who began something he never meant to finish!"

"Yes, I know," Hartwell snapped. "Nobody need tell me that I am black of soul. I have known this for a long time. You, however..." Hartwell softened in spite of himself and had to turn away again. "You are good-hearted. I shall not corrupt you any further. I *must* not."

"*I* will decide if I wish to be corrupted!"

Hartwell whirled. His chest drew tight as he spoke. "You already are." He glanced at the drawers still pooled at Warry's ankles. At the slickness that still clung to the hair about his soft prick. "Just look at you." Hartwell turned away and began searching for his clothes. "Where the devil are my breeches?"

"To hell with you."

"Did you...put them somewhere?"

Warry made no answer, and Hartwell's agitation grew until he finally snapped his gaze up. "Warry—" Warry's glare was fierce and grimly satisfied as he stood there, naked, his hands curled nearly to fists. Hartwell forced himself to take a breath—to keep from saying something he'd regret or to keep from tumbling Warry back onto the bed, he wasn't sure. "You don't understand. You will despise me when sense overtakes whatever you are feeling now." *Where* were his clothes? Surely he had not arrived in just his shirt?

"Will you listen to me?" Warry shouted.

Hartwell stopped dead.

"I do not despise you." Warry stepped closer to him. "Do you hear me? I do not despise you, Hartwell."

The words sank into Hartwell, bringing warmth back into his body, but the sensation lasted only an instant. "You will." He was not even sure he had spoken the words aloud.

Warry sat back on the mattress, not covering himself, and stared at him.

Hartwell knew the only proper choice was to turn away. And yet he could not prevent himself from taking in Warry's mussed and sweat-dampened hair, the hard muscles of his legs, the downy gold hair on his thighs. He gazed hungrily at Warry's prick, imagining it hard again, imagining it in his mouth, its shaft velvet and iron against his tongue.

"Only if you do not get back into bed with me at once."

Good God. What man could resist a request such as that? Or perhaps it was a demand. Still, he hesitated.

"Come, Hartwell." Warry gentled his voice as though he were speaking to a small child. "I know you must think I lack pride, but I assure you I do not. I will not implore you again."

Hartwell could not. He *should* not.

And yet...

Slowly, as though his body were quite independent from his mind, he climbed back onto the bed and obeyed Warry's clumsy attempts to position him so they lay facing each other. His heart pounded, and the tips of his fingers were numb. Oh God, help him.

"I do not despise you," Warry said again.

Hartwell closed his eyes briefly.

"I knew what I was partaking in. You are not responsible for my moral upkeep."

"Where are my clothes?" Hartwell whispered, for that seemed preferable to responding to Warry's statement.

"They are lying outside the door, covered in shit."

Hartwell flinched. Sometimes Warry and his sister were damnably alike in their directness.

Warry stroked his cheek.

"I am sorry."

"Hush." Warry's thumb passed lightly under Hartwell's eye.

Hartwell did not know how many moments of silence passed, only that his own breathing began to slow, and he did not feel quite so panic-stricken. "You know we cannot do this again."

"Stop talking."

Hartwell tried his best. After a few more moments of Warry's thumb drifting hypnotically over his cheekbone and along his jawline, Hartwell placed an arm around him and kissed his brow with resigned tenderness.

Warry exhaled. "I do not despise you…" he trailed off, and Hartwell's stomach tightened. "But I must confess, I am a bit…"

"What?" Hartwell asked finally when Warry could not seem to find the words he wanted.

"Dash it, Hartwell, you must know I'd not done this before."

"Yes, that is precisely the source of my concern."

"I'm a bit nervous."

Damn it all. First he had corrupted Warry, and now Warry was afraid, as he had every right to be, that Hartwell had ruined him. "It is all right," he said, the words coming out in a rush. "I will speak not a word of this. As you said, Balfour need never know. It is not so bad as all that, I promise."

As though Hartwell had not spoken, Warry asked, "Was I…satisfactory?"

Hartwell froze, confused. Then it dawned on him. This was what had Warry nervous? Not the thought of Balfour and the rest of the *ton* learning of his indiscretion but the question of his prowess in bed? Hartwell very nearly laughed, but the sincere anxiety in Warry's expression stopped him. The fellow truly had no idea, did he? That alone was enough to banish the vestiges of Hartwell's earlier panic. This was Warry, with whom Hartwell had shared much of his childhood. And despite some of the mystery Warry held for Hartwell now that he was a grown man, there was much about him that was purely familiar. The way he could be both sweet and sharp—all but demanding Hartwell stay, calling him a coward, but now looking at him with an uncertainty that might have burst Hartwell's chest had he been a more sentimental man.

Hartwell smiled gently. "God help Society if you ever learn your own power." He brushed Warry's hair from his forehead. "I envy Balfour, but I cannot blame him. He is a fortunate man."

A shadow passed over Warry's face then. A second later, his expression reverted to that inscrutable mask Hartwell had seen too often of late. Hartwell's first thought was that the reminder of Balfour had prompted a flood of remorse within Warry after sharing a bed with Hartwell. But perhaps that was not it? Perhaps what Warry regretted was his choice to court Balfour in the first place? There was something quite satisfying in that thought, though it was likely wishful thinking.

"The courtship has been…to your liking?" Hartwell asked awkwardly.

"I…"

That was hardly a resounding yes. "I apologise. We should not speak of it."

"I do not mind."

And yet he clearly did. Or else…Warry was holding something back, and damned if Hartwell didn't want to shake him until it came forth. He thought of that night in the library. Warry's vehement denial that Balfour's overture at the Four-in-Hand had been unwelcome. But Warry was not happy. He was not! Of that, Hartwell was sure.

"You may break it off, you know," Hartwell said on an impulse. "It is okay to court someone and then realise they are an unsuitable match. It is not too late to reclaim your freedom." He tried to grin. "Unlike me. If you are correct, and there is a path for me back into Becca's good graces, well…I suppose it is my fate to be a husband."

Warry sat up, winding his arms around his knees.

Hartwell slowly sat up as well. "Warry?"

There was nothing but stony silence, silence Hartwell did not dare break.

"If I did, would…?"

Warry did not finish, and Hartwell was left to imagine that perhaps the unspoken question matched the one in his own heart. *Would you have me?*

Would he? Ah, the idea of it…

Yet the thought of his father's displeasure quelled the hope rising in his chest. "You know I could not."

"Nor could I!" Warry said savagely. "Really, Hartwell, what did you think I meant?"

Chagrin and no small amount of frustration welled in him. Was it not just as he had said? Warry was beginning to see the potential consequences of their dalliance, and now he regretted it. God forbid Hartwell attempt to comfort or advise the temperamental little devil. This was precisely why he had stopped their kiss at the Marchland ball and sent him back to Balfour, and yet instead of a *Thank you, Hartwell, for urging me to do the right thing*, he got, *You're such a coward.*

Warry spoke at last. "He *is* suitable. I wish our engagement had not been quite so sudden, but he—"

"Engagement?" Hartwell interrupted, stunned.

Warry might as well have clapped a hand over his mouth in dismay.

"You are engaged?" Hartwell repeated.

"I—Yes. We have not—publicly—"

"You did not feel this was something I needed to know before I shared a bed with you?"

Warry appeared at first stricken, but then fire returned to his gaze. "Would it have stopped you?"

No. Hartwell had to admit defeat there. Nothing would have stopped him once they'd started, save word from Warry.

"That is irrelevant." He rose and went to the door. Opened it, grabbed his pile of shit-stained clothes, then shut it roughly again. He began to dress, trying to ignore the smell. He could feel Warry watching him.

"Hartwell…"

It was a bit difficult to maintain any sort of dignity as he pulled on his soiled breeches, but he did succeed in not looking at Warry. "Seems to me I am not the one who cannot decide what he wants, Warry."

"You said there could be nothing between us!"

Hartwell faced him now. "And I did not know at the time how much I meant it. You are not merely courting another man. You are engaged!"

Warry's face took on its familiar flush of shame. He hugged his knees tighter. "If the knowledge would not have dampened your desire, then…then is this really about propriety, Hartwell? Or is it jealousy?"

Hartwell tried not to let the truth show on his face. "Ah, yes," he said sarcastically. "That must be it. I am jealous of Balfour's engagement to a man who takes his promise as lightly as he takes the matter of his own good name."

Warry and Becca both had the same wide-eyed expression of betrayal when dealt a verbal blow. It was enough to make a man feel utterly wretched, even when he was in the right. Hartwell would concede he had perhaps not needed to say anything quite so harsh—yet his feelings raged within him in such a conflicted jumble, he knew not what to do. He stamped out his fantasy about Warry breaking off his courtship with Balfour with violent haste.

The little fool wished to ruin his life by binding himself to Balfour? Very well. It was not as though Hartwell had desired him for anything more than a tumble in the sheets. Warry wished to jeopardize what he apparently shared with Balfour by lying with Hartwell? That was none of Hartwell's concern either.

"As lightly as you took your promise to my sister?" Warry demanded.

"She broke off the engagement, not I." Hartwell stumbled a bit pulling a stocking on, and quickly righted himself. "Do you even love this man, Warry?"

"Of course I do! We have tremendous affection for one another."

"Oh, good Lord." Hartwell reached for a shit-covered shoe, somehow resisting the urge to lob it at Warry's head. "You are beyond anything. And that is not a compliment."

"Hartwell, will you not…stay a minute and let us just talk?"

"I have already far outstayed my use."

"Your *use*?"

"Did I not just crawl back into bed with you and assure you of what a good lad you are so that you may now slink back to your *fiancé* secure in the knowledge that your moral laxity shall not cost you the marriage you so crave?"

"That's not—"

"That is precisely what happened. You assured me you would not despise me, that you were fully complicit in our little tryst, and yet I see regret tormenting you. You shall get no further reassurance from me, Warry. You are your own master. At least until you stand before a priest and hand Balfour the end of your leash."

"You disgust me," Warry snapped.

Hartwell winced inwardly but continued jamming his foot into his shoe. He wished the feeling were quite mutual.

"I called you a coward before only because I knew no stronger word. But you are something far worse. And I hope that I never speak to you again as long as I live."

"Throw your tantrum," Hartwell said, tying his shoe. "You have a child's understanding of how the world works. Go play with your colicked goats and your poor dumb cows."

"And you go on living a life where you love no one truly except yourself. I am not the child here, Hartwell."

"I am not the one betraying the trust of a man I supposedly have *tremendous affection* for."

That silenced Warry so abruptly Hartwell promptly regretted the words—true though they were.

He straightened. "I am sorry I pushed you away at the Marchland ball. I have cursed myself for a fool ever since. And I am sorry, that for all the years of our childhood, I did not see you as I do now. That I did not take you in my arms long before Balfour crossed your path and tell you how absolutely enchanting you are. But what I have done I have done to protect you. To keep you from feeling shame and to prevent myself from standing in your path to happiness. If that makes me a child in your eyes, Warry, then you win. I shall trouble you no further."

He had not quite been able to meet Warry's gaze through much of his speech, but when he turned for the door, he was not fast enough to avoid a last glimpse of Warry's folded-up figure, straw-coloured hair now touching bare knees. The image nearly compelled him to return to the bed. To offer the very reassurances he had just vowed to deny the lad. But the sooner he left this wretched room, the sooner the pain would start to fade. He yanked his other shoe on and hurried out, shutting the door hard behind him.

CHAPTER 14

The letter arrived from Balfour a little after noon, requesting Warry's presence in Hyde Park for a carriage ride. Warry's stomach soured, but at least Balfour had suggested a public meeting place. With Balfour's ball coming up, more members of the *ton* were arriving in London. And with the weather so fair, many of them would be promenading. Perhaps Balfour would not make a scene about last evening.

Even if he did, what did Warry care? What did he care about anything? He'd gone home and slept dreamlessly for two hours. He'd eaten a late breakfast without tasting a bite. And now he saw the park and its inhabitants as though from a great distance. Balfour awaited him, not with his curricle but with a closed carriage. The thought of being closed in with Balfour was unpleasant, but he attempted a smile as he accepted Balfour's hand and climbed up. It was as though the flesh Balfour touched was not even Warry's.

"I do apologise for last night," he remarked with more heartiness than he'd thought himself capable of. "My friend was feeling quite ill. I wanted to see him safely home."

He adjusted himself on the seat as the carriage rolled forward. He waited for Balfour's lecture, knowing he would hear none of it.

Balfour sat across from him and regarded him with chilly, dark eyes.

"What sort of game do you think you're playing?" the man asked.

"I'm not playing any game." It felt good to be so far away and to know that nothing and no one could hurt him ever again, for he understood now that what Balfour had first seen in him—that capacity for love—had been a falsehood.

"Do not lie to me."

Balfour had drawn the curtains. Sunlight tried without much success to filter in through the wine-coloured fabric.

"I saw the way you touched him last night. And then this morning, Lord Wendell tells me he saw you and Hartwell leaving an accommodation on Russell Street. One after the other. Do you think me stupid?"

"I have no opinion of your intelligence."

"Why were you there?"

"He was ill. From the spirits. I stayed to ensure his safety. I slept in a chair."

Memory roared inside him like a flame. He could feel Hartwell's touch, could taste his skin and hear his groans of pleasure.

No. No, he must put all that from his mind.

Balfour slapped the wall of the carriage, and Warry nearly flinched.

"You have promised yourself to me, and yet you have no thought for my reputation. What did I tell you about loyalty?"

Warry nearly laughed out loud. Where had loyalty got him? A memory of placing the jug before Hartwell so he could be sick. Curling around Hartwell so the man might sleep. Assuring Hartwell he did not despise him. All so that Hartwell might once again find his weakest places and strike him just there.

And yet, however ill-used he felt by Hartwell, had there not been truth in the man's words? *I am not the one betraying the trust of a man I supposedly have tremendous affection for.* He owed Balfour nothing—neither honesty nor loyalty. But how had he failed to realise the wrongness of withholding the fact of his engagement from Hartwell? Hartwell had no way of knowing the engagement was a sham. No wonder he despised Warry. Warry did not possess a unique capacity for love. He possessed a unique capacity for manipulation and wickedness. For covering up his sins with more lies.

"I am sorry," Warry said, his focus on the curtained window.

"Low as you might be willing to sink, I will not sink with you. Are we clear?"

Warry looked Balfour directly in the eye, the way Balfour had taught him to in conversation. He straightened his neck and lifted his chin. "Let me go then if I do not please you."

Balfour was staring but not into Warry's eyes. Warry realised too late what he was seeing.

"What is that?" Balfour asked with deceptive calm.

Warry wanted, for some reason, to reach up and touch the mark on his neck. To press on it and make it hurt.

He leaned forward and hissed, right in Balfour's face, "A bit of fun."

The slap came so fast the sound of it was at first greater than the smart. Warry put his hand to his cheek, anchored quite firmly now in reality, and dreading the moment the numbness would fade and he would be forced to confront humiliation as well as pain.

"I will have your obedience," was all Balfour said.

Warry stifled another laugh. Hartwell was right. He was undone. He might have found saving grace in the fact that Balfour was willing to wed a ruined thing like him, except he suddenly understood, fully and with alarming clarity, that Balfour would make the whole of his life hell. He had thought to seek solace with Hartwell, to grasp onto something that was his choice alone, and to be loved, even if it could only be in hidden places or under the cover of darkness. Instead, he had only given Balfour more power over him.

For Balfour knew everything, not just about sherry and horses. He knew Warry's lies for what they were. And he knew how to deal with a wicked thing like Warry.

You are your own master. At least until you stand before a priest and hand Balfour the end of your leash.

He stared at his knees as the carriage bumped along. His cheek throbbed. Could what Hartwell had said be true? That he'd rejected Warry in order to protect him? That he'd held Warry at the Marchland ball and demanded to know Warry's feelings for him, and then, when Warry had made his feelings *very* clear, pushed him away because he thought of *Warry's* shame? Ironic that Hartwell had fallen into horseshit when he was already full of it. Hartwell had been afraid of scandal and afraid of disappointing his father. That was all.

How close he had come that morning to telling Hartwell the truth. About the letter, Balfour, the blackmail…all of it. But what would Hartwell think of Warry having endangered Becca in the first place and then endangering her further by betraying Balfour? Hartwell and Becca might be at odds now, but Hartwell still loved Becca above anyone in the world; Warry was sure of it.

He was still studying his own body as though it were someone else's when Balfour's hand settled on his thigh. He jerked away reflexively, but Balfour yanked his leg back into place. "Don't," Balfour said quietly and without looking at Warry. "I'm certain you allowed Lord Hartwell more liberties than this. Do not play the innocent now."

Warry allowed Balfour's hand to remain.

He began to feel sick, realising just how trapped he was and just how much he deserved his fate. Balfour would never stop holding his indiscretion over him, even once they were married. And if Warry refused to marry him, then it was his sister's reputation that fell to ruin.

He nodded, and Balfour squeezed his thigh almost affectionately.

"Look at me," Balfour said. When Warry glanced up, the other man's eyes held as much longing as Warry had ever seen in Hartwell's.

"Come," he said. "I am sorry I lost my temper. In fact, I'm glad to see that you are not the innocent I thought. It was all a bit much, that wide-eyed act. I will be pleased, on our wedding night, to lie with one who clearly has some *experience*, someone who likes a bit of fun." He ran his thumb over Warry's knee, then moved his hand higher. "Of course, knowing that you are secretly as insatiable as I am is driving me quite mad. It will not be long until I may finally take what I am owed for my discretion." He pushed his thumb into Warry's inner thigh.

Warry shoved his hand away, and Balfour withdrew, laughing.

~

In the late afternoon, Warry had hoped for peace, but instead he joined his father for lunch at the earl's club—a dull, staid place nowhere near as welcoming, to Warry's mind, as the Bucknall Club. *Of which he would probably never be a member now*, he thought wanly, for even if Balfour intended to allow him such freedoms once they were wed, he had no doubt Hartwell would block any of his attempts to join.

His father was in a sour mood too; he usually was when the first big events of the Season were approaching, like a child who had to be bullied into participating in some game but then enjoyed himself immensely. Warry would leave the bullying to his mother; he didn't have the stomach for it today. Instead, he pushed his luncheon around on his plate with a silver fork and tried his hardest to prove a decent dining companion.

"I must say, all this business with Hartwell is perplexing," Earl Warrington grumbled over his asparagus.

Warry jolted, scraping the tines of his fork across the plate with a screech. "The business with Hartwell?"

Earl Warrington waved his hand. "He and your sister. Your mother and I thought it'd be a perfect match. Why, Becca and Hartwell have been thick as thieves since they were still in leading strings. Who'd have guessed she'd be so set against him just because he almost shot you."

Warry smiled a little at that, despite himself. "I'm rather glad, actually, that she's not tripping over herself to marry someone who almost killed me."

"Pish posh," Earl Warrington said, stabbing a piece of carrot. "*Almost*, my boy, *almost*. It's all water under the bridge now, isn't it?"

Yes, it was. He had more to worry himself about than his shattered pride and his bruised heart. The spectre of Balfour loomed large after their carriage ride. Warry could still feel his skin prickling in revulsion as Balfour had slid a hand up his thigh. It was astonishing to think he'd very recently considered the man a friend and a confidant, not that Warry had shared any true confidences with him during that part of their friendship. He'd spoken perhaps a little about his anxiety for the future and his uncertainty about, well, *everything*, and he'd been so happy to find a friend who didn't laugh at him for his insecurities. And a friend who didn't roll his eyes and sigh, the way Becca and Hartwell often did, when he talked about agriculture and animal husbandry and the effects of enclosures on smallholders. Balfour had even listened intently when Warry had spoken—haltingly at first and then with greater confidence—about the Corn Law. The price of a loaf of bread didn't matter a whit to most of the *ton*, and talks of rioting and unrest weren't tolerated in polite company, but Balfour had listened, and Warry had been fool enough to think that meant he had won the man's respect. Instead, it seemed Balfour had only been thinking of ways that, when they were married, he would teach Warry to shut his mouth.

Well then, no declaration of love by Hartwell had saved Warry, so he supposed that, unless he wanted to live a life of abject misery, he would have to save himself. He just didn't know how. He could *not* marry Balfour; nothing was clearer to him now. But in order to escape the man, he had to first deal with the fact that Balfour had Becca's letter in his possession, and Warry didn't doubt he'd use it. Extracting himself from the engagement would be impossible without first securing, and destroying, that letter.

"Are you going back to the house after this?" Earl Warrington asked.

"Yes, I expect so. You?"

No." His father shook his head, his jowls shaking. "Good Lord, no. While you were out earlier, Morgan came around looking for you. When he couldn't find you, he trapped me in my library with a thousand questions about ribbons." His expression darkened. "*Ribbons.* Really, that boy is a menace."

"Father," Warry said chidingly.

"I mean it," Earl Warrington said. "His head is so stuffed full of buttons and ribbons and buckles and hats there's no room for any other thoughts at all. They'd want to get him married off quickly, I tell you, because the boy's a scandal waiting in the wings."

"I rather think that's the plan," Warry said, and it was a plan that Morgan seemed delighted about. Warry was sure Morgan was hoping very much for a wife or a husband who would enjoy dressing him like a doll in the latest fashions and pandering to his every whim. Warry hoped, for Morgan's sake, that he wed someone wealthy and indulgent enough to make him happy. His cousin was a popinjay, but Warry wished him happiness.

Earl Warrington eyed him keenly over the top of his spectacles. "It's the plan of all parents, of course." He paused to attack his mutton briefly and then looked at Warry again. "To make *good* marriages for their children."

Warry wondered if he had imagined the slight emphasis in his father's words. He cleared his throat. "I...I think Becca and Hartwell would make a good marriage."

"Hmm." Earl Warrington studied his face for a long moment and then stabbed a pea. "It wasn't Becca I was talking about, my boy."

Warry took a sip of port and screwed his courage. "Do you think Balfour is not a good match, sir?"

His father tilted his head. "He's rich, and your mother says his nose is not the worst she has seen. I suppose that makes him a good match."

Warry tensed, knowing his father wasn't finished with his assessment yet.

"I have heard nothing concrete about his reputation that would make me question it," the earl said, swirling the contents of his glass. "And if he makes you happy, then I am happy."

Warry nodded sharply. "Thank you."

Earl Warrington waved for a footman to come and take his plate away. "I remember when I first met your mother," he said at last. "She was surrounded by suitors clamouring for her notice, of course, a flock of bright popinjays, and I thought she would never notice a plain brown sparrow like me. And then, one evening after I'd known her a little while, I walked up to her at the theatre, and she smiled, and her smile lit up the entire world. I knew, in that moment, that we would be happy together because she never smiled at all those popinjays the way she smiled at me."

Warry felt an ache in his heart. They had not been happy ever after, though. They were, as he'd told Balfour, often like strangers. His father spent an increasing amount of his time gambling, and his mother spent her time worrying about the family finances. This was some tidy, charming little story his father told himself to deflect life's cruel realities.

"You don't smile when you talk about Balfour," Earl Warrington said quietly.

"I have never been the most demonstrative," Warry said.

"Tell me, then," his father said. "Tell me that he makes you happy."

Warry swallowed, nodded, and held his father's gaze. "He makes me happy."

Earl Warrington exhaled slowly. "Well, then I am happy too."

They sat silently for a long while, their lies festering between them.

CHAPTER 15

Hartwell had received the invitation to Balfour's ball with all the pleasure of a man receiving an offering of a dead bird from a cat. In fact, he may have preferred the dead bird because at least he could appreciate the spirit in which such a gift was intended. But Hartwell was no fan of balls, at least not lately. Perhaps Gale's jaded misanthropy was contagious, or perhaps Hartwell was tired of being prodded about when he would find a match. A ball at Balfour's house meant he would have to watch Warry with the man. Watch them together in conversation, watch Balfour brush a curl of Warry's hair behind his ear. And wonder whether any of it was the truth. If Warry truly loved Balfour, then what of the feelings he'd claimed he harboured for Hartwell? What of the way he'd responded to Hartwell's touch? The way he'd smiled afterward, looking dazed and thoroughly pleased?

Good Lord, what a nightmare.

Hartwell's parents were attending. Both of them. Even his father, who was much more at home at his club than he was in the social whirl, would not miss the first official event of the Season.

His father's mood since learning the engagement was off had been...Hartwell was not sure how to describe it. His father no longer seemed disappointed in him. Rather, it was as if Hartwell had ceased to exist. There was no mention of cutting the purse strings, which ought to have been a relief, but his father's coldness bothered him more than he'd expected. Attending Balfour's ball with his parents would not solve the problem, but Hartwell maintained some childish desire to be in his father's presence, to test the bounds of how thoroughly the elder Hartwell could ignore him.

Balfour's London home was as chilly and polished as the man himself. The entry hall had narrow walls of deep blue and opened into a large, open room with a high ceiling. The walls were lined with tall, dreary portraits with dark wood frames and darkly attired subjects.

Hartwell scanned the ballroom for Becca and was at once relieved and annoyed not to find her. He wanted to put things right with her, yet he dreaded making the attempt. She was by far the quicker wit, and if she did not intend to forgive him, her rejection would be swift and public. His goal tonight was simple, he decided. He would dance with any young lady available, and at the end of the night, he would select the least offensive one and propose to her. That way he would be assured of his father's money if not his affection. And whoever his wife was, he vowed to be the kindest, most attentive husband to her in all the world so that Becca might see what she had missed.

And Warry. Let Warry see that I am no failure. He pushed the thought away, wondering what on earth was the matter with him. He deserved neither of them. He never had.

Allowing Warry into his thoughts seemed to have conjured the little devil, for he soon spied Warry and Balfour off in a corner, deep in conversation.

How jolly for them. Hartwell did not care one whit how close they stood or of what they spoke. He took a step he had not meant to take toward their corner and bumped into someone who cried in a familiar voice, "Lord Hartwell! Oh, Hartwell."

He faced Lady Warrington with a ready smile. "My lady. It is good to see you." How easily he brought forth the smile. How easily he pretended that he had not made the truest wreck imaginable of his life.

Lady Warrington clasped her hands beneath her bosom and tittered anxiously. "Yes, Hartwell, it is always good to see you." And yet her eyes darted in a way that suggested the statement was a strain on her ability to tell a social lie. Hartwell's stomach flipped. Surely Warry would not have said anything to his parents about…

"Becca is over at the punchbowl!" Lady Warrington's face collapsed in the next instant. "Well, how foolish of me. You are not looking for Becca. Unless you are?"

"No," Hartwell said quickly, despising the hope in her gaze. "No, I am not looking for Becca."

"I must confess, I had rather hoped tonight would be a happy one for both of you."

"Yes, I had hoped the same. But sometimes these things do not work out."

"I tried to explain to Becca that you did not fire that arrow at our Warry on purpose."

Ah, yes. The arrow. "With all due respect, my lady, Becca and I have discovered that our incompatibility goes beyond a misfired arrow. But please do accept my apologies once more regarding the near miss with Warry."

I should not have missed, he thought bitterly.

At once, the guilt was on him again.

I should have protected him.

Lady Warrington nodded. "Of course. It was but an accident, though Becca took it quite personally. I hope you will not…Well, I must say, sometimes it is the very person we consider ourselves to be least compatible with who is our best match." She cast her eye across the room. "Why just look at Warry and Lord Balfour." Hartwell had never heard her tone so sour.

"Lady Warrington, I am sorry for causing you pain. I know you wished for the opportunity to announce an engagement tonight. Perhaps Warry will not disappoint you as I have."

By the expression on Lady Warrington's face, Warry already had.

"Will you look at Lord Balfour's nose?" Lady Warrington said softly, almost to herself. "The more I consider it, the more I think it is not the nose of a gentleman. No, no, I hardly think it is."

∽

Warry fairly jumped when Balfour's hand came toward him. Balfour paused, frowned, then reached forward again, straightening Warry's cravat. "I do not like to see you flinch from me," he said.

"I'm sorry," Warry replied woodenly. "I shall endeavour not to in the future."

Balfour tugged his cravat lightly. "You have been skittish all night."

"I suppose I am thinking about our announcement. This is such a large group. I am nervous about the attention our news will draw."

Balfour slid his hand to Warry's shoulder, and Warry tried not to wince. "There is nothing to be frightened of. I will make the announcement. You need not say anything."

Warry nodded. "Thank you." He was to be the same silent prop before the *ton* that Balfour would expect him to be as a husband. Very well. He hesitated, his heart pounding. If he did not act now, he never would. "I should like to speak with my mother for a moment if that is all right."

"Certainly." Balfour squeezed his shoulder. "Be back by my side on the hour."

Warry attempted a smile and a nod, then hastened away. He did his best to lose himself in the crowd. He was not certain if Balfour still watched him, and he knew he mustn't take the chance. He passed behind clusters of revellers, making his way ever closer to the stairs. There were a few people gathered on the staircase, and he hurried past them, using them for cover when he could. At the top of the staircase, he ducked under a thin, tasselled rope, and entered a darkened hallway. Somewhere up here was Balfour's study. Balfour had given him the grand tour earlier before anyone else arrived. If he could just remember which door...

Even through the dimness, he recognised the door he sought—thick, carved oak with an enormous brass handle. He held his breath as he pulled, praying there would be no creak, and then slipped as quietly as a mouse into the dim room.

There was a lamp on the desk, turned down so low that it was almost entirely extinguished, and Warry hurried forward and twisted the mechanism to allow the flame more wick to climb. Then, holding the lamp as gingerly as if he were Aladdin from *Arabian Nights*, afraid of the genie inside, he turned his attention to Balfour's desk.

He hoped that tonight's subterfuge would be simple. He meant to retrieve Becca's letter and thus break Balfour's hold over him before the man announced their engagement. Warry didn't even care if Balfour said vile things about him in Society afterward. He couldn't imagine anything more vile than being married to the man. Even a tarnished reputation, if Balfour wanted to sink so low, would be easier to bear than matrimony. Perhaps Warry would travel to some distant corner of the world and fake his own death like the rake Slyfeel in volume three of *The Maiden Diaries*, except he wouldn't return a few chapters later to reveal himself dramatically. No, he'd make a life for himself somewhere that he wasn't known and be nothing more than a footnote in the Warrington annals.

He realised with a jolt as he began to search Balfour's desk drawers that marrying Balfour would lose him his claim on the title anyway. Balfour's rank was greater than his, and their marriage would not produce heirs, so Earl Warrington's title would pass to his younger brother Thomas in any case, to preserve it. It was the reason marriages between men were reserved for younger sons. The reason, he recalled, or one of them, why Hartwell never would have wanted to marry him at all. Not that Hartwell would lose his title—the son of a duke outranked the son of a mere earl—but because any union between them could never produce an heir. So, it didn't matter if Hartwell wanted him or not because, even if Warry extricated himself from Balfour's grasp, and Hartwell never got re-engaged to Becca, and they both put aside their ridiculous dedication to wounding each other and expressed instead a mutual and lasting affection, it would never happen.

Except that it mattered, just a little, to Warry's bruised heart.

He closed one drawer in the desk and checked the next one down, stubbornly ignoring the wall full of books that faced him and the fact that the letter could be tucked into any of the hundreds of covers there if it was even in the study at all. What if Balfour had hidden it someplace else entirely? Like in his bedroom, or the sitting room, or in the bottom of a tub of potatoes in the kitchen pantry? Good Lord, this really was hopeless, but Warry couldn't stop looking now, both for his sake and Becca's.

And then the door was pushed open, and Balfour stood there, a sneer on his cold face.

"Well, my dear," he said. "What have we here?"

Warry set the lamp down on the desk and stared back at him. It seemed pointless to come up with yet another lie. He could think of none that would explain away his very obvious transgression, and Balfour was no fool.

Balfour closed the door. "We're not married yet. I hardly think my private papers are of any concern of yours, do you?"

Warry lifted his chin. "It is not your private papers that concern me, sir, but my sister's."

Balfour raised his eyebrows and tilted his head. "Ah, and to think I mistook you for a gentleman of good breeding when here you are trying to cheat your way out of our arrangement."

Warry felt his face grow hot, and he hated Balfour for his ability to sting him with his words when he was not the one at fault. "An arrangement you blackmailed me into!"

Balfour rolled his eyes. "What a tiresome little prig you truly are. If you didn't want to be blackmailed, Joseph, you should have counselled your dear sister to keep her legs closed. Or at least not to be so witless as to write down her indiscretions!"

"Why do you want to marry me?" Warry asked hotly. "You don't even *like* me!"

Balfour waved a hand as though batting away an irritating gnat. "I don't like your newfound impertinence, certainly, and as your husband I shall enjoy taking you in hand and reminding you of your manners, but I like you well enough."

"You mean you find me malleable enough!" Warry hated himself because he knew it was the truth.

Balfour's smirk grew into a smile. "You are pleasingly docile. It's true."

"You may find I have more spine than you imagine."

"Oh! Really?" Balfour folded his arms across his chest. "Where have you been hiding it all the time I've known you?"

Warry straightened his shoulders. "You do not really know me at all." His voice sounded weak to his own ears.

"I will soon enough," Balfour replied, unfolding his arms. He reached out, stroking Warry's cheek with the back of one finger. "You know, for a time, I thought I wanted what my father had. When you fell into my lap, as it were, I thought *this will solve all my problems*. My grandmother will be satisfied that I have made a good match, and I will be husband to someone I truly desire. Yet the more I reflect, the less I believe marriage capable of bringing about lasting happiness. It is that word, 'desire', that has become key to me. I *crave* you, Joseph. My thoughts of you seem branded on my body like plague sores, and every way I toss and turn, I am in an agony of wanting you." His finger trailed over the line of Warry's jaw. "So now, marrying you is simply a way to ensure your compliance in all that I wish to do to you."

Warry closed his eyes, humiliation rising in his throat with all the acidity of bile.

"I must say…" Balfour brushed his finger down his throat and pressed the bruise that still lingered there. "Seeing how much Hartwell desires you has spurred me like nothing else. I wish for him to know, whenever he looks at you, that I have claimed you thoroughly, in body and in spirit."

Now Warry did pull back—so sharply he nearly stumbled.

"Ah, you desire Hartwell in return? No matter. You will forget him entirely once we are wed and I have given you pleasure you could never have imagined."

Warry's blood roared. He had already known pleasure beyond anything he had ever imagined. If he married Balfour, he was not just condemning himself to a lifetime of cruelty, but he was cutting himself off from any chance of a match borne of mutual passion. Even if he could not have Hartwell—even if he did not *want* Hartwell, he reminded himself—there might be others he would feel such fire for. And he had wanted for so long to know what it was to love and be loved without feeling shame for it.

The idea landed softly but ominously—the feather of a raven swaying down from the sky to light in the brim of his hat. It was a foolish plot, born of desperation and no rational thought whatsoever. But he was a fool, was he not? So it was a fool's plan.

He met Balfour's gaze, not giving himself time to doubt. "One night."

Balfour tilted his head. "What did you say?"

"You do not truly wish to wed me. You could wed anyone at all to satisfy your grandmother's requirement. And I would not make a good husband to you, no matter how you tried to mould me. The whole reason you desire me—this body—will grow old. You will not always hunger for it. Then I will become extraneous, a nuisance, as I am to everyone. So I offer you instead one night with me. I will tell no one. And I will do anything."

Something sparked in Balfour's eyes. A moment later, he burst out laughing. Which was not precisely the reaction Warry had hoped for. "Joseph," he said between gasps. "Oh, I should like to dismiss this nonsense at once. What sort of fool must you be to think I would take one night in bed with you in place of a lifetime of possessing you? I—"

Warry forced himself on. "When we are wed, I will give you nothing. You will take what is due to you as my husband, I'm certain, but I will offer nothing in return. I will lie there like a corpse, I swear it. But if you take me now, tonight, I will do anything you wish. I will do it…willingly. I will be whatever you wish me to be." He paused, his throat tightening. "Whatever you think I have done with Lord Hartwell, you do not know the truth of it. I am still a…"

"Still a what?" Balfour was no longer laughing. "I want to hear you say the word."

"A virgin."

Balfour stared, his eyes alight.

A shiver passed through Warry. "You may take that from me any way you like. You do not have to saddle yourself with me as a husband. At the end of the night, you give the letter back, and we part ways."

Balfour clucked his tongue. "You did not allow me to finish, Joseph. Bad manners indeed. Although that was a pretty speech, I must admit. I was going to say that I am not opposed to what you suggest simply because you have suggested it."

Warry tried not to let his confusion show.

"Never did I imagine you had it in you to make such an offer. It is quite the most delightful thing I've witnessed in some time, and it is made all the more delicious by the fact that I don't think you truly know what you are offering."

Once again, Warry's face burned. "I know enough."

"Whatever you don't know," Balfour said quietly, "I will teach you."

Wasn't that what Warry had wanted once, to be schooled in this way? He shut his eyes briefly, wishing one last time for it to be Hartwell who might educate him. Then he banished the thought from his mind and nodded.

"All right, then. At the end of the night, as my guests disperse, you will make your way discreetly to the bedchamber at the end of this hall. I will meet you there."

"And you will have the letter?"

"Certainly, I will have the letter."

"Then we are agreed," Warry said, his heart pounding so wildly he was afraid it might fail at any moment.

"We are agreed," Balfour echoed, his gaze surprisingly soft, holding a near-religious fervour. "Shall we shake hands like gentlemen?"

Warry extended his hand cautiously, trying not to flinch when Balfour grasped it. Instead of shaking, Balfour took his hand and turned it, bringing it up to his mouth. Then, instead of kissing it, he dragged his tongue along it like a dog might.

Warry tugged his hand free, disgusted.

Balfour laughed, the sound chilling and hungry at once. "Oh, my dear," he said, "what a delight you shall be."

And then he swept from the study, leaving Warry sick with fear at what he had agreed to do.

CHAPTER 16

"There really are only so many times a man can be expected to watch a quadrille without resorting to violence," Christmas Gale said, sounding as bored and weary of life as ever. "Hartwell." His voice sharpened. "Hartwell, are you even listening to me?"

"Hmm?" Hartwell pulled his gaze away from the pretty couples on the ballroom floor, moving in perfect synchronicity, frills and ribbons flying. "I beg your pardon, Gale. What did you say?"

Gale narrowed his eyes. "You've grown tiresome of late. I don't like it."

"How fortunate that I exist for more than your pleasure, then," Hartwell said, and won himself a rare, wry smile from his dour friend. "What was it you said?"

Gale waved his hand. "Quadrilles and inevitable violence. Nothing of note."

"I cannot see Warry." Hartwell scanned the crowd again. He caught a glimpse of Becca, trapped in conversation with several other ladies. Her smile looked false but only because he knew her so well. Or had known her. A pang of guilt bit at him, and he wondered if there was any way to repair their tattered friendship.

He loved Becca too dearly to imagine a life without her. Of course, a repaired friendship with Becca would mean seeing Warry far too often, and Hartwell had no interest in such an outcome—which certainly didn't explain why he kept staring around looking for the wretched fellow. Or at least it was no explanation that Hartwell wanted to admit to.

Gale arched a brow. "Yes, you are quite tiresome. Why don't you just admit to yourself that you are head over heels for your dull little Warry and ask him to marry you?"

"What?" Hartwell laughed, and the sound was more strangled than he would have liked. "I certainly am not head over heels for Warry, and even if I were…"

"Even if you were?" Gale prompted.

"Even if I were," Hartwell said, his stomach sinking, "my father would never approve of a marriage with a man."

"Why not?" Gale asked. "You have cousins, do you not? You're hardly the last Hartwell in the world, and Warry's not the last Warrington. I mean, it would be a terrible match but *equally* terrible, which ought to count for something."

Hartwell snorted. "My father would not see it so."

"Well, assuredly not." Gale waved his hand as though it didn't matter a whit. "But he would hardly disown you over such a thing, would he?"

"I wouldn't like to gamble on it, actually."

"Ah," Gale said. "But what's the worst thing that would happen if he called your bluff?"

"The worst…" Hartwell's brow creased. "Well, that is the worst thing. He would disown me. I would no longer be the Marquess of Danbury or the next Duke of Ancaster."

"Oh." Gale downed his glass of sherry. "That is all."

"That is *all*?" Hartwell exclaimed, reeling.

"Yes," Gale said. "That is all. You have an income via your mother's side, don't you?"

"I…Yes." Hartwell frowned. "How do *you* know that?"

"I know most things," Gale said with a tired shrug. "But this is all nothing more than an exercise in hypotheticals, of course, since your father would never disown you."

"Now that you *cannot* know."

"Good Lord, Hartwell." Gale sighed. "A man as proud as your father?"

"Exactly so!"

"Remind me to play faro with you more often. You are so easily bluffed. My dear Hartwell, a man as proud as your father would never disown you over a marriage with another peer, man or not, because to do so would be to publicly admit he has no control over you, as a father ought to have over his son."

"What? No, that's utter nonsense."

"He would be a laughingstock." Gale's mouth quirked. "Well, that is what I think at least. Besides, as I said, this is all nothing more than a game of hypotheticals because of course you don't even want to marry little Joseph Warrington at all, do you?"

Hartwell glared at him. "No, of course I do not."

"Well then. I suppose it doesn't matter that a quarter of an hour ago he went into a private part of the house and Balfour followed him."

Hartwell's blood ran cold. "What?"

"Oh, no," Gale said, craning his neck. "There he is again, looking like a startled little rabbit. And right on his heels again is our host."

Hartwell whirled, then immediately cursed himself. He could *feel* Gale smirk behind him.

"The little fool is determined to ruin himself," Hartwell snapped.

"Good thing he is not your problem."

"Yes, good thing."

But Hartwell's stomach would not unclench as he watched Warry cross the ballroom, Balfour behind him.

"What of you?" he asked, determinedly focusing his attention on Gale. "I should never have thought you'd attend a gathering of this size except under duress. Are you here for Clarissa or Anne-Marie?

Or is your presence something to do with that tall fellow you've been exchanging glances with all night?"

"Ah, so you are capable of having a thought without Warrington's name attached to it? That, my friend, is an arrangement that is strictly business."

"Your case?"

"I have told you, Hartwell—"

"Your enquiry. Your research. Your mild espionage."

"I am not at liberty to confirm or deny. What do you remember of the du Bourg hoax?"

"The what?" Hartwell asked.

"The du Bourg hoax," Gale said with the long-suffering sigh he reserved for those he considered his intellectual inferiors. Which was everyone. "Lord Cochrane and the stock exchange fraud? Good Lord, Hartwell, it was only four years ago. It was in all the papers!"

Hartwell wrinkled his nose.

"Bonaparte is dead!"

Hartwell jolted. "Is he? *When?*"

"No, that was the *hoax*!" Gale rolled his eyes. "And certain investments were made on the strength of the rumour, do you remember?"

"It's not ringing any bells," Hartwell said. His attention wandered back to Warry and then to Balfour. No man in all the world ever looked like such a self-satisfied toad. Why *were* the Warringtons supporting this match, especially when Lady Warrington seemed so bitter about it? What was it his mother had said about Balfour and the Warringtons' former valet? *Warry's* former valet? That she didn't see why the Warringtons would allow their son to marry an associate of the man who'd stolen from them. He recalled the day last year when Wilkes had been dismissed. Warry had gone on and on about it, talking excitedly of the silverware and the snuff box that were missing, and how his father had raged at Wilkes loudly enough for the whole house to hear until Becca told him to keep private matters private.

Wilkes. Hartwell suddenly recalled seeing the weasel-faced man at the Four-in-Hand that night, hovering near Balfour as Hartwell had dragged Warry away.

His head buzzed. Something was not right. Something had not been right for a very long time, but he had been too thick-skulled to see what.

Gale drained the last of his sherry. "Yes, well, it was quite a—"

"Excuse me," he murmured, stepping away. He held up one finger to Gale. "I do want to hear all about it. I do. I'll be back." He did not know what he meant to do as he followed Warry's path. He heard a commotion nearby—some fellow had spilled punch on his coat, apparently—but he ignored it. Hartwell might not have a mind like Gale's, capable of putting pieces together to make some sordid whole, but the disjointed fragments of this puzzle were troubling enough.

And yet the puzzle, whatever it was, was not his business. He had promised to stay away from Warry in the future.

He stopped, his legs no longer sure whether to obey him.

"Lord Hartwell?" Hartwell turned to see Sylvie Lancaster peering up at him. A sweet-tempered eldest daughter from a good family, her smile was not unappealing, and he imagined Lady Warrington would approve of her small, straight nose. He reminded himself of his vow that he would choose a wife tonight. He was hardly in the mood to socialise, and yet every moment he spent concentrating on Sylvie Lancaster was a moment he did not spend concentrating on Joseph Warrington, who somehow, over the course of the last minute, had disappeared again.

Hartwell must not pursue him. Whatever choices he had made, Warry was an adult, not the boy Hartwell had once known.

Let him go.

"Miss Lancaster." Hartwell bowed. "It is a pleasure to see you again."

Sylvie's smile was so bright it cleared the shadows from his mind. Perhaps whatever was troubling him about Warry and Balfour and that night at the Four-in-Hand was the design of his overactive imagination. At the very least it was none of his concern.

Let him go, Hartwell. For Christ's sake.

Soon he and Sylvie were dancing. He hoped Gale was not watching. The man would have no choice but to resort to violence if he spied Hartwell dancing the quadrille.

He was surprised to find he enjoyed his time with Sylvie, and he realised, quite breathlessly, that his stress of late—his melancholy, his short temper—all of it was the fault of the Warringtons. He had bound himself so tightly to that family for so long. Now that he was no longer of consequence to Becca or her brother, he found himself oddly free.

When the quadrille finished, he danced with Emily Pearson and after that, Olivia Wilton. As he danced with Olivia, he noticed Becca was now dancing with Emily Pearson, a bright smile on her face. Another pang went through him, but he was in such fine spirits that he felt wonderfully happy for her. He danced and laughed and drank punch until he looked up in surprise to see throngs of people leaving. A sour-faced butler was directing traffic out the front doors. Hartwell pulled out his watch. Good Lord, the hour was late. He had not sought out the fathers of any of his dancing partners to ask permission to propose, so that was a bit of a failure on his part, but he had drunk vast quantities of punch and was much in need of relief. Balfour had made his life hell these past few weeks. The least the man could do was allow Hartwell to linger to use the privy.

He glanced around, a bit disoriented. A gaggle of young ladies called goodnight to him, and he called it back to them. With a start, Hartwell spied Warry hovering in a corner near the staircase and quickly turned away. Where was the room he sought?

When he turned again, Warry was slinking upstairs. What the devil? Hartwell's bladder was near to bursting, and yet he wavered between finding the privy and finding out where Warry was skulking off to.

"Hartwell!" Becca approached, weaving through the tide of people heading out. Hartwell cast another glance over his shoulder as Warry ducked under the rope at the top of the stairs and disappeared down the dark hall. Hartwell's earlier vow to let the brat go yielded to the sense that watching Warry disappear into that black hall was troublingly similar to watching him disappear beneath the water of the frog pond all those years ago.

"Have you seen my brother?" Becca asked.

"I..." Hartwell did not know what to say. He swayed on his aching feet.

"He said he would go to Bucknall's after this. I was hoping to catch him before he left."

"I do not know," Hartwell heard himself say. Why had Warry told his sister he was going to Bucknall's when he was in fact trespassing once more in the private area of Balfour's home?

"Hartwell, do not stand there staring like a dumb beast. It does not suit you."

"I did not know we were on speaking terms," he said, for that at least was the truth.

She coloured up slightly. "We are not. I only wanted to ask you that question." And yet she stood there, gazing at him as though there was much she wanted to say. There was much he wanted to say as well, and if he had any sense left in him, he would open his mouth and say it.

But no sooner had his lips parted when he saw Balfour cross the emptying ballroom, headed for the stairs. His heart began to pound as a memory returned to him. That night by the theatre. Hartwell had been covered in shit and nearly too drunk to stand. The gas lamps had flickered, casting winged spectres on the street before him. And Warry had defied Balfour and got in a hack with him. Hartwell could recall feeling the coldness coming off Balfour as though it were a physical chill. "If you accompany that filthy drunk anywhere," Balfour had said to Warry, "you will regret it."

That was not something a man said to someone for whom he held tremendous affection. To someone he meant to care for as a husband. And while Hartwell knew he himself had said many things to Warry that a man ought not to say to one he cared for, he had never made a threat such as that.

Had Balfour already made Warry regret it? Or was that what he meant to do now?

"Becca," he began. But then a new voice cut the air.

"Lord Hartwell! It was *such* a pleasure dancing with you tonight." Olivia Wilton extended a gloved hand to him. "I am most excited about our excursion tomorrow."

Hartwell turned his blank gaze to Olivia. He did vaguely recall promising to take her for a drive through the park tomorrow afternoon. That conversation seemed to have taken place ages ago. His mind raced as a hare set upon by hounds.

"If I did…?" Warry had asked in response to Hartwell's assurance that he could break his courtship with Balfour if he so wished.

For weeks now, he had watched Warry and Balfour together, unable to concentrate on anything but his own jealousy. He had missed what was right before him. Warry was afraid. And not merely afraid because he believed God would smite him for so much as looking at the cut of Balfour's coat with admiration but well and truly afraid of Balfour himself.

How could he have been so blind?

Warry's ill-fated trip to St. Giles. The robbery. Warry's sudden interest in gaming hells and his encounter with Balfour at the first one he visited. Wilkes's presence there. There could be no doubt about it: Balfour was pulling Warry's strings as he might a marionette.

"Yes," he said faintly, trying to focus on Olivia. "Tomorrow. Excursion."

Olivia shot a cool glance at Becca. "Lady Rebecca. It is good to see you still making an effort to participate in Society, even after having sat so long on the shelf."

She beamed again at Hartwell and waved her gloved fingers. "Until tomorrow!" she called gaily.

Becca glared at Hartwell for a moment, then turned and stalked away.

"Becca, wait!" Hartwell chased her through the crowd but kept getting snagged on small groups wishing each other good night and making plans for the morrow. He finally battled his way outside, just as Becca was climbing into her carriage. "Becca!"

She did not even glance through the window at him. The carriage door was shut behind her. One of the harnessed bays snorted. All around him, hooves clopped, and people chattered and laughed. Any moment now, Becca's carriage would depart.

"I think he is in trouble!" Hartwell shouted over the heads of the revellers. Several people turned toward him. Becca turned too. He stared at her helplessly as her driver flicked the reins and her carriage trundled forward. He stood there for a moment, panting, and then spun and made for the house once more.

"Is somebody in trouble?" inquired a small, frail voice behind him. He turned. Lady Agatha Watson tottered toward him, leaning on her walking stick.

"No, Lady Agatha, everything is fine."

"I have simply been dying for a scandal to start the Season," Lady Agatha declared. "This evening was so very dull. I documented not a single indiscretion."

She clearly hadn't been looking hard enough. Hartwell started forward again but stumbled upon another bit of commotion. His own mother was propped on the shoulders of two of her friends, singing "No One Shall Govern Me," while one of the friends laughed nervously and attempted to shush her.

Well. That was a mess that could hopefully be sorted without him. Hartwell ducked his head, dodged past the group, and reached the front door. The sour-faced butler stood there, looking highly unimpressed. "My Lord," the man said with a lack of affect that would have made Gale envious. "Did you forget something?"

Hartwell racked his mind for an excuse. His bladder twinged again. "No, not exactly. This is quite…You see, I desperately need the privy. I mean *desperately*."

The butler's small eyes shifted sideways. He sighed loudly.

Hartwell gathered himself. "Please, my good man, I beg you."

The butler exhaled once more and then stepped aside. "Down the main hallway, make a left-hand turn."

Hartwell raced inside, past the rows of elongated portraits. He did not turn to see whether the butler watched him as he passed the door the man had indicated and entered the ballroom, hastening toward the staircase.

CHAPTER 17

Balfour's bedroom was as chilly as a mausoleum. That was the excuse Warry gave for his shaking hands as he unknotted his cravat under Balfour's intent gaze. The room was a good size with most of the space taken up by the bed. Wide windows looked outside into the darkness, but Warry couldn't see the view, only the flickering lamp light reflected in the glass panes. He wished a servant had drawn the curtains or that Balfour would. To do it himself would only draw attention to his shame, and he didn't want to show more of that than he could possibly avoid. He knew instinctively that Balfour would mock him for it.

A washstand stood against the far wall, bookended on either side by a pair of large armoires. There was a small table beside the bed with nothing on it except a lamp. Perhaps Balfour took tea in bed in the mornings and that was where the servants set the cup. Warry thought of his own bedroom and the stack of books piled up on his bedside table because he never knew which one he might want to read before bed, or in the morning, or even in the middle of the night if he woke and couldn't immediately fall asleep again.

The walls of the bedroom were papered in light blue with flocked damask stripes running vertically. Warry imagined the colour would look vibrant in the morning light, but he was glad he would never know. He would not stay in the room a moment longer than was necessary. As soon as he had Becca's letter in his possession, he would never step foot in Balfour's foul house ever again.

Balfour crossed to the table and turned the lamp up. The wick spluttered for a moment, throwing strange shadows on the walls, and then the light settled, brighter than before.

"Does it always take you so long to undress?" Balfour asked curiously.

Warry didn't answer, only wrenched his cravat free and set to work on the buttons of his waistcoat. His coat, which he'd shrugged off upon entering the room, had been discarded on a chair by the door. His shoes lay nearby.

He tried not to think of the last time he'd been intimate with a man. With Hartwell. Hartwell, who had spent the evening dancing with young ladies. Warry had tried not to notice him, but he hadn't been able to help himself, his gaze drawn unerringly back to Hartwell at every moment. He'd seen Hartwell smiling and talking and laughing as he danced, and he'd burned with both anger and humiliation. He *hated* Hartwell.

He tugged too hard on a button and the threads snapped. The button landed with a ping on the floor, then bounced off somewhere into the shadows.

"Leave it," Balfour said with a lazy wave of his hand. "I should like a little keepsake of our tryst tonight."

"This is not a tryst," Warry said. "This is merely an exchange."

"Oh," Balfour said, "then you'd rather I treated you as a whore than a lover?"

Warry pressed his mouth shut.

"I offered you love, didn't I?" Balfour asked. "But no, you refused me. You would rather I treat you as a cheap molly. Well, of course, that aligns very happily with my desires." Balfour's thin mouth curled in a hateful smirk.

Warry shrugged his waistcoat off, his fingers trembling on the fabric. Then, holding Balfour's gaze in a manner he hoped was proud rather than alluring, he tugged his shirt over his head and dropped it to the floor.

Balfour arched an eyebrow, his gaze fixed on the buttoned fall front of Warry's silk breeches. Warry felt a rush of cold flow through him as he reached behind him to loosen the gusset ties. He tugged the laces loose and then paused for a moment with his fingers on the buttons of his waistband.

"Tease." Balfour stepped closer.

Warry screwed his courage and dropped his breeches, leaving him standing in nothing but his drawers and his clocked stockings.

"Very nice," Balfour said and began to untie his cravat. "What pretty pale skin you have, Joseph. I do look forward to discovering every inch of it."

Warry's stomach clenched, and bile rose in his throat at the thought of the hours to come.

Balfour yanked his cravat free and threw it to the floor. He circled Warry, and Warry gave himself credit for not bolting. But then Balfour lunged, grabbing Warry by the shoulders and sinking his teeth into the mark Hartwell had left. The pain was so great that Warry cried out through clenched teeth.

At that moment, he heard hurried footsteps from somewhere outside and then, before he could even make a grab for his discarded shirt, the bedroom door was shoved open, and Hartwell, his expression fiery, burst inside.

"Warry!" he exclaimed as he stared in disbelief at Warry's state of undress, then at Balfour and back to Warry again. And then, just as Warry realised with growing horror that Hartwell wasn't alone and that other people were crowding through the door as well, Hartwell dashed forward and punched Balfour in the face.

Balfour dropped to the floor with a howl.

"Well," said Lord Christmas Gale from the doorway where he was standing with Lady Agatha as well as a tall man Warry did not recognise and—Good Lord, no!—*Becca*, "I said it would all end in violence, didn't I? Too many quadrilles, my dear Hartwell. Too many quadrilles."

"Warry!" Hartwell roared. "What the hell is going on here?"

Warry had no answer for that at all. He could only shake his head and clap his hands to his mouth to keep his sudden, panicked sobs from escaping him.

~

"I'm sorry." Becca momentarily paused in her pacing, her eyes flashing to Warry with such ferocity that Hartwell almost pitied him. "You must recount this tale again, in its entirety, for I cannot comprehend what I am hearing."

"Ah, Becca," Hartwell said. "You're normally so sharp. Warry has simply told us that in a deeply misguided attempt to preserve your reputation, he promised himself to Balfour first as a husband and then, when he realised how dreadful it would be to spend a lifetime called to heel by that disgraceful excuse for a man, he decided the next best thing would be to offer his body to the fellow for one night. Hoping, naturally, that a single night of carnal pleasure would prove an adequate substitute in Balfour's eyes for a lifetime of matrimonial bliss."

Hartwell ought to have kept the sarcasm from his voice. Just as he ought not to have shouted at Warry in Balfour's bedchamber. In Hartwell's defence, Warry's self-described actions of the past two weeks were, it turned out, quite beyond belief. And, in his further defence, Hartwell had ceased thundering when he'd witnessed Warry's vain attempt to contain his sobs. At that moment, he had, with no regard for the huddle of witnesses, crossed the room to Warry, giving Balfour a good kick in the head as he passed to render him satisfactorily unconscious, and taken Warry in his arms.

Warry was now propped in the guest bed at Hartwell house

before a roaring fire, a very large quilt pulled over him. He had attempted to push it down moments ago and had received such a bark from Becca that he had immediately tugged it back up to his chin. He did not flinch at Hartwell's words. He'd seemed in a trance since they'd left Balfour's home. This worried Hartwell, which made him increasingly sarcastic, as though perhaps enough sharpness could spur Warry back into normalcy.

He himself could not cease revisiting the events of an hour ago, when he had stood in Balfour's bedchamber, Warry pressed shaking to him, heat and cold both seeming to emanate from his bare skin. He had turned them so his own body sheltered Warry from the onlookers.

Lady Agatha, whose short stature and aging eyes kept the nuances of the situation from her, believed the scandal in progress had to do with Warry and Hartwell, and had crowed about this being precisely the sort of gross impropriety she had been awaiting all evening. When she saw Balfour on the floor with his cravat beside him, she could have soared through the roof in her excitement.

"The Warrington boy caught up in a web of lust with Lord Balfour *and* Lord Hartwell! Oh, his name will be bandied about for years to come!"

"I will wed him myself before that happens!" Hartwell snapped over his shoulder, paying no mind to Gale's groan.

Lady Agatha had turned her attention to Balfour, declaring with a cry of alarm that the man looked to be dead.

Then Becca had raced forward and fairly pried Warry from Hartwell's arms, taking him in her own and demanding answers with a speed and fervour that Hartwell found dizzying. He'd listened with vague gratitude as Gale urged Lady Agatha out of the room, assuring her that Balfour had not been murdered. Gale then informed Hartwell that he and his tall companion, a Bow Street Runner, were there to confront Balfour on charges of stock fraud, having finally obtained the last bit of proof they'd needed over the course of the ball, but that they would wait outside until Warry was decent and Balfour was conscious.

Hartwell had located Warry's clothes and managed to prise him from Becca's grasp just long enough to guide the shirt over his head and help him into his breeches. Balfour had moaned on the floor but did not rise, and Warry had made weak protest that he could put on his own shoes, though one attempt to do so with shaking hands, and Hartwell had taken over the task.

They had left the room, Warry supported between Hartwell and Becca, his face buried in Hartwell's shoulder as though if he could not see anyone, it followed that they could not see him. Hartwell had nodded his thanks to Gale, who had managed to store Lady Agatha somewhere out of sight. Becca's assertion that she and Warry were going home had brought on another paroxysm of panic from Warry, and Hartwell had his hands quite full calming him. Gale had leaned toward him and whispered, "I would say you may take him to my private apartment, but the last time I permitted that, something unspeakable happened to a jug I was rather fond of. If you take him to Hartwell House, I have it on good authority your father intends a late night at Bucknall's, and your mother is on her way home to bed where even cannon fire would be unlikely to awaken her before noon."

"Hartwell House?" came Becca's sharp rejoinder. "Do not be absurd. Warry will come home and be looked after there. Warry, I will handle any questions from Mama. You have nothing to be concerned about."

Yet Warry's terror at the idea of facing his household came from a place quite beyond reason, and in the end, Becca had to concede —under the condition that she too would come to Hartwell House.

And there they were.

"Do I have it about right?" Hartwell demanded, still unable to keep the sharpness from his tone.

Warry nodded mutely.

Becca stepped to the bed and leaned forward. Warry appeared

to be fighting the urge to squirm under her gaze. "He tried to blackmail you into marrying him, and you decided you would endure a lifetime with him in order to save me some embarrassment?"

"It would have ruined you!"

Becca sat down on the bed and clasped Warry's hands. "No, Warry! No! If I am to be ruined in the court of public opinion, then let it be so! I am responsible for my own actions, always, and I am not afraid of a bit of gossip."

"A *bit* of gossip? Becca that letter was…It was *unspeakable*! The things people would say about you…You would not be able to brush it off. It would affect your entire future and—"

"You mean that no one would wish to marry me? I have never in the whole of my life wanted to marry. Not even for one second. And now, more than ever, I am certain that I would die first."

"Our family—"

She huffed. "Oh, so it was your own reputation for which you were concerned? Now we come to the truth of it."

"No, Becca! I feared for you. But—"

"Have mercy, Becca," Hartwell said quietly. "He did what he thought was right. He was only trying to rescue you."

Becca said nothing for a long moment, merely studied her brother with her formidable blue eyes. Then she reached out and flicked him sharply on the forehead. "If ever you feel the compulsion to rescue me again, please consult me first, and I will let you know whether or not I am in need of rescue. Are we very clear?"

Warry glanced away and nodded.

"No, look at me."

Hartwell could see the effort it took for Warry to comply.

"I told you not a few days past that I could see you were not yourself, and I wished to know why. You could have told me then."

"I did not know what to do," Warry muttered to the quilt. "I feared you would despise me."

"When I told you that I would still love you whenever you were ready to be truthful with me, did I say, 'unless the truth is something very unpleasant'?"

Warry squeezed his eyes shut, and the last of Hartwell's own anger fled. How confused Warry must have been, he thought. How frightened. He'd been as shocked by Warry's tale as Becca, but the more he thought on it, the easier it was to see how it had all unfolded. In fact, it suddenly seemed more or less inevitable that Joseph Warrington would have done the thing he feared most—risk his reputation, pollute his body—in order to save the sister he loved so dearly.

Warry gulped as though it pained him to breathe, then opened his eyes, a new anguish in them. "You do not understand. It was my fault."

"What was?"

"That Wilkes was able to get hold of that letter!"

Hartwell started, but he remained silent, waiting for Becca to proceed.

She allowed Warry an attempt to even out his breathing, then said quietly, "Explain."

Warry cast a glance at Hartwell, who was not certain whether the panic in his gaze pled for rescue or for Hartwell to leave and not bear witness to what he was about to say. "I took the letter from your bedroom. I meant to return it. I had taken your diary to give you a scare. I don't even remember what I was angry about. But the letter fell from it. I…I did not mean to read it."

She held up a hand. "If you had not wanted to read it, you would not have read it."

Warry paused, his mouth open. "You are right. I started to read it, and I could not stop. It shames me that I read it, and—and honestly, it was quite shocking, quite horrifying, to think of my sister doing any such…"

"Yes, yes," Hartwell waved his hand, urging him on. "We are all aware that Becca's way with the written word can be…disconcerting."

Becca fixed Hartwell with a glare, and he went silent at once.

Warry took a breath. "I did not know how, precisely, two women could…as a man and a woman do. And though I did not fully understand myself then, I was beginning to awaken to the truth that I wished one day to do such things with a man. With a husband," he added quickly. "But I did not know what it would be like for two men either, and I—Oh, I cannot explain!"

"I think I understand." Becca spoke quietly. "I suppose, when there is no other information available to you besides your sister's sordid, half-finished letter to a former governess—"

"Or your sister's lewd novel collection," Hartwell added helpfully.

Warry shot him a look that Hartwell supposed was intended to strike him dead. Hartwell might have grinned if it weren't so painful to imagine Warry's confusion. Perhaps the same confusion he himself had felt when his father had slapped him and declared that kissing a boy was not acceptable for his only son. The same confusion Becca had felt when she'd first realised what she wanted from Miss Lilley went beyond French lessons.

Becca blinked rapidly several times. "Well, yes, I knew Warry snuck into my room to thumb the pages of my copy of *The Maiden Diaries*."

"And perhaps to thumb something else." Hartwell raised his brows. He did not know why he continued to prod at Warry, just that he felt so very useless at the moment.

"I never did!" Warry shouted.

"You, hush," Becca snapped at Hartwell. "You are nowhere near back in my good graces."

"I saved your brother!"

"Stop!" Warry shouted, his eyes on Hartwell, his voice damn near loud enough to wake the duchess from her drunken slumber. "Is it not enough that you have made me feel small all these years? Was it not enough to tell me how morally destitute I am yesterday after we lay together?"

Becca's gaze shot to Hartwell, and she hissed, "You *what?*"

"And is my disgrace tonight not enough for you? Still you must mock me? I cannot…I cannot stand the sight of you!"

The words cut so deeply that Hartwell could make no response. Perhaps this was what it was like to receive a fatal wound on the battlefield—so much damage done so quickly one did not know the scope of it until one looked down and saw the severed limb, the excised entrails. He did not wish to be the boorish creature Warry described. Had he not also been a rescuer? Had he not—no. What he had been, first and foremost, was unkind. Cowardly. Jealous. And too proud to admit it.

With his sight turned so far inward, he had missed the glaring truth of how much he cared for Warry and how much Warry was suffering, caught in the trap Balfour had laid. Yes, Warry had lied to him, kept the truth from him, but Hartwell had never presented himself as a confidant to Warry. Quite the opposite. He had overlooked his own cruelty in teasing Warry without outwardly tempering it with the admiration he felt, in pushing the pup away in a misguided attempt to protect him. From what, precisely? From scandal? Or from Hartwell's own inconstancy? He now recalled the Gilmore rout in far more detail than he wished to. The way his tongue—normally quick to tease but just as quick to soothe the sting away—had sharpened to a blade, and he had spoken with the veriest intent to wound Warry. To punish him for Hartwell's own inability to say what he felt.

Becca turned on him. "If you feel you have done quite enough damage, you may leave the room. Otherwise please, do stay, and let us see what else you manage to botch." She turned back to her brother. "It is all right, Warry. I knew that you sometimes snuck my books of late, and I was rather proud of you for it. I did not realise you had seen that letter. So you kept hold of it…"

Slowly, Warry tore his livid gaze from Hartwell's and faced Becca. "I truly meant to give it back, but I left it in my bureau, and Wilkes must have…I did not know what had become of it, and I was terrified. Months went by, and nothing happened, so I thought perhaps…perhaps it was simply lost. It must have been during that time that Wilkes and Balfour concocted their plan."

"Wilkes and Balfour," Becca mused.

"I did not know they had an association. Honestly, I had no opinion of Wilkes. He was never friendly with me, and when Father called him a thief and dismissed him, I thought no more of him except that it made for quite a story. But he is an old associate of Balfour's. And Balfour told me he…he used to pay Wilkes to snoop through my possessions and send details to him."

Hartwell half expected Becca to rise off the ground and unfold great wings like an avenging angel. Balfour would do well to sail for the Continent as quickly as possible before Becca tracked him down. "When Wilkes was still with our household?"

Warry nodded, and his cheeks needed no help from the firelight to burn red. "Balfour noticed me at the end of last Season. Desired me from the first he saw of me, he claimed. I…thought highly of him at first. That is the most ludicrous part. If he had not tried to blackmail me, if he had simply courted me…I might have been enamoured. I am such a fool."

Becca tilted her head first one way, then the other, like a bird. Warry visibly braced himself for her censure, and Hartwell held his breath, hoping she would not be too harsh with him. "I wish that you had not taken my private property. I wish that you had possessed more sense than to leave something of such a personal nature lying about, but what Wilkes and Balfour did with that letter is not your fault. And a man like Balfour…He did not want your willing attendance, do you understand?"

Hartwell could not read Warry's expression. The fire let loose a spray of sparks.

Finally, Warry spoke. "I do now."

"He wanted you under his thumb. And he would have found a way to achieve that with or without that particular letter."

"Because I am so weak?" Warry blurted furiously.

"Because a man like Balfour *practises* manipulating people."

Warry looked for a moment as though he might break and begin to shout out all his misery and anger and shame, but then he sagged back against the headboard. "I am sorry." His voice was hoarse, and he looked very, very small underneath the quilt. Hartwell should have liked to come up with even just one thing to say to ease his pain, but he did not trust himself not to make it worse.

"It is Balfour who should be sorry. Though he never will be." Becca's tone did little to hide her rage. "At least he is the Continent's problem now and not ours. It's a shame that people may never know the truth of why he was overtaken by a sudden urge to travel at Gale's very strong suggestion. I would quite like the entire world to know what a snake he is."

The weight of memory struck Hartwell as he saw a very young Becca holding and rocking an even younger Warry at the edge of the frog pond while the boy shivered, water dripping from his mop of hair. In the memory, Hartwell dripped water too. He had pulled Warry from the pond, driven by a terror so vast he could not quantify it. Terror of what his parents would say, what the Warringtons would say, if they knew Warry had nearly drowned under his and Becca's watch. But the terror went deeper than that. It was his own —his fear of losing Warry. The same terror he had felt tonight, throwing open that door and seeing Warry in Balfour's grasp. He let out his breath in a rush.

Warry was staring helplessly at Becca. "Do you despise me now?"

She touched his quilt-covered arm. "No. But do you have any idea why I'm furious with you, brother?"

"For nearly allowing Balfour to ruin my reputation. Our family's reputation. For trying to rescue you when you did not wish—"

"For putting yourself in danger!" she barked, making both Warry and Hartwell jump. "When William told me you were in trouble, I have never known such fear. I shouted to the carriage driver, and I was out before the vehicle had fully stopped. Warry, I do not even know how I reached the top of Balfour's stairs as fast as I did. You mean the world to me. You are my younger brother, and it is my job to protect you, not the other way around." Her voice shook slightly, and she dashed her fist under her eyes.

Hartwell's chest contracted. Even more the fool Warry for not realising, as he sought Balfour's attention and approval, as he listened to the man go on and on about sherry, that he already had someone who cherished him completely.

"Should it not work both ways?" Warry made a valiant, if unsuccessful, effort to steady his own voice. "I would not sit back and let that man decide your future. You did not deserve to be publicly humiliated. What you wanted with Miss Lilley—I know it is impossible because of your different statuses—but you should not ever have to be ashamed of it."

"I am not," Becca said simply.

"He would have made you ashamed of it."

"Nobody can make me anything."

Then Warry did snap, and Hartwell watched it from what felt like a vast distance. "Are you not ever scared? Do you always know precisely what to do? It is not so simple for me. I have always been ashamed of what I want. Trailing after you and Hartwell reminds me perpetually of what I am lacking. Balfour made me feel as though I mattered, completely separate from either of you. Up until he made his bargain with me, I dreamed of being his husband. So you see, I am just as stupid as you have always believed. People can make me anything they want. I have no backbone."

Hartwell at last found his voice, though he was unsure of its welcome. "You have always stood up to me."

Warry and Becca both turned toward him. Hartwell continued, surprised by how calm he suddenly felt.

"Around me, you have been yourself—sweet, vexing, goat-obsessed." He attempted a smile, but the moment held too much truth for jesting. "Until you began spending time with Lord

Balfour, that is. Then you closed yourself off, and it was…it was unbearable to me."

Hartwell slid his hands deep into his pockets.

"I…I have been cruel, I know. You are right to despise me. I teased you all these years for two reasons. First, because I feared to examine my own flaws, and so it was easier to pick apart yours. And second, because I knew I would never change you. No taunt of mine could have stood up to a spirit such as yours. It is not an excuse for the way I treated you. But I would like you to know right now, I cannot imagine ever having meant a single unkind word I spoke about you."

He took a step closer, and Warry stared at him, the fire casting fingers of shadow over his throat, darkening the bruise on his neck. "Whether you meant your words or not, you still spoke them."

"I know. And Warry, I am so very sorry for it."

Becca smoothed the quilt over Warry, then stood up. "You two are both such idiots. I fear for your futures." There was no rancour behind the words. "I am going home. You two may discuss whatever you need to discuss. And remember, Warry dear, if you ever endanger yourself so again, especially for my sake, I shall put an arrow clean through you. And I will not miss."

Hartwell was glad for the dimness of the room, for he could feel himself colour up nicely. "Take my carriage," he said to Becca.

"Oh, I intend to. I will see you both on the morrow."

She left, still muttering about idiots.

CHAPTER 18

When the door shut after Becca, Warry fully expected to find himself tongue-tied. Instead, he surprised himself by looking Hartwell directly in the eye and saying what he should have said long ago. "I care for you a great deal. But I do not trust you. Nor am I certain right now that I even like you."

Pain flashed across Hartwell's face, although Warry had not spoken the words to wound. He only wanted Hartwell to know where they stood.

"I do not fault you for that," Hartwell said.

"You fault me for much else."

Hartwell stepped forward. "No." He sat on the edge of the bed. "The fear Becca spoke of, I knew it too tonight. When I thought you might come to harm, I…there are no words, Warry. And to know that it was my doing…"

That startled Warry. "Your doing?" he asked with suspicion. "You credit yourself with far too much influence on the universe, Hartwell."

"Had I paid any attention these past few weeks, I would have known something was wrong. I saw only my dissatisfaction with the life I was being pushed toward. I saw my jealousy over your match with Balfour. My fear that I would bring about your ruin with my desires. My behaviour toward you has been unpardonable, and you ought to reserve your affection for someone who has earned it. After tonight, I promise, you and your sister may have nothing more to do with me."

Warry straightened, livid once again. "Is that what you think I wish?" Hartwell was not a stupid man, but good Lord, he could play the part well enough.

"I…am afraid I do not know what you wish?"

"You planted a facer on Balfour like none I've ever seen. And yet now, when it matters, you will not truly fight for me, is that it?"

Hartwell appeared utterly desolate. "I have hurt you."

"And I you."

"You were never such a coward as I."

"I certainly was. Becca is right. I could have told her at any time. I could have told you the truth of my desires. You *did* know something was wrong. You did see. You asked me to tell you, and I stayed silent. Time and time again, I chose to lie because shouldering the burden on my own seemed preferable to needing help. To proving yet again that I was mere baggage."

"You have never been that."

Warry listened to the crackle of the fire, frustrated beyond all reason. Hartwell's whipped-dog look brought him no satisfaction. The man's apologies were something, but was he willing to carry the two of them past the bleakness of tonight? Would he not, like the rake Slyfeel, take Warry in his arms and kiss him bruisingly until Warry could have no doubt that his love was returned and that things would be different between them henceforth?

He supposed there was a reason Slyfeel existed only on the printed page.

When no bold declaration was forthcoming, Warry changed the subject, ignoring the bitterness in his stomach. "Lord Christmas said they were arresting Wilkes, and that Balfour is in such disgrace he must leave for the Continent at once. The letter…"

"I have no doubt Gale will locate it and return it to Becca."

He nodded, trying to assemble his thoughts. His next words were sure to disgust Hartwell, and he was not certain he could bear any more censure tonight. "It was a relief, in a way, to…to tell Balfour I would go to his bedroom tonight." He was aware of the jerk of Hartwell's shoulders, but he pushed on. "I am tired of being naive. I don't…I don't know what duties will be expected of me on my wedding night. I have read *The Maiden Diaries*, yes, but many of those scenes do not seem at all realistic. I thought at least through Balfour I would gain some idea of…of the act…"

"If you marry for love, it is not a matter of what duties you are expected to perform or what services you can provide. It is about what feels right to both of us. To both of you," Hartwell corrected hastily. "You and whomever you end up marrying."

"I shall never marry for love," Warry said severely. "It is my second Season, and the only people who have offered are Balfour, in order to humiliate me, and you, in order to silence Lady Agatha. To everyone else, I am not worth looking at."

Hartwell appeared scandalised in a way he had not when Warry had confessed his shameful hope that a night with Balfour would have educated him. "How can you speak such madness? Did I not just say that I care for you?"

"No. I told you I cared for you, and you implied I should not."

Hartwell shifted forward, making the bed creak. "I have cared for you all our years together. A fine job I have done of showing it, and I fear any apology I can make now will lack even the weight of air, my sins are so many. But I did not say what I said to silence Lady Agatha."

Warry's ribs seemed to tighten around his heart. "You did not?"

Hartwell reached out and tucked Warry's hair behind his ear, just as Balfour had done that afternoon on the terrace. Except there was no guile in Hartwell's gesture. It was pure tenderness, and Warry's throat tightened painfully.

"Warry." Hartwell seemed not to know what to say. He simply

breathed the name again. And then again. Warry thought he would never tire of hearing it. "Do you wish me to leave?"

"No," Warry whispered.

"Might I make a promise to you then, with the understanding that you are under no obligation to trust my words until I act to fulfil them?"

Warry nodded slowly.

Hartwell reached under the quilt and found Warry's hand, pulling it out from under the covers to kiss first the back of it, and then, ever so gently, Warry's palm. "I vow never again to make you feel small. To make you feel as though you are a burden rather than a treasure."

Warry prayed it was not the product of his chronic naivete that he believed Hartwell. For never in his life had he felt such wild, dangerous hope. "I promise to tell you..." He stopped, unable to think what he wanted to say. "I promise to tell you," he repeated with more finality.

"Yes," Hartwell kissed his palm again, the sensation sending a jolt between Warry's legs. "You will tell me if you are sad or hurting. You will tell me the moments that you adore me and the moments you cannot stand the sight of me."

Warry tried to laugh. "There will be many of those."

"A great many," Hartwell agreed with the shadow of his familiar grin.

Warry shifted, suddenly aware of Hartwell's thumb resting lightly on his pulse. He did not know that desire could be so *forceful*. He had thought it, up until now, a relatively passive sensation. Something a man resigned himself to, a secret. But the feeling inside him held all the power of a pending storm. "You were right. I ought not to have lain with you when I was engaged to another man."

"Stop that. You did not owe Balfour any such loyalty or honesty."

"No. But I owed it to you."

Hartwell rubbed his thumb along Warry's skin. "I wish I had known."

Warry nodded, and they were silent a few more moments while Warry gathered his courage. "Hartwell—William—Could we...?" He licked his lips.

Hartwell looked surprised at Warry's use of his given name. Then he seemed to realise what Warry was asking, and even by the light of the fire, Warry could swear he saw the man's cheeks pinken. Then Hartwell smiled ruefully and reached out to brush the mark on Warry's neck with a gentleness that stilled the storm inside Warry for an instant.

Warry swallowed, letting Hartwell touch the spot.

"Much as I desire you...I do not feel it would be right so soon after your ordeal. Give yourself time, Warry."

"But I want to forget him," Warry said fiercely. "That is what I want. I am telling you what I desire."

Hartwell moved his hand to Warry's cheek, and Warry flinched in spite of himself, a sudden memory of Balfour seeing Hartwell's mark for the first time and the slap that had followed clouding his mind. He could not allow that memory to make its home within his body. Hartwell paused with his fingertips just above Warry's cheek. His gaze softened further, a shadow of regret passing through his eyes. "No," he said quietly. "None of that. It is me, Warry. It is only me." He stroked Warry's cheek, and Warry released the breath he'd been holding.

"I know," Warry said with no small amount of embarrassment.

Hartwell kept his hand there, and Warry forced himself to hold the man's gaze. Hartwell said, "I would not have you regret this later. It is not your reputation I fear for now. Simply the strength of your conscience. I will not take advantage when you have had such a disorienting night."

"You mistake your own uncertainty for mine." Warry clasped Hartwell's hand, easing it from his face and lowering it to the quilt over his lap. There, he gripped it tightly, and spoke with quiet urgency. "Make me remember your touch again, not his."

Hartwell studied him for a long moment, shadows from the fire flickering over his face.

"Please?" Warry whispered. His courage nearly retreated in the face of Hartwell's silence.

"Ah, come here," Hartwell spoke at last, and it was as though he had reached some place of peace within himself where inner torment acquiesced to the truth of what he craved. "And allow me to show you how very much I care for you."

Warry slipped the quilt down and leaned into Hartwell's embrace, and for several moments, that was all it was. An embrace. He rested his forehead on Hartwell's shoulder, afraid he would begin sobbing and be unable to stop. Hartwell tightened his arms around him and rubbed his back with a warm palm until prickles of pleasure crept up Warry's spine to his scalp.

Then Warry turned and kissed Hartwell softly on the neck. Hartwell sighed and dipped his head to meet Warry's mouth with his own. Warry was struck nearly dumb by the warmth that poured through him. It seemed such an immense discovery, the knowledge of how it felt to be touched by one he desired and to know he was desired in turn. How could this act ever have seemed a shameful thing? Hartwell kissed the corner of Warry's lips, the line of his jaw, the edge of his ear. He slowly began to undo Warry's dressing gown, pausing in his kisses to rest his forehead against Warry's and regain his breath.

The gown slid easily from Warry's shoulders. He tensed for an instant, but Hartwell's palms swept his bare chest, raising gooseflesh in their wake and taking away any fear he had of being exposed in front of this man. Hartwell placed his hands on his shoulders and ran them down his arms as they kissed.

"You are so very beautiful," Hartwell whispered. "Have I said that already? I feel as though I could never say it enough."

The kisses continued down Warry's chest to his navel. Warry

sighed and lay back on the bed, his spine bowing as the man's tongue flicked out, tracing a line from navel to hip. Hartwell's touch was new and yet somehow wonderfully familiar. For even when they had done this in Gale's room, when they had been at each other's throats before and after, Warry had been able to feel the affection in Hartwell's touch. He felt it now too, as though Hartwell were sculpting him from clay, pouring his whole soul, his love, into this work of art.

Hartwell planted a soft kiss on Warry's hip bone, making Warry shiver so hard it drew a laugh from his companion. Deft fingers undid the string of Warry's drawers and helped him slip out of them. He didn't dare breathe as Hartwell gazed at his erect prick. Warry simply bit his lip, letting Hartwell look his fill.

"So very beautiful," Hartwell repeated, his voice low and gentle. He eased Warry's legs apart, and Warry gasped. It was too much, the newness of it, the pleasure, the shock of Hartwell opening him up like this. He tensed again, his belly knotting as Hartwell leaned down once more. Teeth grazed his hip, and another sharp inhale was lost in the crackle of the fire.

Hartwell licked very lightly at the sore spot he'd left, then glided his tongue across Warry's belly at an angle, to the hair at the base of Warry's prick. "Hartwell!" A chuckle blew warm air against an already sensitive place. Hartwell slipped one thumb behind Warry's balls, and then lowered his head to press a series of kisses to Warry's inner thighs. His hair was soft against Warry's cock, and Warry feared he was about to embarrass himself by spending too quickly.

He could think on it no further as Hartwell went to work again, lightly nibbling the tender spot on the innermost part of Warry's thigh. He squirmed so hard he nearly jerked his leg out of reach, and then Hartwell bit down, tugging firmly on the skin. Warry bolted upright, his fingers tangling in Hartwell's hair, a whimper nearly becoming a wail. Hartwell's tongue was immediately there to soothe the spot. He stroked behind Warry's balls with his thumb, leaving Warry struggling to contain his choked gasps, concerned that his cries might be enough to wake Hartwell's mother from her stupor.

And then Hartwell took his prick in his mouth.

It was sheer luck that Warry did not immediately lose his battle to contain himself. The pleasure was beyond anything he could have imagined. Hartwell alternated sucking lightly and laving Warry's prick with his tongue. When Hartwell flattened his tongue against the length of his prick and began pressing rhythmically against the side of it, Warry's own tongue finally loosened, and out spilled a great many half-gasped encomiums detailing the wonders of William Hartwell. Hartwell, to his credit, did not lose focus. He continued to roll Warry's balls gently in one hand, occasionally humming around his length, a sound that drew answering, albeit far more desperate, noises from Warry. Warry tightened his thighs around Hartwell's head, struggling not to squeeze. He had no wish to hurt Hartwell, but how on earth was a man supposed to cope with this sensation without gripping something and roaring as though he were being slain?

Hartwell anchored the nails of his other hand in Warry's belly, then dragged upward to his chest. He took one of Warry's nipples between his thumb and finger and rolled it lightly. Then, with no warning whatsoever, he sucked hard on Warry's prick, increased the pressure on Warry's nipple and twisted it firmly as he lapped the very head of Warry's cock.

Warry folded forward, his fingers tangled in Hartwell's hair, his thighs trembling, his throat clamping on a cry torn from the very centre of him. His prick spent itself in Hartwell's mouth, and Hartwell's tongue continued its feather-light beat until it had teased every drop from him.

Hartwell lifted his head, wiping his mouth with the back of his hand, though apparently it was too much to ask that he wipe the smug grin from his face too. Warry could not stop moaning, which would have been humiliating if it did not clearly delight Hartwell so much. After a moment, the moans became whimpers, and he settled back against the pillow. Hartwell rested his head against Warry's hip, his palm warm as he rubbed Warry's quivering belly.

Warry wished he could speak. He did not know what he would say, but it seemed impolite to remain incoherent for so long. Hartwell did not seem to mind, though.

"You are simply splendid," Hartwell whispered, tilting his head back so he could see Warry's face.

Warry's shaking increased. Hartwell's gaze met his with gentle understanding, and he climbed to his knees and rubbed Warry's thighs with both hands, the touch heavy and deeply reassuring. "Will you sleep now?" he asked.

Warry shook his head. He would never sleep again; he was sure of it. Though exhaustion threatened him, his desire to see Hartwell come apart as he himself had was fierce. "You have not had your pleasure," he managed hoarsely.

"Warry." Hartwell smiled. "I am more than satisfied. I have had everything I wanted."

"And what about what I want?" His voice gained strength as he pulled himself to half-sitting.

Hartwell frowned. "Did you not like it?"

"I liked it better than I have liked anything in my life. But now I wish to see you just as I was."

In the flickering light from the fire, Hartwell appeared apprehensive. "You are under no obligation."

"Do you ever listen? I've told you how I feel about you. I have told you what I want. How can you think I wish to undo you out of a sense of obligation?"

Hartwell's laugh was nervous. "You have already undone me. If you undo me any further, well…I do not know what will happen."

"Then let us find out. Undress, William."

Warry did not need daylight to see the combination of awe, terror, and need in Hartwell's eyes, and it pulled a thread of mischievous giddiness through him.

The man stood slowly, his hands going to the buttons of his waistcoat. He hesitated. "I do not think anything has ever made me feel more naked than hearing you say my given name."

"William," Warry said again, loving the feel of it on his tongue. He was only a little anxious, and the nerves were more excitement than anything else. He had never in his life imagined having any sort of command over William Hartwell.

Hartwell undressed in silence, his fingers fumbling with a button or two. At last, he slid his drawers down and stepped out of them, standing naked before Warry, the fire casting shadow in every muscular furrow of his body. Warry nearly lost his reason. How could any sight be so splendid? How could a mere pup such as he be so fortunate as to have a man like William about to climb into bed with him?

He could have remained there for the rest of the night, simply staring. Instead, he forced himself to shift over. He drew back the bedclothes and patted the spot beside him. "Come here."

"As you wish." Hartwell stepped forward. Warry could never recall having seen the man so uncertain. To imagine William Hartwell nervous was a strange thing indeed. It was even stranger to know he was the cause of Hartwell's nerves.

He laughed, the sound genuine and delighted. "What is it you think I mean to do to you?"

Hartwell's answering chuckle was not quite steady. "I do not know," he admitted, climbing onto the bed. "I know only that I am your servant."

"I am the one in thrall to you, my lord," Warry whispered as he wrapped an arm around Hartwell's waist and drew their bodies together. His softened prick rubbed against the stiff length of Hartwell's, and Hartwell closed his eyes and groaned. Warry kissed him, a gesture Hartwell returned eagerly, his hand coming up to cup Warry's face. Warry ran his own hand down Hartwell's back, but lost courage when he came to the base of the man's spine. He stroked the small hollow there with his thumb, relishing the soft sigh Hartwell made into his mouth. Then he gathered his wits and ran his hand over the firm curve of Hartwell's arse.

Hartwell groaned and pressed himself tightly against Warry, their hips grinding for a moment, Warry sucking forcefully on Hartwell's tongue. He used his unoccupied hand to trace the muscles of Hartwell's arm, then his chest. Every plane of Hartwell's body was as hard as packed earth, and Warry revelled in touching him.

He squeezed Hartwell's arse hard enough to elicit another groan, then broke the kiss, placing his fingers in his mouth and wetting them. If *The Maiden Diaries* had taught him anything, it was that the act he was considering was enjoyed by both men and women to a degree that was borderline alarming.

Hartwell stared at him. Warry removed his fingers, slick with spit, from his mouth. "Is it okay?" he asked.

Hartwell gave a half laugh, half groan. "I'll not last more than a second if you try it."

Warry grinned. "That is certainly all right by me." He stuck his fingers back in his mouth, then slipped them out again and reached around behind Hartwell. He trailed his smallest finger down the cleft of Hartwell's arse, attempting to familiarise himself with the territory. When he found what he dearly hoped was the right place, he stroked it with the wet pad of his middle finger. Hartwell whimpered encouragingly, throwing his leg over both of Warry's and spreading himself open. Warry pushed inward, barely containing a gasp at the tightness and heat. Hartwell grunted tersely, his body going rigid for an instant. Warry could imagine this part was uncomfortable, and he despaired at the thought of causing Hartwell even a moment's pain when he wanted nothing more than to give him pleasure. Hartwell's chin dropped to his chest, and on an impulse, Warry kissed the top of his head, hoping to reassure him.

Then the tight muscle gave way, and Warry's finger slid all the way inside. Hartwell buried his face in the crook of Warry's neck, moving himself on Warry's finger, emitting a series of soft cries and sharp pants. Warry attempted to thrust in a way that complemented Hartwell's movements until Hartwell's cries became barely coherent pleas against Warry's skin. With his other hand, Warry rubbed Hartwell's arse, squeezing and kneading. He gripped one of Hartwell's cheeks and dug his nails in, and at the same moment thrust his finger as deeply as he could. Hartwell clenched around him with a force that startled Warry. The other man sank his teeth into Warry's shoulder to muffle a fierce cry, his fingers gouging Warry's side to the point of pain. He seemed to sob, his spine arching then dipping, and Warry's prick was suddenly slick with Hartwell's spilled seed. The sensation was delightful, and Warry could not help rubbing against Hartwell, wondering for a moment if his own prick might get hard again.

"Warry," Hartwell begged. "Warry, please, I cannot bear it."

Warry took pity on him and slowly withdrew his finger, moving his unsoiled hand up to rub Hartwell's shoulders. Hartwell collapsed on him, still breathing hard against Warry's neck.

They remained like that for some time; Warry lazily stroking Hartwell's slick skin as the man's breathing gradually slowed. His mind began to race with future possibilities. What would it be like to enter Hartwell with his prick? To hear how Hartwell would beg him then? And what if Hartwell did as he had done earlier, but this time worshiped every single inch of Warry's body with his lips before taking him to the very height of pleasure?

The fire had died to embers. Hartwell emitted a puff of breath, and Warry heard him lick his lips, then try once to speak before finally gaining his voice. "Are you all right?"

"I have never been better in the whole of my life," he replied honestly.

Hartwell lifted his head and gazed at him. "The same is true of me," he whispered. He rested his head on the pillow, stroking Warry's chest with his fingertips.

"How soon until we can do it again?" Warry asked.

"You must be joking. I shall not be able to move again for hours."

Warry sniggered. "I thought you were my servant?"

Hartwell's eyes caught the last flickers of firelight. "Come here."

Warry tipped his head toward him. "I am already here."

"Come closer. I need to tell you something."

"You're going to belch in my ear, aren't you?"

"What?" Hartwell cried. "How can you even *think* I would—"

"You're going to belch in my ear."

"*No*! We have just shared something beautiful. I can't believe you would think so poorly of me."

Warry relented, feeling a jab of guilt at assuming the worst of Hartwell. They *had* just shared something beautiful. He shifted his head a bit closer, and Hartwell leaned down, lips to Warry's ear.

Warry shot upright, yanking his pillow out from under him and mashing it against Hartwell's face just as Hartwell let out an enormous belch.

Hartwell's laughter was muffled by the pillow.

"I knew it!" Warry exclaimed, forcing Hartwell onto his back, keeping the pillow over his face. "I knew it, Hartwell, damn you!"

"Stop trying to smother me!" Hartwell begged plaintively. "Warry!"

"You deserve it."

"No, listen—" Hartwell groped blindly with one hand, catching Warry's arm and tugging him off balance, then sitting up. The pillow fell into his lap. "Let me say what I really wanted to say." He tried to pull Warry closer.

"William!" Warry jerked away, laughing.

Hartwell got hold of him again and brought his lips to Warry's ear once more. "Listen. Shh, Warry, just listen."

Warry went still except for the occasional fit of sniggers that set his body shaking. "Don't…" he moaned.

"No, listen." Hartwell drew a breath, and then whispered, "You are my heart."

Now Warry went entirely still.

"You are beautiful. I care for you. I love you."

Warry sank back onto the bed, his heart pounding. Hartwell lay beside him again, gazing at him.

"You too," Warry whispered.

The silence that followed was comfortable. Familiar.

Eventually Warry sighed, not wanting to speak the next words, but knowing he must. "I should go home. My parents will worry if I am out all night."

"I imagine Becca will make any excuses that need to be made should you wish to stay here and sleep."

Warry studied what he could of Hartwell's face in the darkness. "I fear what she might tell them."

"She will do nothing to betray your trust. That I know."

It was horrible to imagine what his parents might have already heard of the gossip. If Lady Agatha had spread the word that he had been discovered in a state of undress in Balfour's bedroom, locked in Hartwell's embrace, Balfour lying on the floor with his cravat undone…

Hartwell seemed to read his thoughts. "There is nothing to be done about it for the moment. I will retire to my own room if you wish to sleep alone, but I do not think you should attempt to go home now."

"Do you think my parents would believe that I was helping you organise your father's library?" His attempt at humour was met with a sympathetic snort. Hartwell's hand smoothed his hair. "I think your parents love you and want what's best for you."

"And what of yours?"

"They have always tolerated me. I imagine they will continue to do so."

"Even if we wed?"

"Now that," Hartwell said, and Warry could hear the smile in his voice, "you are in no state to decide tonight. Go to sleep, and things will look better in the morning."

"Things are so nearly perfect right now," he murmured.

Hartwell made a small noise of assent and nuzzled Warry's jaw.

Warry lingered another moment in the embrace, then with a soft groan, got out of bed and went to clean his hands at the washstand. When he climbed back in, Hartwell's breathing had slowed such that Warry wondered if he was asleep, but Hartwell shifted at once, wrapping both arms around Warry and pulling him against his chest once more. "Sleep," Hartwell growled in his ear, "or I shall have to do a more thorough job of tiring you out next time."

Warry smiled and let himself be lulled by the steady beat of the man's heart.

CHAPTER 19

"Demme!" George, the Duke of Ancaster exclaimed.

"Language," the duchess said mildly from across the table, sipping her tea.

"Language?" Ancaster demanded. "*Language?* What, a man can't even say *demme* in his own house nowadays? The world has gone mad!"

"Oh, pish," the duchess said and waved her hand in his direction as though she were trying to shoo away a fly.

"Pish?" Ancaster roared. "*Pish?*"

His wife sighed and ignored him.

Hartwell watched the exchange from the other end of the table, looking from one parent to the other like it was a game of battledore and shuttlecock. He'd have a crick in his neck very soon if they didn't call a truce.

"He's ruined, of course," Ancaster said at last, settling into his chair and deflating like a bladder. His gaze landed on Hartwell. "Warry, I mean. Half the *ton* already knows he was caught in a compromising position with you last night at the ball, and the other half will know by luncheon. Really, William, what the hell were you thinking?"

"Language," the duchess murmured.

"I shall say *hell* if I wish!" Ancaster muttered like a petulant child.

"He's not ruined," Hartwell said, lifting his chin. "Not if I marry him."

"Marry!" Ancaster spluttered. "You will not!"

Hartwell lifted his chin and drew a deep breath. "I shall. I have every intention of doing so, Father, and there is nothing you can say to dissuade me. I know that for some time it has been your greatest wish that I marry, and the reason I have dragged my feet on the subject has recently become apparent to me. I do not wish to marry Becca, or any other woman, no matter how dear she may be. I wish to marry *Warry*, and nobody else, and so I shall. And while I hope to have your approval on the matter, I intend to proceed whether or not it is forthcoming."

His father's jaw dropped. "But your title!"

"Your title, you mean," Hartwell said. "I would be honoured if I were to one day inherit it and become the Duke of Ancaster, but you must know that if you force me to choose between the title and my heart, I will choose my heart, and my Warry, every time."

"Oh!" His mother clutched her hands to her bosom. "George, he is in love!"

Confusion twisted his father's features into a comical mask. "But you don't even like Warry! Your contempt for him of late has been palpable. And you tried to shoot him!"

"I have acted like a fool," Hartwell said, "in an attempt to deny my own feelings. But I can no longer deny that I care deeply for Warry. I love him, and I will marry him. And the shooting," he added, "was an accident."

He had spent so long fearing a conversation like this one that now it was happening he was surprised his voice didn't waver. But the memory of Warry's bravery last night—and his boldness in the bedroom—steeled his nerves. And this morning, when Warry had left in the dull, grey hour before the dawn, Hartwell had kissed him and confessed to him again that he held his heart. Warry, braver and bolder last night but perhaps a little more jaded too, had only smiled and kissed him back and murmured a caution against making any promises. Hartwell had wanted to grab him by the shoulders, shake him, and demand to know where the closeness and affection and, yes, the *love* they had shared the night before had vanished, but he had not. Instead, he had suffered a stab of guilt in the guts because if Warry was suddenly hardening his heart against the hopes of a happy resolution, then Hartwell had played a part in that process. Because Warry hadn't wanted to hear any promises at that moment, Hartwell had made the promise to himself instead, silently. He would marry Joseph Warrington and make everything right between them.

It wasn't Warry's fault that he was once bitten and twice shy, and Hartwell refused to take it as a slight against his pride. No, if Warry had been hesitant this morning to repeat the things they had said last night—both the promises to always say what they were feeling and their talk of marriage—then it was up to Hartwell to prove himself better than Warry's doubts. He had to show he was worthy of Warry's heart. And the first step in that, he knew, was to declare his intentions to his father, even at the risk of being cast out.

Gale might have claimed the duke would never do something so drastic but, holding his father's gaze, Hartwell wasn't as certain.

"But he is *ruined*," Ancaster said helplessly.

"He is not," Hartwell said firmly. "Not if I marry him."

"And if I do not give my permission for such a thing?" Ancaster asked, his gaze narrowing.

"Father," Hartwell said, gentling his tone. "I do not need your permission. I am telling you that I am determined to marry Warry. You may disown me if that is your wish, but that has no bearing on my decision."

The duke passed a hand over his eyes. "Good Lord. But you will have no son, William. What will become of the title?"

"This is not a decision I make lightly," Hartwell said. "I swear that. If I am to be the Duke of Ancaster in due course, then I also swear I will do everything I can to preserve that legacy and make Cousin James the heir, just as he would be if you disowned me."

"Oh!" his mother exclaimed suddenly. "He has you there, George, doesn't he? James is a good boy. We like James. Do you remember when he was three and got a pebble stuck up his nose and almost died? I thought his mama would bring the ceiling down with all her screaming. Well, fortunately he's not so silly anymore." She popped a piece of honey cake into her mouth and added, thoughtfully, "I suspect Elizabeth still is, though."

Hartwell regarded his father curiously. He felt oddly uninvested in his father's decision and at peace with whatever it was. He also felt quite proud of cornering the man and forcing him to make a choice. Either way, James would be Duke of Ancaster. Whether he would be the next one or the one after that was up to the current duke, and entirely out of Hartwell's hands.

"Good Lord," his father repeated at last. He turned his mouth down unhappily. "Well, you are quite decided, I see."

"Quite," Hartwell agreed.

"Then marry him," Ancaster said shortly, and Hartwell warmed to see the grudging respect in his father's eyes. "Marry him and be happy."

Hartwell swelled with pride. "And Ancaster?" he asked.

His father snorted. "Get out, William. Get out, and don't come back until I've yelled at the servants for a while."

"He's not going to yell at the servants," the duchess said airily. She leaned down the table and clasped Hartwell's wrist. Her eyes sparkled. "I wouldn't allow it."

And the wink she gave Hartwell promised that she wouldn't allow him to be disowned either, and that everything, eventually, was going to be just fine between him and his father.

∼

"Well, Hartwell, you've picked a fine day for a picnic," Gale declared sardonically. "It is far too cold to sit near any body of water, even one so stagnant as this. Why has Lady Rebecca cast aside her shawl? I always counted her among the few people of sense I have known."

"Stop your grumbling," Hartwell ordered. "I invited you along because I require some advice."

"Advice?"

Hartwell lowered his voice and said in Gale's ear, "I mean to propose to Warry."

Gale appeared not at all surprised. "What on earth do you need my advice for? I would sooner dive into that frigid, stagnant water than I would propose to anyone."

"Perhaps not your advice, then, but your support." Hartwell surveyed the grassy expanse and the green-brown pond full of lily pads around them. "This is where we used to play as children."

"Good Lord, Hartwell. You rash-minded disciple of that rake Slyfeel. You brought Warry to the very pond you used to throw him into, and you expect to romance him here? My advice is not to do it."

Hartwell ignored that statement. "I am only afraid, now that the moment is here, that he will not have me."

"He has no choice, my friend. If that makes you feel any better."

"It does not," Hartwell said sharply. "Do not say that. He has a choice. I will make sure he knows he has one."

Gale shrugged, watching Becca and Warry shake out the blanket at the side of the pond. "Does she know?"

"Not yet. Although I'm certain she suspects. I must set things right with her before I make my proposal to Warry."

"If I had known what a show I would be getting, I would not have grumbled so about being invited. I think you a fool, Hartwell. But you are, quite literally, the only person I have ever born any love for, so I will do my best to speak words of encouragement instead of derision."

"You exaggerate." Hartwell glanced at him. "You love Clarissa, Ann-Marie, Cordelia, Helene, and Eugenie—"

"Eugenie? Who the devil is Eugenie?"

Hartwell rolled his eyes but humoured him. "Your youngest sister."

"You cannot be serious? Hartwell, my life was nightmare enough when I thought I had only four. Now you tell me I have five?"

"You know precisely how many sisters you have. You know their ages and their likes and dislikes, and you buy them sweets on the regular. You do not fool me."

"Lower your voice, man! If people find out, I will be in greater disgrace than your Warry."

"Then I suppose you also do not wish for me to thank you."

"Thank me for what service, pray tell?

"Why did you start looking into Balfour's finances in the first place? And why did you brave the first ball of the Season to uncover his attempted manipulations of the stock exchange?" Hartwell inquired casually.

Gale would not look at him. "Anyone could see there was something wrong with the man. I merely did a bit of digging."

"Because you knew I loved Warry." Hartwell rendered it a statement, not a question.

Gale did not answer, but Hartwell could swear he saw the man's lips twitch with what might have been a smile or a grimace.

"Thank you for taking the case."

"For pity's sake, I have told you, do not call it a case! Go. Go and apologize to Lady Rebecca and then go propose to that dull little wisp you wish to call husband. Leave me here to become chilled to the point of death."

Hartwell grinned and walked over to the blanket. His heart was going a bit fast, but he was otherwise surprisingly steady, considering the circumstances. Warry was hunting in the picnic basket for something, and Hartwell approached Becca. "Would you walk with me for a moment?"

He thought she might refuse, but then she stepped toward him, and they began a circuit around the pond.

"I do not know what apology I could make," he said, "that would not fall terribly short of what the circumstances require."

"Why don't you start with any apology at all?" Becca suggested.

"I am sorry." Hartwell spoke with complete sincerity. "Nothing feels so terrible as being at odds with you. I never did think ill of you. You will always be the person I admire most in the world."

"Such flattery."

"It is the truth."

She turned to him. "I am sorry as well. To hurt you in retaliation for you hurting me did not help the situation."

"Are we to be friends again?"

"I suppose it would be best to declare ourselves so. Seeing as we will be family soon."

Hartwell attempted to school his face. "Why do you say that?"

Becca's lips curved briefly. "Because you keep looking at my brother as though you mean to sweep him into your arms and carry him to the altar right now. And because the letter you sent me was not so cryptic as you might have liked to think."

"May I ask him?"

She laughed. "You do not need my permission."

"But it would mean very much to me."

Her smile faded. She quickened her pace and so did he.

"You must not hurt him, William."

"I never will."

"You must not act out of guilt or to preserve his reputation."

"I do not. I swear, Becca. I love him."

She sighed. A moment later, she stumbled slightly, then bent down. "The heel of this shoe," she complained, adjusting it beneath the hem of her dress. "It wobbles so." She straightened. "Very well. You have my permission to ask."

"I am, and will forever be, grateful. You are an angel, truly."

"Doing it a bit too brown, William. Have you told your parents?"

He nodded. "The result could have been worse. Are your parents...Are they very angry? About Warry? About us?"

She let out a slow breath. "They are handling things well, considering. They have heard the rumours, but they are not seeking your blood. And they have been gentle with Warry thus far."

"That is good."

"I have distracted them somewhat from Warry's shame by declaring that I will never marry. They are...Well, my mother is... trying to come to terms with it."

"I saw you dancing the other night with Miss Emily Pearson..." He lifted both his voice and his brows suggestively.

She gave him a most unimpressed stare.

"I will admit, I wondered...when you finally declared yourself willing to submit to your parents' wishes and marry me...why not marry instead a woman you have a fondness for? Even if it was done out of expediency, wouldn't it still be better to marry someone you could come to love one day?"

She stopped walking, and he did too. "Of course I thought of that. But it seemed, until recently, too painful to consider even feigning affection for any woman but Miss Lilley. I know you must think what I feel for her is calf love, but—"

"I may not have read the letter, Becca, but I know you. And I assure you, calf love is the very last thing I was thinking."

She laughed, but it trailed off into a solemnity he didn't know what to make of. "If I cannot marry the woman I love because she is a commoner, then I wish to marry no woman. Nor any man, either, though I'll allow that you came close, William. With you, there could be no expectation that I would love you in that way. Marrying you seemed the closest thing to not marrying at all."

"I am flattered."

She snorted, pulling her shawl around her. "Warry asked yesterday if I am ever scared. Of course I am. I do know what people will say about me, about my eternal spinsterhood. And it will hurt, I'm sure, at times. But I cannot live a lie. I *will* not live one. And besides…" She cast a sly glance at Hartwell. "I am thinking of travel."

"Of travel?"

"Yes. To the Continent. If I am to be a spinster, then I am obligated to travel, am I not?"

"Are you?" he asked, confused.

"Yes," Becca said airily. "But of course it would be scandalous to travel unaccompanied. I shall have to hire a companion. A lady of good reputation and modest demeanour." Her mouth twitched. "Perhaps even one already known and thought well of by my parents. Someone who has previously been in their trusted employ."

"Becca, you sly thing!" Hartwell exclaimed admiringly. "I shall expect detailed letters from you so Warry and I might get a map and plot your and Miss Lilley's course across Europe."

Becca smiled. "I should expect nothing less."

They had nearly completed their circuit of the pond, and Hartwell's heart stuttered at the sight of Warry sitting on the blanket, the breeze ruffling his hair.

Hartwell did not realise he had stopped moving. He was not aware of anything except Warry until a moment later when his shirt was pulled back and something wet and wriggling dropped down his back. He shouted, whirling.

Becca grinned at him.

"Dash it, Becca!" He tugged his shirt loose to free the frog, catching it in hand and then setting it gently by the pond's edge. She must have picked the creature up when she feigned to repair the heel of her shoe.

"Now I will consider us even."

Hartwell tried, over the course of the few steps to the picnic area, to compose himself. His cheeks were hot, and it seemed he could still feel the frog hopping about in his shirt.

"Lady Rebecca," Gale called as they drew near. "Will you not come over here with me and help feed these damnably stale seed cakes to the pigeons?"

"I do not even like you," Becca protested.

"Nobody does," Gale assured her. "But these birds look quite hungry."

Hartwell shook his head as his two dearest friends wandered to a spot several yards away—and yet, he noticed, not entirely out of earshot—where pigeons flocked. He knelt beside Warry on the blanket, which had been placed so near the edge of the pond that it felt damp under his knees. "I had hoped it would not be so chilly today." He cursed himself at once for bringing up the weather. He had far more important things to speak of.

Warry made no answer and would not quite look at Hartwell, which was disconcerting.

"It was not your fault," Hartwell said at last. "What Balfour did to you."

Warry tensed visibly, but Hartwell pushed on. "Becca and I were quite shocked by your story last night. And perhaps we made it sound as though we blamed you. I want you to know that it was not your fault. That you are not ruined. That things will be…will be all right."

"Hartwell," Warry said carefully, perhaps a bit bitterly. Hartwell missed 'Willam.' "I am in no need of reassurances. You offered me many last night, which was kind of you, but I am not some fragile thing. I will be fine on my own."

On his own? Hartwell would be damned first.

"Be that as it may, I want to make sure you understand that you are under no obligation to answer my next question with a yes."

Now Warry did turn to him, his tousled hair hanging just over his widening eyes. Hartwell rose and drew Warry with him, taking both of Warry's hands in his.

"In the light of day, the things I said last night have not lost their shape. I care for you deeply, Warry. I cannot imagine loving anyone as I love you. I should like a chance to prove to you that I am better than I have thus far shown myself to be. I wish to live my life by your side, to protect you as best I can from ever being hurt, and to cherish you each day, now and for all the future."

Warry's gaze softened, though Hartwell could not identify the precise emotion it held. Perhaps because it held so many at once: hope, delight, caution, amusement. "What is your question?" Warry asked with a dryness of tone that would have made Gale proud.

Hartwell snorted but studied him with such adoration that he could see the depth of his own feeling begin to echo in Warry's expression. "Will you marry me?"

As Warry stared back at him, Hartwell could not help noticing that Gale and Becca were edging closer. Eavesdropping. He hoped he was not about to be humiliated before both of them.

"That depends," Warry said thoughtfully, and Hartwell braced himself. "Will you love me when I am old?"

"Of course." Hartwell's brow furrowed.

"Good answer," Gale murmured behind him. Hartwell did not recall asking his friend to interfere, but perhaps this was what counted in Gale's mind as being supportive.

Warry asked, "Will you love me no matter how much time I spend talking about goats' digestive systems?"

Hartwell opened his mouth to say yes, absolutely, but Gale whispered, "I would negotiate it down to horses. Goats have four stomachs to be nattered on about, but horses only have the one."

Hartwell said loudly, "I will listen to any description, of any length, of any organ inside any animal. And I will love you more with every word you speak on the subject."

"Hartwell, that is rash," Gale warned.

Warry was struggling increasingly to hide his smile. "Will you love me always, no matter what I put you through?"

"Nothing you could do would sway me from loving you," Hartwell promised.

"Well in that case…" Warry shoved him firmly, and Hartwell toppled backward into the pond.

He rose up, sputtering and circling his arms to keep himself afloat. The water was damnably chilly, but Warry, curse the wretch, laughed with such pure delight it seemed to warm the very air around them.

"Then my answer is yes!" Warry announced. He stuck out his hand to Hartwell. "Come. I will rescue you."

Hartwell coughed out a bit of water and reached up to grip Warry's hand. As soon as he grasped it, he gave a mighty tug and pulled Warry into the water with him. Warry splashed and flailed, laughing so hard that Hartwell feared he would drown from inhaling water. He pulled Warry close to him, aware they were making quite a scene.

Telling himself they were hidden from spectators by the reeds lining the pond, he pressed a quick kiss to Warry's lips.

"You see," Hartwell said. "You are a terrible imp, and I love you all the more for it." He hauled them both back onto the grass, Warry still breathless with laughter as he peered up at Hartwell. "My husband," Hartwell whispered.

Warry stopped laughing then and returned Hartwell's gaze, every bit of him alive, the way Hartwell remembered him. Water dripped from his hair, caught in his eyelashes, beaded in the bow of his lips. "Yes," Warry said. "Yes. Yes, yes, yes."

Hartwell stole another kiss. When he drew back, Warry's eyes were wide.

"We shall have no more scandals, shall we?" he asked hopefully.

"None," Hartwell agreed. "We shall be dull and staid and boring forevermore. Whoever the next scandal of the Season belongs to, it shall not be ours."

"Oh, good," Warry said, his brilliant smile reappearing. "I do like the sound of that." He traced his fingers across Hartwell's palm and gave a thoughtful hum. "Whose, do you suppose, the scandal shall be?"

Hartwell only shrugged, and then leaned in to kiss his Warry again.

AFTERWORD

Thank you so much for reading *A Husband for Hartwell*. We hope that you enjoyed it. We would very much appreciate it if you could take a few moments to leave a review on Amazon or Goodreads, or on your social media platform of choice.

ABOUT J.A. ROCK

J.A. Rock is an author of LGBTQ romance and suspense novels, as well as an audiobook narrator under the name Jill Smith. When she's not writing or narrating, J.A. enjoys reading, collecting historical costumes, and failing miserably at gardening. She lives in the Ohio wilds with an extremely judgmental dog, Professor Anne Studebaker.

You can find her website at https://jarockauthor.com.

ABOUT LISA HENRY

Lisa likes to tell stories, mostly with hot guys and happily ever afters.

Lisa lives in tropical North Queensland, Australia. She doesn't know why, because she hates the heat, but she suspects she's too lazy to move. She spends half her time slaving away as a government minion, and the other half plotting her escape.

She attended university at sixteen, not because she was a child prodigy or anything, but because of a mix-up between international school systems early in life. She studied History and English, neither of them very thoroughly.

Lisa has been published since 2012, and was a LAMBDA finalist for her quirky, awkward coming-of-age romance *Adulting 101*, and a Rainbow Awards finalist for 2019's *Anhaga*.

You can join Lisa's Facebook reader group at Lisa Henry's Hangout, and find her website at lisahenryonline.com.

ALSO BY J.A. ROCK AND LISA HENRY

When All the World Sleeps
Another Man's Treasure
Fall on Your Knees
The Preacher's Son
Mark Cooper versus America (Prescott College #1)
Brandon Mills versus the V-Card (Prescott College #2)
The Good Boy (The Boy #1)
The Boy Who Belonged (The Boy #2)

The Playing the Fool Series
The Two Gentlemen of Altona
The Merchant of Death
Tempest

The Lords of Bucknall Club Series
A Husband for Hartwell
A Case for Christmas
A Rival for Rivingdon

ALSO BY J.A. ROCK

By His Rules
Wacky Wednesday (Wacky Wednesday #1)
The Brat-tastic Jayk Parker (Wacky Wednesday #2)
Calling the Show
Take the Long Way Home
The Grand Ballast
Minotaur
The Silvers
The Subs Club (The Subs Club #1)
Pain Slut (The Subs Club #2)
Manties in a Twist (The Subs Club #3)
24/7 (The Subs Club #4)
Sub Hunt (The Subs Club #5)
"Beauties" (All in Fear anthology)
"Stranger Than Stars" (Take a Chance Anthology)
Sight Unseen: A Collection of Five Anonymous Novellas
Touch Up: A Rose & Thorns Novel, with Katey Hawthorne

ALSO BY LISA HENRY

The Parable of the Mustard Seed
Naked Ambition
Dauntless
Anhaga
Two Man Station (Emergency Services #1)
Lights and Sirens (Emergency Services #2)
The California Dashwoods
Adulting 101
Sweetwater
He Is Worthy
The Island
Tribute
One Perfect Night
Fallout, with M. Caspian
Dark Space (Dark Space #1)
Darker Space (Dark Space #2)
Starlight (Dark Space #3)

With Tia Fielding
Family Recipe
Recipe for Two
A Desperate Man

With Sarah Honey
Red Heir
Elf Defence

Socially Orcward

Writing as Cari Waites

<u>Stealing Innocents</u>